The Mystery of t

E. W. Howe

Alpha Editions

This edition published in 2024

ISBN : 9789361479694

Design and Setting By
Alpha Editions
www.alphaedis.com
Email - info@alphaedis.com

Contents

CHAPTER I.

THE TOWN OF DARK NIGHTS.

Davy's Bend—a river town, a failing town, and an old town, on a dark night, with a misty rain falling, and the stars hiding from the dangerous streets and walks of the failing town down by the sluggish river which seems to be hurrying away from it, too, like its institutions and its people, and as the light of the wretched day that has just closed hurried away from it a few hours since.

The darkness is so intense that the people who look out of their windows are oppressed from staring at nothing, for the shadows are obliterated, and for all they know there may be great caverns in the streets, filled with water from the rising river, and vagabond debris on their front steps. It occurs to one of them who opens the blind to his window a moment, and looks out (and who notices incidentally that the rays from his lamp seem afraid to venture far from the casement) that a hard crust will form somewhere above the town, up where there is light for the living, and turn the people of Davy's Bend into rocks as solid as those thousands of feet below, which thought affects him so much that he closes his blinds and shutters tighter than before, determined that his rooms shall become caves.

The rain comes down steadily, plashing into little pools in the road with untiring energy, where it joins other vagrant water, and creeps off at last into the gutter, into the rivulet, and into the river, where it joins the restless tide which is always hurrying away from Davy's Bend, and bubbles and foams with joy.

The citizen who observed the intense blackness of the night comes to his window again, and notes the steady falling of the rain, and in his reverie pretends to regret that it is not possible for the water to come up until his house will float away like an ark, that he may get rid of living in a place where the nights are so dark and wet that he cannot sleep for thinking of them. When he returns to his chair, and attempts to read, the pattering rain is so persistent on the roof and at the windows that the possibility of a flood occurs to his mind, and he thinks with satisfaction that, should it come to pass, Davy's Bend would at last be as well off as Ben's City; and this possibility is so pleasant that he puts out his light, the only one showing in the town, and goes to bed.

At the foot of a long street, so close to the river that its single light casts a ghastly glare into the water, stands the railroad station, where the agent awaits the arrival of the single train that visits the place daily,—for only a few people want to go to Davy's Bend, and not many are left to move away,—so the agent mutters at the rain and the darkness, and growls at the hard fate that keeps him up so late; for, of all the inhabitants of the place, he is the only one who has business to call him out at night. There are no people in Davy's Bend who are overworked, or whose business cares are so great as to make them nervous or fretful; so they sleep and yawn a great deal, and have plenty of time in which to tell how dull their own place is, and how distressingly active is Ben's City, located in the country below them, and which is admired even by the river, for it is always going in that direction.

Fortunately, on this misty night the agent has not long to wait; for just as he curls himself up in his chair to rest comfortably, certain that the train will be late, there is a hoarse blast from a steam whistle up the road, which echoes through the woods and over the hills with a dismal roar, and by the time he has seized his lantern, and reached the outside, the engine bell is ringing softly in the yard; the headlight appears like a great eye spying out the dark places around the building, and before he has had time to look about him, or express his surprise that the wheels are on time, a few packages have been unloaded, and the train creeps out into the darkness, hurrying away from Davy's Bend, like the river and the people.

There is but one passenger to-night: a man above the medium height and weight, dressed like a city tradesman, who seems to own the packages put off, for he is standing among them, and apparently wondering what disposition he is to make of them; for the agent is about to retire into the station with his books under his arm. Evidently the stranger is not good natured, for he hails the official impatiently, and inquires, in a voice that is a mixture of indignation and impudence, if the hotels have no representatives about, and if he is expected to remain out in the rain all night to guard his property.

The agent does not know as to that, but he does know that the stranger is welcome to leave his packages in the building until morning, which arrangement seems to be the best offering, for it is accepted, after both men have denounced the town until they are satisfied; for no one pretends to defend Davy's Bend, so the agent readily assents to whatever the stranger desires to say that is discreditable to his native place, while he is helping him to carry the trunks and bundles into the light.

When the rays of the single lamp in the station fall upon the stranger, the agent at first concludes that he is middle-aged, for a new growth of whiskers covers his face completely; but he thinks better of this during the course of his inspection, and remarks to himself that the owner of the packages is not as old as he seemed at first glance, but he is a man not satisfied with himself, or with anything around him,—the agent is sure of that; and as he helps with the baggage, of which there is a great deal, he keeps thinking to himself that it will stand him in hand to be more polite than usual, for the stranger looks sullen enough to fight with very little provocation. His quick, restless eyes were always busy,—the agent feels certain that he has been measured and disposed of in a glance,—but the longer he looks at the stranger the more certain he becomes that the packages he is helping to handle contains goods of importance, for their owner is evidently a man of importance.

"There must be gold in that," the agent says, as he puts his end of one of the trunks down, and pauses to rest. "I have been agent here a good many years; but if that is not an excess, I never had hold of one. Now for the rest of them."

The work is soon finished, and after extinguishing the light the agent steps upon the outside, locks the door, and puts the key into his pocket.

"I am sorry," he says, as he stands with the stranger outside the door, on a covered platform, where they are protected from the rain, "but I go in this direction, while the hotel lies in that," pointing the way. "It's a rough road, and you may have trouble in getting them up, but I guess you will get there if you go far enough, for the hotel stands directly at the head of the street. It's a pity that the town does not afford an omnibus, or a public carriage, but it doesn't, and that ends it. I intend to go away myself as soon as I can, for the company does not treat me any too well, though it is generally said that another man could not be found to do the work as I do it for the money."

By this time the agent has his umbrella up, which appears to be as dilapidated as the town, for it comes up with difficulty, so he says good night cheerily, and disappears; and the traveller, after shivering awhile on the platform, starts out to follow the direction given him, floundering in the mud at every step.

There is a row of houses on either side, with great gaps between them, and he is barely able to make out the strip of lighter shade which he judges is the street he is to follow, the night is so dark; but as the hotel is said to lie directly across his path, he argues that he is sure to run into it sooner or later, so he blunders on, shivering when he realizes that he is becoming wet to the skin. After travelling in this manner much longer than was desirable, finding the sidewalks so bad that he takes to the middle of the street, and finally goes back to the walk again in desperation; stumbling over barrels and carts, and so much rubbish that is oozy and soft as to cause him to imagine that everything is turning into a liquid state in order that it may leave the place by way of the gutters, the rivulets, and the river, he becomes aware that a lantern, carried by one of two men, whose legs are to be seen in long shadows, is approaching, and that they are very merry, for they are making a good deal of noise, and stop frequently to accuse each other of being jolly old boys, or thorough scoundrels, or dreadful villains, or to lean up against the buildings to discuss ribald questions which seem to amuse them. Apparently they have no destination, for after one of their bursts of merriment they are as apt to walk up the street as down it; and believing them to be the town riff-raff out for a lark, the stranger tries to pass them without attracting attention when he comes up to their vicinity; but the one who carries the lantern sees him, and, locking arms with his companion, adroitly heads the traveller off, and puts the lantern so close to his face that he dodges back to avoid it.

"Tug," the man says, in an amused way, "a stranger. There will be a sensation in Davy's Bend to-morrow; it hasn't happened before in a year."

Believing the men to be good-natured prowlers who can give him the information he is seeking, the stranger patiently waits while they enjoy their joke; which they do in a very odd fashion, for the man who carries the lantern, and who, the stranger noticed when the lantern was raised, was rather small, and old, and thin-faced, leans against his companion, and laughs in an immoderate but meek fashion. The fellow who had been addressed as Tug had said nothing at all, though he snorted once, in a queer way, which threw his companion into greater convulsions of merriment than ever, and changing their position so that they support themselves against a building, one of them continues to laugh gayly, and the other to chuckle and snort, until they are quite exhausted, as though a stranger in Davy's Bend is very funny indeed.

"There will be a train going the other way in three hours,—for both the trains creep through the town at night, as if they were ashamed to be seen here in daylight," the little man says to the traveller, recovering himself, and with a show of seriousness. "You had better take it, and go back; really you had. Davy's Bend will never suit you. It don't suit anybody. The last man that came here stood it a week, when off he went, and we never expected to see another one. Look at these deserted houses in every direction," he continues, stepping out farther into the middle of the street, as if to point around him, but remembering that the night is so dark that nothing can be seen, he goes back to his companion, and pokes him in the ribs, which causes that worthy to snort once more in the odd way that the stranger noticed on coming up. This reminds them of their joke again; so they return to the building, leaning against it with their arms, their heads, and their backs, laughing as they did before. Meanwhile the stranger stands out in the rain, watching the two odd men with an air of interest; but at last, recollecting his condition, he says,—

"It happens that I am looking for a place that suits nobody, and one that is generally avoided. If you will point out the way to the hotel, I will decide that question for myself to-morrow."

The little man picks up the lantern immediately when the hotel is mentioned.

"I never thought of the hotel," he exclaims, on the alert at once, and starting up the street, followed by his snorting companion, who ambled along like the front part of a wagon pushed from behind. "It is my business to be at the station when the train arrives, to look for passengers," the man continues as he hurries on with the light; "but it seemed like a waste of time to go down there, for nobody ever comes; so I thought I'd spend the time with Tug."

The man says this in a tone of apology, as though accustomed to making explanations for lack of attention to business; and as he leads the way he is not at all like the jolly fellow who laughed so immoderately, while leaning against the building, at his own weak joke; but perhaps he is one thing when on duty, and another when he is out airing himself. However this may be, the stranger follows, taking long strides to keep up, and occasionally stumbling over the person who has been referred to as Tug, and who appears to be unjointed in his legs; for when room is made for him on the left-hand side of the walk, he is sure suddenly to turn up on the right.

Thus they hurry along without speaking, until at length a dim light appears directly ahead of them, and coming up to this presently, the stranger finds that it comes from a building lying across the course in which they are travelling; for the street leading up from the river and the station ends abruptly in that direction with the hotel, as it ended in the other with the station. Another street crosses here at right angles, and the hotel turns travellers either to the right or to the left.

When the three men enter the place, and the light is turned up, the traveller sees that it had formerly been a business place; that it has been patched and pieced, and does not seem to answer the purpose for which it is being used without a protest, for the guests fall down two steps when they attempt to enter the dining-room, and everyone is compelled to go outside the office to get to the stairway leading to the rooms above. In its better days the room used as an office had probably been a provision store; for the whitewash on the walls does not entirely cover price-lists referring to chickens and hams and oats and flour.

"I am the clerk here," the man who had carried the lantern says, as he brings out a chair for the stranger, but condemns it after examination because both the back legs are gone, and it can only be used when leaning against the wall. "I am sorry I was not at the station to meet you; but it is so seldom that anyone comes that I hope you will not mention it to him," pointing his thumb upward, evidently referring to the proprietor sleeping above.

The arrival was thinking that queer little men like the one before him were to be found at every country hotel he had ever visited, acting as clerk during the hours when there was no business, and as hostler and waiter during the day, but he rather liked the appearance of this fellow, for he seemed more intelligent than the most of them, so he turned to listen to what he was saying, at the same time recollecting that he himself had suddenly become very grave.

"This is not much of a hotel," the clerk continues, at last fishing out a chair that seems to be strong, and placing it in front of the guest; "but it is the best Davy affords. The hotel, though, is better than the town; you will find that out soon enough."

A small man, of uncertain age, the clerk turns out to be, now that the light is upon him. He may be thirty, or forty, or fifty; for, judged in some ways, he looks old, while judged in other ways he looks young; but it is certain that he is not jolly around the hotel as he was on the street, for he is very meek, and occasionally strokes his pale face, which is beardless, with the exception of a meek little tuft on either side, as though he thinks that since he has been caught laughing it will go hard with him.

After looking at his companion, with an amused smile, for a moment, the stranger says that he will not mention anything, good or bad, "to him," whoever he may be, and, while thinking to himself that "Davy" is a familiar way of referring to Davy's Bend, he notices that the man who has already been called Tug, and who has found a chair and is sitting bolt upright in it, is eyeing him closely. He also remarks that Tug is hideously ugly, and that he is dressed in a suit of seedy black, which has once been respectable, but is now so sleek, from long use, that it glistens in the lamplight. He has a shock of hair, and a shock of beard, both of which seem to have been trimmed recently by a very awkward person; and the stranger also notices, in the course of his idle examination, that one of Tug's eyes, the left one, is very wide open, while the other is so nearly shut that generally the man seems to be aiming at something. When Tug winks with the eye that is wide open, the one that is nearly shut remains perfectly motionless, but follows the example presently, and winks independently and of its own accord, so that the stranger thinks of him as walking with his eyes, taking a tremendous leap with his left, and then a limp with his right.

Tug continues his observations, in spite of the cold stare of the stranger, and makes several discoveries, one of which is, that the stranger has a rather good-looking face and a large and restless eye. Tug imagines that he can read the man's character in his eye as easily as in an open book, for it has varying moods, and seems to be resolute at one moment, and gloomy and discontented at another. Although he is looking straight at him, Tug is certain that the stranger's thoughts are not always in Davy's Bend; and, while thinking that the stranger has important matters to think of somewhere, the clerk returns from the kitchen, carrying in his arms a great piece of cold beef, a loaf of bread, a half a pie in a tin plate, and a coffee-pot and a tumbler.

Covering with a newspaper a round table that stands in the room, he places the articles upon it, and asks the guest to sit up and help himself.

The stranger declined, but he noticed that Tug, from his position against the wall, was walking toward the table with his eyes, with first a long step and then a short one, and that at a sign from his friend he walked over hurriedly with his legs, and went to work with a ravenous appetite, putting pieces of meat and bread into his mouth large enough to strangle him. This convinced the stranger that the lunch was really prepared for Tug, and that there would have been disappointment had he accepted the clerk's invitation.

"I don't suppose you care to know it," the clerk said, seating himself, and apparently enjoying the manner in which Tug was disposing of the cold meat, "but my name is Silas Davy. I am what is known as a good fellow, and my father was a good fellow before me. He discovered this town, or located it, or settled here first, or something of that kind, and once had a great deal of property; but, being a good fellow, he couldn't keep it. If you will give me your name, I will introduce you to my friend, Mr. Tug Whittle."

"I don't care to know him," the guest replied, somewhat ill-humoredly, his restless eyes indicating that his thoughts had just returned from a journey out in the world somewhere, as they finally settled on Tug. "I don't like his looks."

Tug looked up at this remark, sighted awhile at the guest with his right eye, and, after swallowing his last mouthful, with an effort, pointed a finger at him, to intimate that he was about to speak.

"Did you see any ragged or sore-eyed people get off the train to-night?" he inquired, in a deep bass voice, still pointing with his bony finger, and aiming along it with his little eye.

The guest acted as though he had a mind not to reply, but at last said he was the only passenger for Davy's Bend.

"I was expecting more of my wife's kin," Tug said, with an angry snort, taking down his finger to turn over the meat-bone, and using his eye to look for a place not yet attacked. "Come to think about it, though, they are not likely to arrive by rail; they will probably reach town on foot, in the morning. They are too poor to ride. I wish they were too sick to walk, damn them. Do you happen to know what the word ornery means?"

The guest acted as though he had a mind not to reply again, but finally shook his head, after some hesitation.

"Well," the ugly fellow said, "if you stay here,—which I don't believe you will, for you look too much like a good one to remain here long,—I'll introduce you not only to the word but to the kin. After you have seen my wife's relations, you'll fight when anybody calls you ornery."

Finding a likely spot on the meat-bone at the conclusion of this speech, Mr. Whittle went on with his eating, and was silent.

"There are a great many people who do not like Tug's looks," the clerk went on to say, without noticing the interruption, and looking admiringly at that individual, as though he could not understand why he was not more generally admired; "so it is not surprising that you are suspicious of him. I do not say it with reference to you, for you do not know him; but my opinion is that the people dislike him because of his mind. He knows too much to suit them, and they hate him."

By this time Tug had wiped up everything before him, and after transferring the grease and pie crumbs from his lips and beard to his sleeve, the three men were silent, listening to the rain on the outside, and taking turns in looking out of the windows into the darkness.

"I suppose the shutters are rattling dismally up at The Locks to-night," Silas Davy said. "And the windows! Lord, how the windows must rattle! I've been told that when there isn't a breath of air the shutters and windows at The Locks go on at a great rate, and they must be at it to-night, for I have never known it to be so oppressive and still before."

"And the light," Tug suggested, removing his aim from the stranger a moment, and directing it toward Davy.

"Yes, the light, of course," Davy assented. "They say—I don't know who says it in particular, but everybody says it in general—that on a night like this a light appears in the lower rooms, where it disappears and is seen in the front hall; then in the upper hall, and then in an upper room, where it goes out finally, as if someone had been sitting down-stairs, in the dark, and had struck a light to show him up to bed. There is no key to the room where the light disappears, and those who visit the house are not permitted to enter it. I have never seen the light myself, but I have been to the house on windy, noisy days, and it was as silent on the inside as a tomb. The windows and shutters being noisy on quiet nights, I suppose they feel the need of a rest when the wind is blowing."

The guest was paying a good deal of attention, and Davy went on talking.

"The place has not been occupied in a great many years. The man who built it, and occupied it, and who owns it now, made money in Davy's Bend, and went away to the city to live, where he has grown so rich that he has never sent for the plunder locked up in the rooms; I suppose it is not good enough for him now, for I am told that he is very proud. He has been trying to sell the place ever since, but Davy began going down hill about that time, and the people have been kicking it so sturdily ever since that nobody will take it. And I don't blame them, for it is nothing more than a nest for ghosts, even if it is big, and respectable-looking, and well furnished."

The guest's mind is evidently in Davy's Bend now, for he has been paying close attention to the clerk as he talks in a modest easy fashion, even neglecting his first ambition to stare Mr. Whittle out of countenance. It may be that he is in need of an establishment, and is looking out for one; but certainly he takes considerable interest in the place Silas Davy referred to as The Locks.

"Who has the renting of the house?" he interrupted the clerk to inquire.

The clerk got up from his chair, and, walking over to that portion of the room where the counter was located, took from a nail a brass ring containing a number of keys of about the same size.

"Here are the keys," Davy said, returning to his chair, and holding them up for inspection. "Number one admits you to the grounds through the iron gate; number two opens the front door; number three, any of the rooms leading off from the hall down stairs; number four, any of the rooms opening off from the hall up stairs; and number five and number six, any of the other rooms. *We* are the agents, I believe, though am not certain; but anyway we keep the keys. The place came to be known as The Locks because of the number of keys that were given to those who applied to see it, and The Locks it has been ever since."

The stranger rose to his feet, and paced up and down the room awhile, thinking all the time so intently that it occurred to Tug that he was puzzled to decide whether his family would consent to live in a place which had the reputation of being visited by a ghost carrying a light.

"I would like to see this house," he said, stopping in his walk finally, and addressing Davy. "I may become a purchaser. Will you show me the way to it, now?"

Up to this time, since polishing the meat-bone, Tug had occupied himself by aiming at the stranger, but as if the suggestion of a walk up to The Locks was pleasing to him, he jumped to his feet, and walked towards the door. Silas Davy made no other reply than to put the ring containing the keys on his arm, and, putting out the light, the three men stepped out into the rain together.

The Locks appear to be located towards the river; not down where the railway train stops to take people on who desire to get away from Davy's Bend, but higher up the street running at right angles in front of the hotel, for the men walk in that direction, Davy and Tug ahead carrying the lantern, with their arms locked together, and the stranger behind, who thinks the two men are a queer pair, for they seem to enjoy being out in the rain, and one of them, the smaller one, laughs frequently but timidly, while the other snorts in a manner which the stranger recognizes as signifying pleasure.

Occasionally they stop to light the stranger's steps on reaching a particularly bad place, and when he has passed it they go on again; up hill and down, toward the river, and when they stop at last, it is so dark that the stranger does not know that they have reached a stone wall with an iron gate opening into an enclosure, until he comes entirely up to them.

The lock turns heavily, and Tug condescends to hold the lantern while Silas applies both hands to the key. Upon the inside a long stone walk, leading toward the house, then a flight of stone steps, and a porch is reached, where they are out of the rain.

Silas selects a key from the collection he carries on his arm, and, once more calling upon Tug to hold the light, opens the door, and they all enter the wide hall.

Considering that the house has not been occupied for eight years, it is in good condition. As they walk through the different rooms, Davy opening the doors from the bunch of keys on his arm, the stranger notices that they are decently furnished, everything being plain and substantial; and he hears for the first time, while standing in front of the door that is not to be opened, that an old lady and her grand-daughter live on the grounds in a detached building, who, when she sees fit, airs and dusts the rooms, and that she has lived there for eight years, in the pay of the owner. This explains the good condition of everything, and they continue their investigation by the dim light of the lantern.

There are ten rooms in all, counting the two in the attic, all of them furnished, from the kitchen to the parlor; and the stranger is so well pleased that he inquires the rent asked, and the purchase price. Silas Davy is not certain as to either, but promises that his proprietor will give full particulars in the morning.

"I will take the house," the stranger finally says, after a lamp has been found and lighted, and seating himself in a chair as an intimation that he is ready for the two men to depart. "If I do not buy it I will rent it, and I will stay here to-night."

Tug is willing to depart at once, but Silas lags behind, and seems to be ill at ease.

"Have you any objection to giving me your name, that I may record it at the house?" he respectfully asks.

"Oh, my name," the stranger returns. "Sure enough; I had forgotten that."

It seems to have escaped him, for while Silas stands waiting, he studies for a long time, contracting his brow until he looks so fierce and savage that Tug, who has been aiming at him from the door, steps out into the hall to get out of the way.

"You may register me as Allan Dorris," he said at last, getting up from his chair, and looking confused, "from Nowhere-in-Particular. It is not important where I am from, so long as I am responsible; and I will convince your proprietor of that in the morning. You will oblige me if you will step over to the quarters of the old lady you spoke of, and inform her that there is a new master at The Locks, and that he has taken possession. When you return I will show you out."

"I neglected to mention," Silas says, after making a note of what the stranger has said on an envelope, "that you can open and close the gate from this room, and lock and unlock it. There is also a speaking-tube leading from this room, whereby you can converse with persons on the outside. I will call you up when I go out. It is located here, behind the door."

The two men step over to examine it, and Tug creeps in to look too, and after sighting at it awhile returns to the hall.

The apparatus consists of an iron lever, with a show of chains running over pulleys and disappearing through the floor, and a speaking-tube. Silas explains that when the lever is up the gate is open, and when it is down the gate is shut and locked. Both men try it, and conclude that, with a little oil, it will work very well, leaving it open so that the men may pass out.

There being no further excuse for remaining, Silas and his ugly friend start down the stairs, the stranger holding the light at the top; and after they have passed out of the door and slammed it to work the spring lock, and tried it to see that it is locked, Allan Dorris returns to the room they have just left.

The grate in the room is filled with wood, and there is kindling at the bottom, probably put there years before, judging by the dust; and the stranger lights this, intending to dry his wet clothing. While about it there is a whistle from the speaking-tube, and going over to it and replying, a sepulchral voice comes to him from somewhere to the effect that Mrs. Wedge, the housekeeper, is delighted to hear that the house is to be occupied at last; that she will call upon the new master in the morning to pay her respects, as well as to make her arrangements for the future; and, good night.

The stranger says good night in return, pulls the lever down, which closes and locks the gate, and returns to the fire, which is burning brightly by this time.

"Allan Dorris, from Nowhere-in-Particular," he mutters after he is seated, and while watching his steaming garments. There is an amused look on his face at first, as he repeats the name, but a frown soon takes its place, that grows blacker as he crouches down into his chair, and looks at the fire.

At length he seems to tire of his thoughts, for he gets up and walks the floor, pausing occasionally to look curiously at the pictures on the walls, or at the carpet, or at the furniture. If he returns to his chair, the frown appears on his face again, and once more he walks to get rid of his thoughts.

This is continued so long that the darkness finally gets tired of looking in at the windows, and hurries away at the approach of day. From time to time, as the light increases, he steps to the window and looks out; and when walking away, after a long look at Davy's Bend through the morning mist, he mutters:—

"Allan Dorris, if you are from Nowhere-in-Particular, you are at home again."

CHAPTER II.

THE LOCKS.

From the southern windows of The Locks, Allan Dorris looked with curious interest the day after his arrival, and the week and the month following, for he remained there for that length of time without going out, except to walk along the country roads for exercise, where he occasionally met wagons containing men who cursed the town they were leaving for its dullness.

The dwellings of Davy's Bend were built upon hills sloping toward the little valley where the business houses were, and which poured a flood of water and mud into the long streets in rainy weather through gaping gullies of yellow clay. The rains seemed to be so fierce and frequent there that in the course of time they had cut down the streets, leaving the houses perching on hills above them, which were reached by flights of steps; and this impression was strengthened by the circumstance that it was a wet time, for it rained almost incessantly.

The houses were a good way apart, so far as he could see from his southern windows; and this circumstance caused him to imagine that the people were suspicious of each other, and he noticed that while many of them had once been of a pretending character, they were now generally neglected; and that there was a quiet air everywhere that reminded him of the country visited in his walks.

The houses themselves appeared to look at him with a cynical air, as the people did, as if to intimate that he need not hope to surprise them with his importance, or with anything he might do, for their quiet streets had once resounded to the tread of busy feet, and they had seen strangers before, and knew the ways of men. Some of the dwellings perching on the hills, deserted now except as to bats and owls, resembled unfortunate city men in a village; for there was a conspicuous air of decayed propriety about them, and an attempt at respectability that would have been successful but for lack of means. These in particular, he thought, made faces at him, and sneered as he passed through their part of the town in his walks to and from the country roads.

Several times he heard parties of men passing his house at night, talking loudly to make themselves heard above the jolting of their wagons; and these usually had something to say about the new owner of The Locks, from which he imagined that there was much speculation in the town concerning him. The house in which he lived was such a gloomy place, and he was shut up in it alone for such a length of time, that he came to listen to the sound of human voices with pleasure, and often went to the windows to watch for the approach of wagons, that he might hear the voices of their occupants; for there were no solitary travellers that way, and while the men may have been dissatisfied with themselves and their surroundings, they at least had company. He longed to join these parties, and go with them to their homes, for he thought the companionship of rough men and their families would be preferable to the stillness of his house; but the wagons drove on, and Allan Dorris returned to his walk across the room, and back again.

From the window most patronized by him in his lonely hours he could see a long stretch of the river, and at a point opposite the town a steam ferry was moored. Usually smoke was to be seen flying from its pipes during the middle hours of the day, as it made a few lazy trips from one shore to the other; but occasionally it was not disturbed at all, and sat quietly upon the water like a great bird from morning until night.

From making excursions about his own premises, as a relief from doing nothing, he found that the house in which he lived was situated in a wooded tract of several acres in extent, entirely surrounded by a high stone wall, with two entrances; one in front, by means of a heavy iron gate, which looked like a prison door, and a smaller one down by the stable. The stable, which was built of brick, had been occupied by pigeons without objection for so many years that they were now very numerous, and protested in reels and whirls and dives and dips in the air against the new owner coming among them at all; perhaps they imagined that in time they would be permitted to occupy the house itself, and rear their young in more respectable quarters. There were a few fruit and ornamental trees scattered among the others, but they had been so long neglected as to become almost as wild as the native oaks and hickories. Occasionally a tall poplar shot its head above the others, and in his idleness Allan Dorris imagined that they were trying to get away from the dampness below, for in the corners, and along the stone wall, there was such a rank growth of vines and weeds that he was almost afraid to enter the dank labyrinth himself. There was a quaking asp, too, which was always shivering at thought of the danger that might be concealed in the undergrowth at its feet, and even the stout hickories climbed a good way into the air to insure their safety.

Close to the south wall, so close that he could almost touch it, stood a stone church, with so many gables that there seemed to be one for every pigeon from the stable, and on certain days of the week someone came there to practise on the organ. At times the music was exquisite, and in his rambles about the place he always went down by the south wall to listen for the organ, and if he heard it he remained there until the music ceased. The music pleased him so much, and was such a comfort in his loneliness, that he did not care to see the player, having in his mind a spectacled and disagreeable person whose appearance would rob the spell of its charm; therefore he kept out of his way, though, on the days when the music could be expected, Dorris was always in his place, impatiently waiting for it to commence. There was something in the playing with which he seemed to have been acquainted all his life; it may have been only the expression of weariness and sad melancholy that belongs to all these instruments, but, however it was, he regarded the organ as an old acquaintance, and took much pleasure in its company even when it was silent, for it occupied a great stone house like himself, and had nothing to do.

Between the stable and the house was the residence of Mrs. Wedge, the housekeeper—a building that had originally been a detached kitchen, but the cunning of woman had transformed the two rooms into a pleasant and cozy place. This looked home-like and attractive, as there were vines over it and flowers about the door; and here Allan Dorris found himself lingering from day to day, for he seemed to crave companionship, though he was ashamed to own it and go out and seek it. Instead of dining in the stone house, he usually sat down at Mrs. Wedge's table, which he supplied with a lavish hand, and lingered about until he thought it necessary to go away, when he tried to amuse himself in the yard by various exercises, which were probably recollections of his younger days; but he failed at it, and soon came back to ask the motherly old housekeeper odd questions, and laugh good-naturedly at her odd answers.

A highly respectable old lady was Mrs. Wedge, in her black cloth dress and snowy white cap, and no one was more generally respected in Davy's Bend. During his life Mr. Wedge had been a strolling agent, never stopping in a town more than a week; and thus she lived and travelled about, always hoping for a quiet home, until her good-natured but shiftless husband took to his bed one day, and never got up again, leaving as her inheritance his blessing and a wild son of thirteen, who knew all about the ways of the world, but nothing of industry. Hearing of Davy's Bend soon after as a growing place,—which was a long time ago, for Davy's Bend was not a growing place now,—she apprenticed her son to a farmer, and entered the service of the owner of The Locks, under whose roof she had since lived.

The wild son did not take kindly to farming, and ran away; and his mother did not hear of him again until four years after she was living alone in The Locks, when a little girl five years old arrived, accompanied by a letter, stating that the son had lived a wanderer like his father, and that the child's mother being dead, he hoped Mrs. Wedge would take care of his daughter Betty until the father made his fortune. But the father never made his fortune; anyway, he never called for the child, and Mrs. Wedge had found in her grand-daughter a companion and a comfort, passing her days in peace and quiet. Therefore when the new owner offered her a home there, and wages besides, in return for her agreement to undertake his small services, she accepted—having become attached to the place—and lived on as before.

The house itself, which was built of stone, and almost square, contained ten rooms; four of about the same size below, and four exactly like them above, and two in the attic or half story in the roof. There were wide halls up stairs and down, and out of the room that Allan Dorris had selected for his own use, and which was on the corner looking one way toward the gate in front, and the other toward the town, began a covered stairway leading to the attic.

In this room he sat day after day, and slept night after night, until he almost became afraid of the quiet that he believed he coveted when he came to Davy's Bend; and at times he looked longingly toward the speaking-tube behind the door, hoping it would whistle an announcement that a visitor had arrived; for his habit of sitting quietly looking at nothing, until his thoughts became so disagreeable that he took long walks about the place to rid himself of them, was growing upon him.

But no visitors came to vary the monotony, except the agent on the morning after his arrival, who received a quarter's rent in advance, and afterwards named a price so low that Allan Dorris bought the place outright, receiving credit for the rent already paid.

Had the dark nights that looked in at Allan Dorris's windows, and for which Davy's Bend seemed to be famous, been able to remark it, there would have been much mysterious gossip through the town concerning his strange actions. Whenever he sat down, his eyes were at once fixed on nothing, and he lost himself in thought; he was oblivious to everything, and the longer he thought, the fiercer his looks became, until finally he sprang from his chair and walked violently about, as if his body was trying to escape from his head, which contained the objectionable thoughts. At times he would laugh hoarsely, and declare that he was better off at The Locks than he had ever been before, and that Davy's Bend was the best place in which he had ever lived; but these declarations did not afford him peace, for he was soon as gloomy and thoughtful as ever. That he was ill at ease, the dark nights could have easily seen had they been blessed with eyes; for the dread of loneliness grew upon him, and frequently he sent for Mrs. Wedge, confessing to her that he was lonely, and that she would oblige him by talking, no matter what it was about.

Mrs. Wedge would politely comply, and in a dignified way relate how, on her visits to the stores to purchase supplies, great curiosity was everywhere expressed with reference to the new master of The Locks,—what business he would engage in; where he came from; and, most of all, there was a universal opinion that he had bought The Locks for almost nothing.

"A great many say they would have taken the place at the price themselves," Mrs. Wedge would continue, smoothing down the folds of her apron, a habit of which she never tired, "but this is not necessarily true. The people here never want to buy anything until it is out of the market; which gives them excuse for grumbling, of which they have great need, for they have little else to do. I believe the price at which you took the house was lower than it was ever offered before,—but that is neither here nor there."

Then Mrs. Wedge would tell of the queer old town, in a quaint way, and of the people, which amused her employer; and noticing that, in his easy chair, he seemed to enjoy her company, she would smooth out her apron once more, and continue:—

"They all agree,"—there would be an amused smile on Mrs. Wedge's face as she said it,—"they all agree that you do not amount to much, else you would have gone to Ben's City, instead of coming here. This is always said of every stranger, for Davy's Bend is so dull that its people have forgotten their patriotism. I have not heard a good word for the town in ten years, but it is always being denounced, and cursed, and ridiculed. I think we despise each other because we do not move to Ben's City, and we live very much as I imagine the prisoners in a jail do,—in cursing our home, in lounging, in idle talk, and in expecting that each one of us will finally be fortunate, while the condition of the others will grow worse. We are a strange community."

Dorris expressed surprise at the size of the church near The Locks, and wondered at the deserted houses which he had seen in his walks, whereupon Mrs. Wedge explained that Davy's Bend was once a prosperous city, containing five thousand busy people, but it had had bad luck since; very bad luck, for less than a fifth of that number now remained, and even they are trying to get away. What is the cause of this decrease in population? The growth of Ben's City, thirty miles down the river. The belief which existed at one time that a great town would be built at Davy's Bend turned out to be a mistake. Ben's City seemed to be the place; so the people had been going there for a number of years, leaving Davy's Bend to get along as best it could.

This, and much more, from Mrs. Wedge, until at a late hour she notices that Dorris is asleep in his chair, probably having got rid of his thoughts; so she takes up the lamp to retire with it. Holding it up so that the shade throws the light full upon his face, she remarks to herself that she is certain he is a good, an honorable, and a safe man, whoever he is, for she prides herself on knowing something about men, and arranging the room for the night, although it does not need it, she goes quietly down the stairs, out at a door in a lower room, and into her own apartment.

CHAPTER III.

THE FACE AT THE WINDOW.

Allan Dorris sleeps on, unconscious of the darkness peering in at him from the outside, which is also running riot in the town, and particularly down by the river, where the crazy houses with their boarded windows seem to collect shadows during the day for use at night, robbing the sunlight for the purpose; for there is little brightness and warmth at Davy's Bend, but much of dampness and hazy atmosphere.

There is light and life down this way; a light in the window of the wretched house occupied by Mr. Tug Whittle, and all the neighboring buildings are alive with rats and vermin. Tug occupies his house for the same reason that the rats occupy theirs, for in this quarter of the town the tenants pay no rent. Some of the buildings were once busy warehouses and stores, but they have been turned over to the rats these ten years, and Tug occupies a little frame one from choice, as he argues that if it falls down from old age, there will not be so many ruins in which to bury the tenants. Besides, the big buildings shelter him from the cold north winds in winter, and do not interfere with the southern breezes from the river in summer; therefore the faded sign of "T. Whittle, Law Office," swings in front of the little frame building back from the street, instead of from the more imposing ones by its side.

Everybody knows Tug Whittle, and admits that he is perfectly harmless and hopelessly lazy—always excepting Silas Davy, who believes that his friend is very energetic and dangerous; therefore when Silas is unable to hold a position because he is a good fellow, or because he spends so much time at night with Tug that he is unfit for work during the day, he is also an inhabitant of the little law office, along with the lawyer and the rats, although it is not much of a law office, for it contains nothing but a stove, half cooking and half heating, a bed that looks as though it came from the fourth story of a cheap hotel, a few broken chairs, a box that is the lawyer's table, and a few other articles common to a kitchen, all of them second-hand, and very poor.

There is nothing about the place to suggest a law office save the sign in front, and a single leather-covered book on the inside; a ponderous volume to which Mr. Whittle applies for everything, including kindling. Silas has seen him look through it to decide questions in science, theology, law, and history, and tear leaves out of it with which to start his fire; and while a cunning man would have guessed that Mr. Whittle made up his authority, instead of finding it in the book, Silas Davy, who is not cunning, believes that it is a repository of secrets of every kind, although it is really a treatise on a law which has been repealed many years. When Silas so far forgets himself as to mildly question something his companion has said, Mr. Whittle refers to the book, and triumphantly proves his position, no difference what it may be; whereupon the little man feels much humiliated. Mr. Whittle has even been known to refer to the book to convict his enemies in Davy's Bend of various offences; and Silas has so much respect for the volume that he has no trouble in imagining that the den in which Tug lives is not only a law office, but a repository of profane, political, and sacred history, to say nothing of the sciences and the town scandal.

Like the rats again, Tug lies by during the day, and goes abroad at night, for he is seldom seen on the streets until the sun goes down, and he is not entirely himself until after midnight. Occasionally, on dark, bad days he is to be seen walking about, but not often, and it is known that he sleeps most of the day on the rough bed in his rough office. If he is disturbed by idle boys, which is sometimes the case, he gets up long enough to drive them away, and returns to his bed until it is dark, when he yawns and stretches himself, and waits patiently for Silas Davy, who is due about that hour with his supper.

But for Silas Davy, like the rats again, Tug would be compelled to steal for a living; for he never works, but Silas believes in him, and admires him, and whenever he is employed, he saves half of what he gets for his friend, who eats it, and is not grateful. Indeed, he often looks at Silas as much as to say that he is not providing for him as well as he should, whereupon Silas looks downcast and miserable; but, all in all, they get along very well together.

Up to the present rainy and wet year of our Lord eighteen hundred and no difference what, Tug has never admired anyone, so far as is known; but he admires Allan Dorris, the new owner of The Locks, and frequently says to Silas that "*There* is a man," at the same time aiming his big eye in the direction Dorris is supposed to be. There is every reason why Tug should admire Silas Davy, who is very good to him, but he does not, except in a way, and which is a very poor way; and there is no reason why he should admire Allan Dorris, who is suspicious of him, but he does, and on this night, Silas having arrived early with his supper, he is killing two birds with one stone, by discussing both at the same time.

"By the horns of a tough bull," Tug says, which is his way of swearing, "but there *is* a man. Muscle, brain, clothes, independence, money; everything. What, no butter to-night?"

He says this impatiently after running through the package his companion has brought, and not finding what he was looking for; and Silas humbly apologizes, saying he could not possibly get it at the hotel.

"Well, no matter," Tug continued in an injured way, using a pickle and two slices of bread as a sandwich. "It will come around all right some day. When I come into my rights, I'll have butter to spare. But this impudent Dorris; I like him. He has the form of an Apollo and the muscle of a giant. If he should hit you, you would fall so fast that your rings would fly off your fingers. He's the kind of a man I'd be if I had my rights."

While Tug is munching away at his supper, Davy remembers how unjust the people are with reference to these same rights; how they say he has none, and never will have, except the right to die as soon as possible. The people say that Tug's wife, the milliner, drove him from her house because he would not work, and because he was ugly in disposition, as well as in face and person; that it was soon found out that he was not so dangerous, after all, when men were talking to him, so they have regarded him as a harmless but eccentric loafer ever since. Some of the people believe that Tug does not appear on the streets during the day for fear of meeting his wife, while others contend that he goes out only at night because he is up to mischief; but neither class care to question him about the matter, for he has a mean tongue in his head, and knows how to defend himself, even though he is compelled to invent facts for the purpose.

But Davy knows that Tug can tell a very different story, and tell it well, and he is sure that there will be a genuine sensation when he finally tells it, and comes into his own.

"What a voice he has, and what a eye," Mr. Whittle goes on to say, throwing a leg over a chair to be comfortable. "I usually despise a decent man because I am not one myself, but this fellow—damn him, I like him."

Silas Davy was the sort of a man who is never surprised at anything. Had he been told on a dark night that it was raining blood on the outside, he would not have disputed it, or investigated it, believing that such storms were common, though they had escaped his observation; therefore he was not surprised that Tug admired Allan Dorris, although he knew he had no reason to.

"I have known people to come here and denounce us for a lack of culture who knew nothing about propriety except to eat pie with a fork," Mr. Whittle said again; "but this Dorris,—I'll bet he practises the proprieties instead of preaching them. He don't remind me of the people who come here and call us ignorant cattle because we do not buy their daub paintings at extravagant prices, or take lessons from them; *he* don't look like the cheap fellows who declare that we lack cultivation because we refuse to patronize their fiddle and pianow concerts, therefore look out for Dorris. He's a man, sure enough; I'll stake every dollar I'm worth and my reputation on it."

Although he had neglected to bring butter, the supper Silas had brought was good enough to put Mr. Whittle in a cheerful humor, and he continued,—

"The people around here put me in mind of the freaks in a dime museum; but Dorris's clothes fit him, and he looks well. There are plenty of men so common that they look shabby in broadcloth, and who are so miserably shaped that no tailor can fit their bones; but this fellow—he would look well with a blanket thrown over his shoulders, and running wild. Hereafter, when I refer to my rights, understand that I would be a Dorris sort of a fellow were justice done me. Did you bring me a drink?"

Silas produced a flask from his pocket, and while Tug was mixing the contents with sugar, by means of stirring them together with a spoon in a tumbler, making a cheerful, tinkling sound the while, he delivered a stirring temperance lecture to his companion. He did this so often that Silas regarded himself as a great drunkard, although that was not one of his failings; but he felt grateful to Tug, who drank a great deal, for his good advice. He was so mortified to think of his bad habits and Tug's worthiness, that he turned his face away, unable to reply.

"Dorris reminds me of a young widow two years after the funeral," Mr. Whittle said, after drinking the dram he had prepared. "Handsome, clean, well-dressed, and attractive. I have an ambition to be a young widow myself, but owing to the circumstance that I have been defrauded of my rights, at present I look like a married woman with six children who does not get along with her husband. In short, I am slouchy, and ill-tempered, and generally unattractive, with an old wrapper on, and my hair down. Ben, come here."

The light in the room was so dim that it had not yet revealed to the eyes of Silas the form of a boy seated on a low box at the side of the room farthest from him, who now came over into the rays of the lamp, and looked timidly at Tug.

Silas knew the boy very well; little Ben Whittle, the son of his friend, who worked on a farm three miles in the country, and who came to town occasionally after dark to see Silas, who treated him well, but always returning in time to be called in the morning; for his employer was a rough man, and very savage to his horses and cattle and boys. Ben was dressed in a coat no longer than a jacket, buttoned tightly around his body, and his pants were so short that they did not nearly touch the tops of his rough shoes. He wore on his head a crazy old hat, through the torn top of which his uncombed hair protruded, and altogether he was such a distressing sight that Davy was always pitying him, although he was never able to do him much good, except to treat him kindly when he came to the hotel at long intervals, and give him something to eat.

"Are you hungry?" Tug inquired, looking sharply at the boy, as he stood cringing before him.

"Yes, sir, if you please."

"Then help yourself," his father roughly returned, crabbed because Ben had told the truth, and pointing to the table; whereupon the boy went to nibbling away at the crumbs and bones remaining of the lunch brought by Silas.

Little Ben was so surprisingly small for a boy of eleven that he was compelled to stand to reach the crumbs and bones, but his father regarded him as a brawny youth as tough as dogwood.

"When I was a boy of his age," Tug said to Davy, "they dressed me up in good clothes, and admired me, and thought I was about the cutest thing on earth, but I wasn't."

Davy looked up as if to inquire what he really was at Ben's age, and received an answer.

"I was an impudent imp, and detested by all the neighbors; that's the truth. My father used to go around town, and tell the people the cute things I said, instead of making me go to work, and teaching me industry; but the people didn't share his enthusiasm, and referred to me as that 'worthless Whittle boy.' Ben, what can you do?"

"I can cut corn, sir, and drive the team, and plough a little," the boy replied, startled by his father's loud voice.

"Anything else?"

"I can't remember everything, sir. I do as much as I can."

Little Ben did not look as though he could be of much use on a farm, for he was very thin, and very weak-looking; but apparently this did not occur to his father, who continued to stare at him as though he wondered at his strength.

"Think of that, will you," Tug continued, addressing Silas again. "He can cut corn, and plough, and all that, and only eleven years old. Why, when he gets to be thirteen or fourteen he will whip old Quade, and take possession of the farm! What could I do when I was eleven years old? Nothing but whine, and I was always at it, although I was brought up in a house with three-ply carpets on the floor, and always treated well. I was treated *too* well, and I intend to make a man out of Ben by seeing that he is treated as mean as possible. Look here, you," he added turning toward the boy, "when old Quade fails to lick you twice a day, get your hat and run for me; and I'll try and make you so miserable that you'll amount to something as a man."

It was the opinion of Davy that Ben was meanly enough treated already, not only by his father, but by the farmer with whom he worked; for no one seemed to be kind to the boy except himself, and he made his long journeys to town for no other reason than to hear Davy's gentle voice. But Davy was afraid to say this to Tug, and in his weakness could do nothing to help him. In the present instance he looked out of the window.

"You are a fortunate boy in one respect, at least," the admiring father said to his son again. "Your mother hates you, and you have a prospect of becoming a man. Many a boy at your age has a good bed to sleep on, and plenty to eat, and will grow up into a loafer; but here you are on the high road to greatness. Had my father been a wise man, as your father is, I might have been a storekeeper now instead of what I am; therefore don't let me hear you complain—I'll give you something to complain about if I do. The ways of Providence may be a little mysterious to you now, you robust rascal; but when the Hon. Benjamin Whittle goes to Congress he will tell the reporter who writes him up that his father was a kind, thoughtful man who did a great deal for him."

There was something more than the darkness peering in at the window when Silas Davy looked that way; a good deal more—a strange man's face, which was flattened against the lower pane. At the moment that Silas saw him, the man seemed to be using his eyes in investigating the other corner of the room, for he did not know for a moment that he was detected. When his gaze met Silas Davy's, he quickly drew away from the window, and disappeared; but not until Silas remarked that it was a swarthy, malicious face, and that cunning and determination were expressed in its features. Silas was not at all astonished at the appearance, as was his custom; but when he looked at Tug again, to pay respectful attention to his next observation, he saw that he, too, had seen the face, for he was preparing to go out.

"Another stranger," Tug said, as he looked for his hat. "We are becoming a great town."

Silas asked no questions, but when his companion stepped into the dirty street, leaving little Ben alone, he followed, and walked a few paces behind him, as he hurried along in the direction of the inhabited portion of the town. As they neared the dismal lamps, and while they were yet in the darkness, they saw the figure of a tall man, enveloped in what seemed to be a waterproof cloak, turn into the main street, which ran parallel with the river, and walk toward the hotel where Davy was employed. But the man wearing the cloak did not stop there, except to examine a scrap of paper under the light; after which he turned again, and walked in the direction of The Locks. Silas and his companion followed, as rapidly as they could, for there were no lights now, and they stumbled over the hills, and into the gullies, until The Locks gate was reached, which they found ajar.

This strange circumstance did not deter them from entering at once, though quietly and with caution, and together they crept up the pavement, and up the front steps, through the front door, which was wide open, and up the stairway, until they stopped in front of the door leading into the room occupied by Allan Dorris.

Everything was still; and as they stood there in the dark, listening, Tug was surprised to find that Davy was in front of him, whereas he had believed that he was in his rear. Likewise Silas Davy was surprised, for while he was sure that Tug had passed him, and gone lightly down the stairs, a moment afterward he put his hand on him, and knew that he was bending over, and listening at the keyhole.

But nothing could be heard except the regular breathing of Allan Dorris as he slept in his chair, although they now realized that the mysterious stranger had passed them on the stairs, and was on the outside; so they crept down the stairs, and into the street, closing the door and gate after them.

Over the hills and into the hollows again; so they travelled back to their retreat down by the river, where they greatly surprised little Ben and the rats by opening the door suddenly and walking in upon them.

Silas dropped down on the bed, and Tug into a chair, where they remained a long time without speaking.

"What do you make of it?" Tug inquired at last.

"Nothing," Silas returned.

There was another long silence, which was finally broken by Tug remarking,—

"I make nothing of it, myself. We are agreed for once."

CHAPTER IV.

DAVY'S BEND.

It was generally agreed among the people of Davy's Bend—a thousand in number, the census said; six hundred they said themselves, for they changed the rule, and exaggerated their own situation unfavorably—that the town possessed more natural advantages than any other in the world.

They demonstrated this with great cleverness, by means of maps drawn on brown wrapping-paper inside of the stores, and, after looking at their maps, they triumphantly exclaimed, with a whack of their fists on the counter, "There are the figures; and figures won't lie." But in spite of their maps showing valleys occupied with railroads (which Capital neglected to build), Ben's City, below them, continued to prosper, whereas Davy's Bend continued to go steadily down the hill.

The people did little else than wonder at this, and curse Capital because it did not locate in a town where nature was lavish in the matter of location, instead of going to a place where it would always find the necessity of contending against odds confronting it. Such a town was Ben's City, in the estimation of those living at Davy's Bend; but they must have been mistaken, for great houses and institutions grew up where little had been planted, and men with money trampled upon each other in their mad haste to take advantage of the prosperity that seemed to be in the air. Those who drew the maps declared that a crash was soon to come, when the capitalists who did not know their own interests would trample upon each other in their haste to get away; but those who bought Ben's City property, no difference at what price, soon sold out again at an advance; and the prosperity of the place was quite phenomenal.

Never was Capital so thoroughly hated as in Davy's Bend. It was cursed a thousand times a day, and shown to be fickle and foolish and ungrateful; for evidences of these weaknesses on the part of Capital abounded on every hand. There were railroads to be built out of Davy's Bend that would pay immensely, as had been demonstrated times without number by the local paper; but Capital stubbornly refused to build them, preferring to earn a beggarly per cent elsewhere. There were manufactories to be built in Davy's Bend that would make their owners rich, as every child knew; but Capital, after a full investigation, was so dull that it could not see the opportunity. The town was alive with opportunities for profitable investments, but Capital, with a mean and dogged indifference, refused to come to Davy's Bend; therefore Capital was hated, and bullied, and cursed, and denounced; and it was generally agreed that it deserved no better fate than to go to ruin in the general crash that would finally overtake Ben's City.

The people of Davy's Bend were a good deal like a grumbling and idle man, who spends the time which should be devoted to improving his condition to grumbling about his own ill luck and the good luck of his industrious rival, who is steadily prospering; and as men frequently believe that the fates are against them when they are themselves their only opposition, so it was generally believed in this wretched little town that some sort of a powerful and alert goddess was in league with Ben's City. While they readily admitted their own points of advantage, even to the extent of giving themselves more credit than they deserved, they refused to be equally fair with their competitor, as men do, and contended, with an ignorant persistency, that Ben's City was prosperous because of "luck," whereas they should have known that there is no such thing, either good or bad.

But, in course of time, when they found that they would always be in the rear, no difference whether they liked it or not, the people of the Bend, in order to more thoroughly denounce their own town for its lack of ability to attract Capital, began to exaggerate the importance of Ben's City. A four-story building there became seven stories high, and those who visited the place vied with each other in giving vivid and untruthful accounts of its growth and prosperity on their return; all of which their acquaintances repeated over and over, though they knew it to be untrue, even adding to the exaggerated statements, in order to bully their own meek town.

Probably they were not proud of the greatness of their rival; for they talked of it as a cowardly man might exaggerate the strength of the fellow who had whipped him, using it as an excuse for defeat. Indeed, they were proud of nothing, except their own accounts of the greatness of Davy's Bend a long while before, when the huge warehouses were occupied, and before Capital had combined against it; of this they talked in a boastful way, magnifying everything so much that many of the listeners who had not heard the beginning of the conversation imagined that they were talking of Ben's City; but of bettering their present condition they had no thought,—by common consent it was so very bad that attempts to become prosperous again were useless, so the Bend was a little worse off every year, like an old and unsuccessful man.

Most of the business men of Davy's Bend had been clerks in the days of the town's prosperity, making their own terms when their energetic employers wanted to get away, and in spite of the general dullness and lack of success, they entertained very good opinions of themselves; for no difference what a citizen's misfortunes were, he loaded them all on the town, and thus apologized for his own lack of ability. But for the circumstance that he was tied to Davy's Bend, he would have been great and distinguished; they all said the same thing, and in order to get his own story believed, every man found it necessary to accept the explanations of the others, or pretend to; so it happened that the people did not hold themselves responsible for anything,—the town in which they lived was to blame for everything that was disagreeable, and was denounced accordingly.

The esteem with which the people regarded themselves was largely due to the manner in which they were referred to in the local paper, a ribald folio appearing once a week. None of the business men were advertisers, but they all gave the publisher free pardon if he referred to them in complimentary terms in his reading columns, and sent in his bill. Thus, the merchant who did not own the few goods he displayed was often referred to as a merchant prince, with an exceedingly shrewd business head on his shoulders. Sometimes notices of this character were left standing from week to week by the shiftless editor; a great number of them would occasionally get together on the same page, referring to different men as the shrewdest, the wisest, the most energetic, etc.; and it was very ridiculous, except to the persons concerned, who believed that the people read the notices with great pleasure.

So great was the passion for puffery among them that designing men who heard of it came along quite frequently, and wrote the people up in special publications devoted to that kind of literature. There would be a pretence that the special edition was to be devoted to the town, but it really consisted of a few lines at the beginning, stating that Davy's Bend had more natural advantages than any other town in the world, and four pages of puffs of the people, at so much per line; whereupon the men made fun of all the notices except their own, believing that its statements were true, and generally accepted as a part of the town's history. A few of those who were able had engravings inserted, and the puff writers, in order to make the notices and bills as large as possible, told how long and how often the subjects had been married; how many children they had, together with their names, where they came from, and much other mild information of this character.

It was known that many of the complimentary sketches were written by the persons to whom they referred; but while Harrisonfield, the grocer, gave wide circulation to the fact that Porterfield, of the dry-goods store, had referred to himself as an intellectual giant, and a business man of such sterling ability that he had received flattering offers to remove to Ben's City, he did not know that Porterfield was proving the same indiscretion with reference to himself.

Every new man who wrote up the town in this manner was more profuse with compliments of the people than his predecessor had been; and finally the common language was inadequate to describe their greatness, and they longed for somebody to come along who could "write," and who could fully explain how much each one was doing for the town; but although they all professed to be doing a great deal constantly for Davy's Bend, there was no reason to believe that any of them were accomplishing anything in this direction, for it could not have been duller than it was in the year of our Lord just referred to.

But there was an exception to this rule, as there is said to be to all others,— Thompson Benton, the merchant; the dealer in everything, as the advertisements on his wrapping-paper stated, for he advertised nowhere else. But he was reliable and sensible, as well as stout and surly; so it was generally conceded that he was the foremost citizen of the Bend.

Not that he made a pretence to this distinction; old Thompson was modest as well as capable, and whatever good was said of him came from the people themselves. Had there been new people coming to Davy's Bend occasionally, it is possible that old Thompson would not have been the leading citizen, for it was said that he "improved on acquaintance," and that people hated the ground he walked on until they had known him a dozen years or more, and found out his sterling virtues; but they had all known him a great many years, and therefore admired him in spite of themselves.

Thompson Benton had been a resident of the town in the days of its prosperity, and ranked with the best of those who had moved away; but he preferred to remain, since he had become attached to his home, and feared that he could not find one which would suit him equally well elsewhere. Besides, he owned precious property in the Davy's Bend cemetery, and lavished upon it the greatest care. Hard though he was in his transactions with men, the memory of his wife was sacred to him; and many believed that, had she lived, he would have been less plain-spoken and matter-of-fact. This devotion was well known; and when the people found it necessary to forgive him for a new eccentricity,—for it was necessary to either forgive him or fight him,—they said he had never recovered his spirits since the day a coffin was driven up to his house.

His store was always open at seven in the morning, and the proprietor always opened it himself, with a great iron key that looked as venerable and substantial as the hale old gentleman whose companion it had been so many years; for it was not a key of the new sort, that might lock up a trifling man's affairs, but a key that seemed to say as plainly as could be that it had money and notes and valuable goods of many kinds in its charge. At six in the evening his store was closed, and the proprietor turned the key, and put it into his pocket. At noon he ate his frugal dinner while seated on a high stool at his desk, and he had been heard to say that he had not eaten at home at midday in fifteen years; for on Sundays he dined in state at five o'clock.

There were no busy days in Davy's Bend, therefore he got along without a clerk, and managed his affairs so well that, in spite of the dulness of which there was such general complaint, he knew that he was a little richer at the close of every day, and that he was probably doing better than many of his old associates who were carrying on business with a great deal of noise and display in Ben's City. Certainly he was reputed to be rich, and those who were less industrious said that he should have retired years before, and given others a chance.

Thompson Benton was known as a plain-spoken man, and if he thought one of his customers had acted dishonestly with him, he said so at the first opportunity, and gruffly hoped it wouldn't happen again; by which he was understood to mean that if it *did* happen again, there would be a difficulty in which the right would triumph. Indeed, he had been known to throw men out of the front door in a very rough manner, two and three at a time; but the people always said he was right, and so it usually turned out, for he was never offended without cause. If an impostor came to the town, the people were fully revenged if he called at Benton's store, for the proprietor told him what he thought of him, and in language so plain that it was always understood.

Thompson Benton's principal peculiarity was his refusal to be a fool. The men who threatened to leave the town because they were not appreciated received no petting from him; indeed, he told them to go, and try and find a place where they would not grumble so much. The successors of the business men who had moved away were always trying to invent new methods as an evidence of their ability, and some of them did not pay their debts because that was an old, though respectable, custom; they rejected everything old, no matter how acceptable it had proved itself, and got along in an indifferent manner with methods invented by themselves, though the methods of their inventing were usually lame and unsatisfactory. For such foolishness as this old Thompson had no charity, as he believed in using the experience of others to his own profit; so he raised his voice against the customs of the town, and though he was usually abused for it, it was finally acknowledged that he was right.

But notwithstanding his austere manner, the people had confidence in old Thompson, and many of the town disputes were left to him. If the people had spare money, they asked the privilege of leaving it in his iron safe (which had belonged to the last bank that moved away), and took his receipt for it. When they wanted it again, it was always ready; and if the Ben's City cracksmen ever came that way to look at the safe, they concluded that the proprietor would prove an ugly customer, for it was never disturbed.

His family consisted of a maiden sister almost as old and odd as himself, and his daughter Annie, who had been motherless since she was five years old. The people said that old Thompson never smiled during the day except when his pretty daughter came in, and that his only recreation was in her society during two hours in the evening, when she read to him, or played, or sang. They were all certain that he was "wrapped up" in her, and it was also agreed that this devotion was not without cause; for a better girl or a prettier girl than Annie Benton was not to be found in all the country round.

The house in which he lived was as stout as brick and mortar could make it; for the people said that he inspected every brick and stick as it was used; and when it was completed, his prudish sister, whom he referred to as the "Ancient Maiden," was equally careful in the furnishing, so that it was a very good house, and kept with scrupulous neatness. The Ancient Maiden's drafts were always honored, for nothing was too good for Thompson Benton's home; and those who went there never forgot the air of elegant comfort which pervaded everything. Though Thompson Benton went down town in the morning with the men who worked by the day, and carried a lunch basket, he dined in the evening in state, surrounded by silver and china both rich and rare; though he worked ten hours a day, and ate a lunch at noon, he slept at night in a bed and in a room which would have rested a king; and his house was as good as any man's need be.

Very early in life Annie Benton learned, somehow, that it had been one of her father's pleasures, when he came home at night, to listen to her mother's piano-playing, when that excellent lady was alive; and, resolving to supply the vacant place, she studied so industriously with the poor teachers the town afforded that at fifteen she was complimented by frequent invitations to play for the glum and plain-spoken merchant. If she selected something frivolous, and played it in bad taste or time, and was not invited to play again for a long while, she understood that her music did not please him, and studied to remedy her fault. In course of time she found out what he wanted, though he never gave her advice or suggestion in reference to it; and he had amply repaid her for all the pains she had been to by saying once, after she had played for him half an hour in a dark room, while he rested on a sofa near her, that she was growing more like her mother every day.

"There were few ladies like your mother, Annie," old Thompson would say, when the girl thanked him for his appreciation. "It pleases me that you remind me of her, and if you become as good a woman as she was, it will be very remarkable, for you have had no mother, poor child, to direct you in her way."

Annie would try harder than ever, after this, to imitate the virtues of the dead woman, and bothered the Ancient Maiden a great deal to find out what she was like. She was not a drone, that much was certain; therefore the daughter was not, and tried to be as useful in the hive as she imagined her mother had been, in every way in which a worthy woman distinguishes herself.

In like manner the girl learned to read to please her father, and every day he brought home with him something he had come into possession of during the day, and which he wanted read; a book, a pamphlet, or a marked paragraph in a newspaper,—he seemed to read nothing himself except business letters; but none of these, or any mention of his affairs, ever came into his home.

Annie Benton's mother had been organist in the big stone church near The Locks, which the first residents had built in the days of their prosperity, and the girl learned from family friends that her father regularly attended both services on Sunday, to hear the music; perhaps there were certain effects possible on the great organ which were not possible on a more frivolous instrument; but it was certain that he never attended after her death until two or three years after his daughter became the organist, and after she was complimented on every hand for her voluntaries before and after the services, and for her good taste in rendering the hymns; for old Thompson was not a religious man, though he practised the principles of religion much better than many of those who made professions.

But one summer morning the girl saw her father come in, and occupy the seat he had occupied before her mother's death, and regularly after that he came early and went away late. Except to say to her once, as they walked home together, that she was growing more like her mother every day, he made no reference to the subject, though he pretended to wonder what the matter was when she threw her arms about his neck after they reached the house, and burst into tears.

One Sunday afternoon he had said to her that if she was going down to the church to practise, he would accompany her, and after that, every Sunday afternoon he was invited to go with her, although she never had practised on Sunday afternoons before. Arriving there, an old negro janitor pumped the organ, and the girl played until she thought her father was tired, when they returned home again, where he spent the remainder of the day alone; thinking, no doubt, of his property in the cemetery, and of the sad day when it became necessary to make the purchase.

CHAPTER V.

A TROUBLED FANCY.

It was Annie Benton's playing which Allan Dorris occasionally heard as he wandered about the yard of The Locks, for she came to the church twice a week in order that she might pretend to practise on Sunday afternoons, and please her father's critical ear with finished playing; and Dorris was so much impressed with the excellence of the music that he concluded one afternoon to look at the performer.

In a stained-glass window looking toward The Locks there was a broken square, little larger than his eye, and he climbed up on the wall and looked through this opening.

A pretty girl of twenty, a picture of splendid health, with dark hair, and features as regularly cut as those of a marble statue, instead of the spectacled professor he expected to see. Allan Dorris jumped down on the outer side of the wall, and, going around to the front of the church, entered the door.

The player was so intent with her work that she did not notice his approach up the carpeted aisle, until she had finished, and he stood almost beside her. She gave a little start on seeing him, but collected herself, and looked at him soberly, as if to inquire why he was there.

"I hope you will pardon me," he said in an easy, self-possessed way, "but I live in the place next door called The Locks, and having often heard you play of late, I made bold to come in."

"All are welcome here," the girl replied, turning the leaves of the book before her, and apparently paying little attention to Dorris. "You have as much right here as I, and if I can please anyone with my dull exercises, I am glad of the opportunity."

Allan Dorris seated himself in a chair that stood on the platform devoted to the choir, and observed that the girl had splendid eyes and splendid teeth, as well as handsome features.

"Do you mind my saying that I think you are very pretty?" he inquired, after looking at her intently as she turned over the music.

Allan Dorris thought from the manner in which she looked at him that she had never been told this before, for she blushed deeply, though she did not appear confused.

"I don't say it as a compliment," he continued, without giving her an opportunity to reply; "but I enjoyed the playing so much that I was afraid to look at the performer, fearing he would be so hideously ugly as to spoil the effect; but you are so much handsomer than I expected that I cannot help mentioning it."

"You are a surprise to me, too," the girl replied, avoiding the compliment he had paid her, and with good nature. "I imagined that the new occupant of The Locks was older than you are."

There was a polite carelessness in his manner which indicated that he was accustomed to mingling with all sorts of people; for he was as much at his ease in the presence of Annie Benton as he had been with Mrs. Wedge, or with Silas and Tug.

"I am so old in experience that I often feel that I look old in years," he replied, looking at the girl again, as though about to repeat his remark concerning her beauty. "I am glad I do not appear old to you. You have returned my compliment."

The girl made no other reply than to smile lightly, and then look intently at her music, as an apology for smiling at all.

"How old are you?" he asked abruptly.

Annie Benton looked a little startled at the question, but replied,——

"Twenty."

"Have you a lover?"

This seemed to require an indignant answer, and she looked at him sharply for that purpose, when she discovered that there was not a particle of impudence in his manner, but rather a friendly interest. He made the inquiry as an uncle might, who had long heard of a pretty niece whom he had never met; so she compromised the matter by shaking her head.

"That's strange," he returned. "It must be because the young men are afraid of you, for you are about the prettiest thing of any kind I have ever seen. It is fortunate that you live in Davy's Bend; a more intelligent people would spoil you with flattery. Will you be kind enough to play for me?"

The girl was rather pleased than offended at what he said, for there was nothing of rudeness in his manner; and when she had signified her willingness to grant his request, he went back to the pews, and sat down to listen to the music. When the tones of the organ broke the silence, Dorris was satisfied that the girl was not playing exercises, for the music was very beautiful, and rendered with excellent judgment.

Her taste seemed to run in the direction of extravagant chords and odd combinations; the listener happened to like the same sort of thing, too, and the performance had such an effect upon him that he could not remain in his seat, but walked softly up and down the aisle. The frown upon his face was very much like that which occupied it when he walked alone in his own room, after permitting himself to think; for there were wild cries in the music, and mournful melodies. When it ceased, he walked up to the player, and asked what she had been playing.

"I don't know myself," she answered, looking at him curiously, but timidly, as if anxious to know more of him. "It was a combination of many of the chords I have learned from time to time that pleased me. My father, who is a very intelligent man, likes them, and I thought you might. It was made up from hymns, vespers, anthems, ballads, and everything else I have ever heard."

"The performance was very creditable, and I thank you for the pleasure you have afforded me," he said. "Would you care if I should seat myself here in this chair while you play, and look at you?"

The girl laughed quietly at the odd request, and there was a look of mingled confusion and pleasure in her face as she replied,—

"I wouldn't care, but I could not play so well."

"Then I will go back to the pews; I don't wish to interfere with the music. If you don't mind it, I will say that I think you are very frank and honest, as well as pretty and accomplished. Many a worse player than you are would have claimed that the rare combination of chords I have just heard was improvising."

"It is my greatest fault," the girl answered, "to let my fancy and fingers run riot over the keys, without regard to the instructions in the book, and of which I am so much in need. The exercises are so dull that it is a great task for me to practise them; but I never tire of recalling what I have learned heretofore, and using the chords that correspond with my humor. I have played a great deal, lately, with The Locks in my mind, for I have heard much of you, and have known of the strange house all my life. Perhaps I was thinking of you when you were listening."

"If you will close up the book, and think about me while you are playing, I will go back to the door, and listen. The subject is not very romantic, but it is lonely enough, Heaven knows. I should think the old organ might have sympathy with me, and do the subject justice, for it is shut up from day to day in a great stone house, as I am."

Allan Dorris went back by the door, and the organ was still for such a length of time that he thought it very correctly represented the silence that hung over his house like a pall; but finally there was the thunder of the double-bass, and the music began. The instrument was an unusually good one, with a wide range of effects in the hands of such a player as Annie Benton proved to be; and Allan Dorris thought she must have learned his history somehow, and was now telling it to whoever cared to listen. Dirges! The air was full of them, with processions of mourning men and women. The girl seemed to have a fondness for odd airs, played in imitation of the lower and middle registers of the voice, with treble accompaniment, and the listener almost imagined that a strong baritone, the voice of an actor in a play, was telling in plain English why Allan Dorris, the occupant of The Locks, came to Davy's Bend, and why he was discontented and ill at ease.

The actor with the baritone voice, after telling everything he knew, gave way for a march-movement, and a company of actors, representing all the people he had ever known, appeared before him under the magic of the music. Some of them looked in wonder, others in dread and fear, as they passed him in procession; but the march kept them going, and their places were soon taken by others, from the store in his memory, who looked in wonder, and in dread and fear, at the strange man in the back pew, though he was no stranger to them. Not by any means; they knew him very well. What an army! They are still coming, flinging their arms to the time of the march; but the moment they arrive they look toward the back pew, and continue looking that way, until they disappear; as though they have been looking for him, and are surprised at his presence in that quiet place. After a pause, to arrange the stops, the music sounded as if all those who had appeared were trying to make their stories heard at once. Their hatred, their dread, their fear,—all were represented in the chords which he was now hearing, but in the din there was nothing cheerful or joyous. If any of the actors in the play he had been witnessing knew anything to the credit of Allan Dorris, their voices were so mild as to be drowned by the fiercer ones with stories of hate and fear and dread.

The music at last died away with the double-bass, as it began, and the player sat perfectly still after she had finished; nor did Dorris move from his position for several minutes.

The music seemed to have set them both to thinking, for nothing could be heard for a long time except the working of the bellows; for the old janitor was so deaf that he did not know that the music had ceased.

"What have you heard about The Locks?" he asked, after he stood beside the girl, feeling as though there was nothing concerning him which she did not know; for she had expressed it all in the music.

"Everything about The Locks, and a great deal about you," she answered.

"I didn't suppose that you had ever heard of me. Who talks about me?"

"The people."

"What do they say?"

"I wouldn't care to tell you all they say," she answered; "for in a dull town, like this, a great deal is said when a mysterious man arrives, and takes up his residence in a house that has been regarded with superstitious fear for twenty years."

She was preparing to go out now, and he respectfully followed her down the aisle.

"Whatever they say," he said, when they were standing upon the outside, "there was a great deal more than art in the piece you dedicated to me. You know, somehow, that I am lonely, and thoroughly discontented. Do the people say that?"

"No."

"Then how did you know it?"

"I saw it in your manner. Anyone could see that."

"A perfectly contented man would become gloomy were he to live long in that house," he replied, pointing to The Locks. "When the stillness of night settles upon it there never was a scene in hell which cannot be imagined by those so unfortunate as to be alone in it. I believe the wind blows through the walls, for my light often goes out when the windows and doors are closed; and there is one room where all the people I have ever known seem collected, to moan through the night. Did you ever hear about the room in The Locks into which no one is permitted to look?"

"No."

"Even the new owner was asked to give a promise not to disturb that room,—it adjoins the one I occupy,—or look into it, or inquire with reference to it; and if I look ill at ease, it must be because of the house I occupy. I am sincerely obliged to you for the music. May I listen to you when you practise again?"

"Certainly," she answered. "I could not possibly have an objection."

She bowed to him, and walked away, followed by the limping negro janitor, who turned occasionally to look at Dorris with distrust.

CHAPTER VI.

PICTURES IN THE FIRE.

Allan Dorris was seeing pleasant pictures in the cheerful fire which burned in his room, for he watched it intently from early evening until dusk, and until after the night came on.

The look of discontent that had distinguished his face was absent for the first time since he had occupied the strange old house. Perhaps a cheerful man may see pleasant pictures in a fire which produces only tragedies for one who is sad; for it is certain that Allan Dorris had watched the same fire before, and cursed its pictures, and walked up and down the room in excitement afterward with clenched fists and a wicked countenance. But there was peace in his heart now, and it could not be disturbed by the malicious darkness that looked in at his windows; for the nights were so dark in Davy's Bend that they seemed not an invitation to rest, but an invitation to prowl, and lurk, and do wicked things.

When Mrs. Wedge brought in the lamp, and put it down on the mantel, he did not look up to say a cheerful word, as was his custom, but continued gazing into the fire; and she noticed that he was in better humor than he had ever been before during their acquaintance. Usually his thinking made him frown, but to-night he seemed to be enjoying it.

The worthy woman took pleasure in finding excuses to go to his room as often as possible, for he seemed to bless her for the intrusion upon his loneliness; but for once he did not seem to realize her presence, and he was thinking more intensely than usual.

Mrs. Wedge had come to greatly admire the new occupant of The Locks. That he was a man of intelligence and refinement there was no doubt; she believed this for so many reasons that she never pretended to enumerate them. Besides being scrupulously neat in his habits, which was a great deal in the orderly woman's eyes, he was uniformly polite and pleasant, except when he was alone, when he seemed to storm at himself.

There was a certain manly way about him—a disposition to be just to everyone, even to his housekeeper—that won her heart; and she had lain awake a great many nights since he had come to The Locks, wondering about him; for he had never dropped the slightest hint as to where he came from, or why he had selected Davy's Bend as a place of residence.

She often said to herself that a bad man could not laugh as cheerfully as Allan Dorris did when he dropped in at her little house to spend a half-hour, on which occasions he talked good-humoredly of matters which must have seemed trifling to one of his fine intelligence; and she was certain that no one in hiding for the commission of a grave offence could have captured the affections of Betty as completely as he had done, for the child always cried when he returned to his own room, or went out at the iron gate to ramble over the hills, and thought of little else except the time when she could see him again.

Mrs. Wedge had heard that children shrink from the touch of hands that have engaged in violence or dishonor, and watched the growing friendship between the two with a great deal of interest.

Mrs. Wedge believed that he had had trouble of some kind in the place he came from, and that he was trying to hide from a few enemies, and a great many friends, in Davy's Bend; for Mrs. Wedge could not believe that anyone would select Davy's Bend as a place of residence except under peculiar circumstances; but she always came to the same conclusion,—that Allan Dorris was in the right, whatever his difficulty had been. She watched him narrowly from day to day, but he never gave her reason to change her mind— he was in the right, and in the goodness of her heart she defended him, as she went about her work.

"Were it Betty's father come back to me, instead of a stranger of whom I know nothing," the good woman would say aloud, as she swept, or dusted, or scoured in her little house, "I could not find less fault with him than I do, or be more fond of him. I know something about men, and Allan Dorris is a gentleman; more than that, he is honest, and I don't believe a word you say."

"Grandmother," the child would inquire in wonder, "who are you talking to?"

"Oh, these people's tongues," Mrs. Wedge would reply, with great earnestness, looking at Betty as though she were a guilty tongue which had just been caught in the act of slandering worthy people. "I have no patience with them. Even Mr. Dorris is not free from their slander, and I am tired of it."

"But who says anything against Mr. Dorris, grandmother?"

Sure enough! Who had accused him? No one, save his friend Mrs. Wedge, unless his coming to Davy's Bend was an accusation; but she continued to defend him, and declared before she went to sleep every night; "I'll think no more about it; he is a worthy man, of course."

But whatever occupied his thoughts on the evening in question, Allan Dorris was not displeased to hear an announcement, from the speaking-tube behind the door, of visitors, for they were uncommon enough; and going to it, a voice came to him from the depths announcing that Silas and Tug were at the gate, and would come up if he had no objection. Pulling the lever down, which opened the gate, he went down to admit them at the door, and they came back with him.

During his residence in the place he had met the two men frequently, for they took credit to themselves that he was there at all, since his coming seemed to please the people (for it gave them something to talk about, even if they did not admire him); and when he returned to his house in the evening, he often met the strange pair loitering about the gate. He had come to think well of them, and frequently invited them to walk in; but though they apparently wanted to accept his invitation, they acted as though they were afraid to: perhaps they feared he would lose the little respect he already entertained for them on acquaintance. But they had evidently concluded to make him a formal call now, induced by friendliness and curiosity, for they were smartened up a little; and it had evidently been arranged that Silas should do the honors, for Tug kept crowding him to the front as they walked up the stairs.

Apparently Tug did not expect a very warm reception at The Locks, for he lagged behind, and sighted at Allan Dorris with his peculiar eyes, as though he had half a mind to try a shot at him; and when he reached the landing from the level of which the doors opened into the rooms of the second story, he looked eagerly and curiously around, as if recalling the night when he traced the shadow there, but which had escaped him.

Allan Dorris invited both men into the apartment he usually occupied, and there was a freedom in his manner that surprised them both. The pair had decided to visit him from a curiosity that had grown out of their experience with the shadow; and although they expected to find him stern and silent, and angered at their presence, he was really in good humor, and seemed glad to see them; perhaps he was so lonely that he would have welcomed a visit from a ghost. They both noticed that the ragged beard which he had worn on his face when he first arrived was now absent; for he was clean shaven, and this made him appear ten years younger. He looked a good deal more like a man in every way than he did on the night of his arrival, when he sat moping in the hotel office; and Silas and Tug both wondered at the change, but they were of one mind as to his clean face; it was a disguise.

Tug's suit of black glistened more than ever, from having been recently brushed; and as soon as he had seated himself, he set about watching Allan Dorris with great persistency, staring him in the face precisely as he would look at a picture or an ornament. Silas seated himself some distance from the fire, and seemed greatly distressed at his friend's rudeness.

"I like you," Mr. Whittle said finally, without moving his aim from Dorris's face.

- 39 -

Dorris seemed amused, and, laughing quietly, was about to reply, when Tug interrupted him.

"I know you don't like me, and I admire you for it, for every decent man despises me. I am not only the meanest man in the world, but the most worthless, and the ugliest. My teeth are snags, and my eyes are bad, and my breath is sour, and I am lazy; but I like you, and I tell you of it to your teeth."

Tug said this with so much seriousness that his companions both laughed; but if he understood the cause of their merriment, he pretended not to, for he said,—

"What are you laughing at?" glaring fiercely from one to the other. "I am not trying to be funny. I hate a funny man, or a joky man. I have nothing for a funny man but poison, and I have it with me."

Dorris paid no more attention to his fierce companion than he would to a growling dog, and continued laughing; but Silas shut up like a knife, as Tug took from his vest pocket a package carefully wrapped in newspaper, and after looking at it a moment with close scrutiny, continued,—

"Whenever you find me telling jokes, expect me to giggle at my own wit, and then pour the contents of this package on my tongue, and swallow it; and it will be no more than I deserve. I have but one virtue; I am not funny. You have no idea how I hate the low persons who advertise themselves as comedians, or comediennes, or serio-comic singers, or you would not accuse me of it."

Silas had often seen this package before, for Tug had carried it ever since they had been acquainted, frequently finding it necessary to renew the paper in which it was wrapped. From certain mysterious references to it Tug had dropped, Silas believed the powder was intended for a relative more objectionable than any of the others, though he occasionally threatened to use it in a different manner, as in the present instance. Indeed, he seemed to carry it instead of a knife or a pistol; and Silas had noticed on the night when they were following the shadow that his companion carried the package in his hand, ready for instant use.

"You are the kind of a man I intended to be," Tug continued, putting away his dangerous package with the air of a desperado who had been flourishing a pistol and took credit to himself for not using it. "I might have been worthy of your friendship but for my wife's relations, but I admire you whether you like it or not. Do your worst; I am your friend."

Tug had not taken his huge eye from Dorris's face since entering, except to look at the poison; but he removed it as Mrs. Wedge came in to prepare the table for the evening meal.

Dorris was a good deal like Tug in the particular that he did not sleep much at night, but he slept soundly when the morning light came up over the woods to chase away the shadows which were always looking into his window; therefore he frequently ate his breakfast at noon, and his supper at midnight.

There was a roast of beef, a tea urn, a pat of butter, and a loaf of bread, on the platter carried by the housekeeper, while Betty followed with the cups and saucers, and the potatoes, the napkins, and the sugar.

"I am obliged to you for your good opinion," Dorris said, while the cloth was being laid, "and if you will remain to supper with me, we will become better acquainted."

It occurred to Silas that Dorris looked at Tug, in spite of his politeness, as he might look at an amusing dog that had been taught to catch a bacon rind from off his nose at the word of command, and wondered that Tug felt so much at home as he seemed to; for he was watching the arrangements for supper with great eagerness. Silas was sure the invitation to supper would be accepted, too, for Tug had never refused an invitation of any kind in his life, except invitations to be a man and go to work, which the people were always giving him.

At a look from Dorris, Mrs. Wedge went out, and soon returned with additional plates, besides other eatables that seemed to be held in reserve; and during her absence the master had been placing the chairs, so that by the time the table was arranged, the three men were ready to sit down, which they did without further ceremony. Among other things Mrs. Wedge brought in a number of bottles and glasses, which were put down by the side of Dorris, and these now attracted the aim of Tug.

"If you offer us drink," he said, "I give you fair warning that we will accept, and get drunk, and disgrace you. We haven't a particle of decency, have we, you scoundrel?"

This, accompanied by a prodigious poke in the ribs, was addressed to Silas Davy, who had been sitting meekly by, watching the proceedings. Tug had a habit of addressing Silas as "his dear old scoundrel," and "his precious cut-throat," although a milder man never lived; and he intently watched Dorris as he opened one of the bottles and filled three of the glasses. Two of them were placed before Tug and Silas, and though Silas only sipped at his, Tug drank off the liquor apportioned to him greedily. This followed in rapid succession, until two of the bottles had been emptied, Dorris watching the proceedings with a queer satisfaction.

He also helped them liberally to the roast beef and the gravy, and the potatoes, and the bread and butter, to say nothing of the pickles and olives;

but Tug seemed to prefer the liquor to the tea, for he partook of that very sparingly, though he was anxious to accept everything else offered; for he occasionally got up from the table to tramp heavily around the room, as if to settle that already eaten to make room for more.

Allan Dorris enjoyed the presence of the two men, and encouraged the oddities of each by plying them with spirits. Although the drink had little effect on Silas, who was very temperate, Tug paid tribute to its strength by opening his wide eye to its greatest extent, as if in wonder at his hospitable reception, and closing the other tighter, like a man who had concluded to give one side of his body a rest.

As the evening wore away, and the liquor circulated more freely through his blood, Tug recited, between frequent snorts, what a man he had been until he had been broken up and disgraced by his wife's relations, Silas earnestly vouching for it all, besides declaring that it was a shame, to which their host replied with enthusiasm that it was an outrage that such a bright man and such a good-looking man as Tug had been treated so unjustly, at the same time filling up the glasses, and proposing that they drink to the confusion and disgrace of the relations. Neither of them seemed to realize that Dorris was making game of them; for Tug listened to all he said—and he said a great deal—with an injured air that was extremely ludicrous; and when Davy related that when Mr. Whittle was in practice, the judges begged the favor of his opinion before rendering their decisions on difficult legal questions, Dorris regretted that he had not known the judges, for he felt sure that they were wise and agreeable gentlemen. But at the same time Dorris felt certain that if he should be invited to attend the man's funeral, he would laugh to himself upon thinking how absurdly dignified he must look in his coffin.

Silas had never known Tug when he was great, of course, for he had flourished in the time of Silas's father; but he nevertheless believed it, and seemed to have personal knowledge of the former magnificence of the rusty old lawyer. Indeed, but few of the present inhabitants of Davy's Bend had known Tug when he was clean and respectable, for he always claimed that his triumphs were triumphs of the old days, when Davy's Bend was important and prosperous, and among the energetic citizens who had moved away and made decay possible.

"I don't amount to anything except when I am drunk—now," Tug said, getting on his feet, and taking aim at his host, "but fill me with aristocratic liquor, and I am as cute as the best of them. Have you ever heard the story of the beggar on horseback? Well, here he is, at your service. Will the rich and aristocratic owner of this house oblige the beggar by pouring out his dram? Ha! the beggar is at full gallop."

Dorris good-naturedly obeyed the request, and while Tug was on his feet, his aim happened to strike Silas.

"Silas, you greatest of scoundrels," he said, "you thoroughly debased villain, loafer, and liar, I love you."

Reaching across the table, Tug cordially shook hands with his friend, who had been doing nothing up to that time save enjoying Tug's humor, and indorsing whatever he said. Whether Silas enjoyed being called a scoundrel, a villain, a loafer, and a liar, is not known, but he certainly heard these expressions very frequently; for Tug seemed to tolerate him only because of his total and thorough depravity, though the other acquaintances of Silas regarded him as a mild-mannered little man without either vices or virtues.

"I have but two friends," Tug said again, seating himself, and gazing stiffly at his host, "Rum and Davy; rum cheers me when I'm sad, and Davy feeds me when I'm hungry, though the splendid thief does not feed me as well as he might were he more industrious. Rum has a bad reputation, but I announce here that it is one of my friends. I am either ravenously hungry, or uncomfortable from having eaten too much, all the time, so that I do not get much comfort from victuals; but rum hits me just right, and I love it. You say it will make me drunk. Very well; I *want* to get drunk. If you argue that it will make me reckless, I will hotly reply that I *want* to be reckless, and that a few bottles will make me as famous as a lifetime of work and success will make a sober man. Therefore I hail rum as my best friend, next to the unscrupulous rascal known for hailing purposes, when there are boots to be polished, or errands to run, as Hup-avy."

The eminent legal mind hurriedly put his hand to his mouth, as though thoroughly humiliated that he had hiccoughed, and, looking at Dorris with the air of a man who commits an unpardonable indiscretion and hopes that it has not been noticed, continued with more care, with a great many periods to enable him to guard against future weakness.

"Although I have but two friends, I have a host of enemies. Among them Tigley. My wife's cousin. When I was a reputable lawyer, Tigley appeared in Davy's Bend. Tigley was a fiddler. And spent his time in playing in the beer halls for the drinks. The late Mrs. Whittle believed him to be a great man. She called him a mastero, though he played entirely by ear; and excused his dissipation on the ground that it was an eccentricity common to genius. If Tigley ever comes in my way again there will be something to pay more disagreeable than gold. He taught me to like rum."

Silas, who acted as a kind of chorus, intimated to Dorris that his friend referred to a word of four letters beginning with an "h," and ending with an "l."

"That's *one* reason why I am a drunkard," the victim of too many relatives added, after a moment's thought. "The other is that I could never talk up to the old women except when I was drunk, and it was necessary to talk up to her so often that I finally craved spirits."

Tug crooked his elbow and produced the package from his vest pocket, which he waved aloft as an intimation that Tigley's nose should be held, when next they met, until he swallowed its contents.

"By-the-way," Tug said, as if something new had occurred to him, "I warn you not to believe anything I say; I lie because I enjoy it. Drinking whiskey, and lying, and loving Davy, are my only recreations. Then there was Veazy Vaughn, the Vagrant—my wife's uncle—he is responsible for my idleness. When he came here, twenty odd years ago, I tried to reclaim him, and went around with him; but he enjoyed vagrancy so much, and defended his position so well, that I took a taste of it myself. I liked it. I have followed it ever since."

There was not the slightest animation about Tug, and he sat bolt upright like a post while he talked with slow and measured accent, to avoid another hiccough, and his great eye was usually as motionless as his body.

"The late Mrs. Whittle treated her relatives so well that other worthless people who were no kin to her began to appear finally, and claim to be her cousins and nieces and nephews," Tug said. "And she used my substance to get up good dinners for them. They came by railroad. By wagon. On foot. And on horseback. I was worse than a Mormon, for I married a thousand, at least, on my wedding-day. Some of them called me 'Uncle W,' while others spoke of me as their 'Dear Cousin T;' but when the last dollar of my money was invested in dried beef, and the relatives had eaten it, I protested, and then they turned me out. The relations have my money, and I have their bad habits. I have nothing left but the poison, and they are welcome to that."

He once more produced the package, and as he laid it on the table, Dorris half expected to see a troop of ill-favored people come dashing in, grab up the paper, and run away with it. But none of them came, and Tug went on:

"I was a polite man until my wife's relations made me selfish. We always had gravy when they were around, and good gravy at that; but by the time I had helped them all, there was none left for me. I now help myself first. Will the Prince pass the Pauper the fresh bottle of rum?"

The bottle was handed over, and the rare old scoundrel helped himself to a full glass of its contents, drinking as deliberately as he had talked, apparently taking nine big swallows without breathing, at the same time thinking of the one he loved the best, as a means of curing the hiccoughs.

"I like Mrs. Wedge," Tug said, looking at that excellent woman with a tipsy grin, as she came into the room with some new delicacy for her employer's guests. "She looks so common, somehow, and I don't believe she knows any more about manners than I do. Whenever you see her eating her dinner, you'll find that she puts her arms on the table, as I do, though it's not polite. Polite things are not natural, in my opinion; mind I don't assert it as positive. I hate cold water, but it's polite to bathe; and your respectable shirt-collars rub all the hide off my neck. And anything that's good for me, I don't like. There's oatmeal, and graham grits, and such like—they are healthy, therefore I don't like their taste; but give me milk gravy, or salt risin' bread, or fried beef, or anything else that's not good for me, and you'll find me at home, as the man who had the party said on his cards."

During this discourse Mr. Whittle's great eye was following Mrs. Wedge about the room, but when she disappeared it lit on Dorris.

"I'm with the crowd, though, when it comes to my wife's kin," he said, eyeing his host in an impudent way. "A good many don't say so; but it makes them all hot to fill their houses with their relations. Whenever you go to see your relations, depend upon it that they are glad when you are gone. They may pretend to like you, but they don't, except when you are away from them. But in all other respects I'm common. Common! I'm so common that I like boiled cabbage; and the olives you blow about—I'd as soon eat green pignuts soaked in brine. *Common!*" He yelled out the words as though he were calling some one of that name in the cellar. "If men were judged by their commonness, I would be a chief with plumes in my hat."

Allan Dorris and Silas Davy were seated with their backs to the windows overlooking the town, while Tug sat opposite them, and in transferring his gaze from one to the other, in dignified preparation for resuming his conversation, which both his companions were enjoying, he saw the mysterious face he had seen once before peering into the room, and which was hastily withdrawn.

Tug jumped up from his chair at sight of it, and hurried to the window with such haste that the table was almost upset; but the face, as well as the figure to which it belonged, had disappeared. Throwing up the sash, Tug found that he could step out on to a porch, and from this he dropped into the yard with a great crash through the vines and lattice-work. Silas Davy quickly followed, by way of the stairs, suspecting the cause of Tug's disappearance; and Dorris was left alone.

All this had occupied but a few moments, and he probably thought of the circumstance as one of the many eccentricities of the two odd men; for after pulling down the lever to close the gate (it is a wonder that he was not surprised to find it open) he sat down before the fire and engaged in the pleasant thoughts that were interrupted early in the evening.

Silas did not come up with Tug until he reached the vicinity of the hotel, where a single street lamp burned all night, and while they were hurrying along without speaking, the figure they were pursuing passed quickly on the opposite side of the street from the hotel. The rays of the lamp were so feeble that the figure was only a shadow; but they easily recognized it as the one seen before—that of a man above the medium height, enveloped in a long cloak, not unlike those worn by women in wet weather, with a slouch hat pulled down over his face.

The two men hurried after it, but in the darkness they were frequently compelled to stop and listen for the footsteps of the pursued, in order to detect his course. Each time the echoes were more indistinct, for the fellow was making good use of his legs; and in this manner they traced his course to the river bank, near the ferry landing, where the ferry-boat itself was tied up for the night. They concluded that the fugitive had a skiff tied there somewhere, which he intended to use in leaving the place, and, hurrying on board the ferry-boat, they rapped loudly at the door of the little room on the upper deck where the crew usually slept, with a view of procuring means of following.

The fellow who had charge of the ferry, a native of the low lands lying along the river, was known as "Young Bill Young," although he greatly desired that the people call him "Old Captain Young;" therefore both men pounded vigorously on the door, and loudly called "Captain Young," as a tribute to his vanity. "Captain Young" soon appeared, for he always slept in a bunk with his clothes on, which he said reminded him of his sea days, although he had never really seen any other water than that on which he operated his ferry. As the two hurriedly explained to him that they wanted a boat, Young Bill Young went to the lower deck, and unlocked one that floated at the stern, and soon Tug and his friend were pulling down the river with long strokes, for there were two pairs of oars. Occasionally they stopped rowing to listen, but nothing could be heard save the gentle ripple of the current; whereupon they worked with greater vigor than before.

They had rowed in this manner for an hour or more, when, stopping to listen again, the plash of oars was indistinctly heard on the water ahead of them. Lying down in the prow of the boat, Tug could see the boat and its occupants low down on the water, between him and the first rays of light of the coming morning. There was a heavy fog on the river, which was lying close to the water, but this had lifted sufficiently to permit an inspection through the rising mist. There were two figures in the boat; one rowing, who was evidently the man they had twice seen looking in at them, and the other a much smaller person, who was seated in the stern, and steering. This fact Tug regarded as so remarkable that he told Davy to lie down, and take a look, and when Davy returned to his oars, after a long inspection, he said:—

"I make out two."

"A big one and a little one," Tug replied, bending to the oars, and causing the boat to hurry through the water. "Earn your supper up at The Locks, and I'll introduce you to them."

On the left hand a smaller stream put into the main river, and at its mouth there was an immense growth of willows, besides a chute, an island, and a bend. Into this labyrinth the boat they were pursuing effectually disappeared; for though Tug and Silas rowed about until broad daylight they could find no trace of it or its occupants.

A short distance up the smaller stream was a lonely station on a railroad that did not run into Davy's Bend, and while rowing around in the river, the roar of an approaching train was heard, and the fact that this stopped at the station, with a blast from the engine-whistle indicating that it had been signalled, may have been important; but it did not occur to either Silas or Tug, who pulled their boat back to town in silence.

CHAPTER VII.

THE LOCKS' GHOST.

There was general curiosity in Davy's Bend with reference to the new occupant of The Locks, and when the people had exhausted themselves in denouncing their own town more than *it* deserved, and in praising Ben's City more than it deserved, they began on Allan Dorris, and made him the subject of their gossip.

Whoever was bold enough to invent new theories with reference to him, and express them, was sure of a welcome at any of the houses where the speculation concerning his previous history went on from day to day; and, this becoming generally known, there was no lack of fresh material for idle tongues. Whenever he walked into the town, he knew that the stores turned out their crowds to look at him, and that in passing the residences which were occupied, the windows were filled with curious eyes. But although there were a hundred theories with reference to him, it was only positively known that he one day appeared at his gate, two months after his arrival, and tacked up a little sign on which was inscribed in gold letters:

DR. DORRIS.

This curiosity of the people brought Dr. Dorris a great deal of business, for many of them were willing to pay for the privilege of seeing him, and he applied himself to practice with such energy that he was soon in general demand. As the people knew more of him, their curiosity became admiration; and many of them defended him from imaginary charges as warmly as did Mrs. Wedge, for there was every reason that the people should admire him, except that he had located at Davy's Bend.

That he was skilful and experienced as a physician became apparent at once, and it was therefore generally believed that he was only there temporarily; for certainly no one who was really capable would consent to remain long in Davy's Bend.

His heart was not in his work; this was a part of the gossip concerning him, though it is difficult to imagine how the idea originated; for he appeared to be pleased when he was called out at night, as though the companionship of even those in distress suited him better than the solitude of his own house; but though he was always trying to be cheerful, he could not disguise the fact that his mind was busy with matters outside of his work. Perhaps this was the excuse of the people for saying that his heart was not in his work, and the charge may have been true. While busy, he gave whatever was in hand careful and intelligent attention, but as soon as he was idle again, he forgot his surroundings, and permitted his mind to wander—nobody knew where.

When addressed, he good-naturedly remembered that he was in Davy's Bend, and at the service of its people, and did whatever was expected of him with so much gentleness and ability that he won all hearts. This was his brief history during the summer following his arrival, except as shall be related hereafter.

The sun, which had been struggling for mastery over the mist and the fog, had triumphed after a fashion, and the pleasanter weather, and his business, served to make him more cheerful than he had been; and had he cared to think about such matters, the conviction would no doubt have forced itself upon his mind that he was doing well, and that he had every reason to feel contented, though he was not.

Still there were times when he was lonely in spite of his rather busy life, and nights when he sent for Mrs. Wedge and Betty to keep him company; for there were strange sounds through his house, when the summer air was still and oppressive, and the doors and windows rattled in the most unaccountable manner.

Thus it came about that they were with him one night long after their usual time to retire, Dorris being particularly nervous and restless, and having asked them to come up to his room rather late in the evening.

Mrs. Wedge had told him of Annie Benton a dozen times already, but she made it a baker's dozen, and told him again of her simple history; of her popularity in the town, though the people all seemed to be shy of her, and of her gruff father, who, in Mrs. Wedge's opinion, would resent the appearance of a lover in the most alarming manner. Mrs. Wedge thought she observed that Dorris was fond of this subject, and kept on talking about it; for he was paying close attention as he lounged in his easy chair. Dorris laughed in such a way at the accounts of Thompson Benton's jealousy of his daughter that Mrs. Wedge believed that he regarded him as he might regard a growling mastiff, which growled and snapped at whoever approached, knowing it was in bad taste and not expected of him.

Mrs. Wedge was sure her employer was not afraid of old Thompson,—or of any one else, for that matter,—so she added this declaration to the great number she was constantly making in his defence, and repeated it to herself whenever he was in her mind.

She was pleased with the circumstance that he admired Annie Benton, and though she said a great deal in her praise, it was no more than the truth, for she was a girl worthy of admiration and respect. But the subject was exhausted at last, and when she got up to go out, Dorris roused himself from one of his reveries, and asked her to tell him the history of The Locks, as a last resort to induce her to keep him company.

The worthy woman seated herself again, smoothed down the folds of her apron, and began by saying,—

"Betty, open the door leading into the hall."

The child did as she was directed, and, coming back, brought up a low chair, and rested her head on her grandmother's knee.

"Listen," Mrs. Wedge said again.

They were all perfectly quiet, and a timid step could be distinctly heard on the stair; it came up to the landing, and, after hesitating a moment, seemed to pass into the room into which no one was to look. The little girl shivered, and was lifted into her grandmother's lap, where she hid away in the folds of her dress.

Dorris was familiar with this step on the stair, for he had heard it frequently, and at night the thought had often occurred to him that some one was in the house, going quietly from one room to another. A great many times he had taken the light, and looked into every place from the cellar to the attic, but he found nothing, and discovered nothing, except that when in the attic he heard the strange, muffled, and ghostly noises in the rooms he had just left.

"It is not a ghost to frighten you," Mrs. Wedge said, looking at her employer, "but the spirit of an unhappy woman come back from the grave. Whenever the house is quiet, the step can always be heard on the stair, but I have never regarded it with horror, though I have been familiar with it for a great many years. I rather regard it as a visit from an old friend; and before you came I often sat alone in this room after dark, listening to the footsteps.

"Jerome Dudley, who built The Locks, was a young man of great intelligence, energy, and capacity; but his wife was lacking in these qualities. Perhaps I had better say that he thought so, for I never express an opinion of my own on the subject, since they were both my friends. I may say with propriety, however, that they were unsuited to each other, and that both knew and admitted it, and accepted their marriage as the blight of their lives. Differently situated, she would have been a useful woman; but she was worse than of no use to Jerome Dudley, as he was contemptible in many ways towards her in spite of his capacity for being a splendid man under different circumstances.

"The world is full of such marriages, I have been told; so I had sympathy for them both, and was as useful to them as I could be. When I came here as housekeeper, I knew at once that they were living a life of misery, for they occupied different rooms, and were never together except at six o'clock dinner.

"Mr. Dudley always went to his business in the morning before his wife was stirring, and did not return again until evening; and, after despatching his dinner, he either went back to his work, or into his own room, from which he did not emerge until morning. He was not a gloomy man, but he was dissatisfied with his wife, and felt that she was a drawback rather than a help to him.

"The management of the house was turned over to me completely, and when I presided at the table in the morning, he was always good-natured and respectful, (though he was always out of humor when his wife was in the same room with him) and frequently told me of his successes, and he had a great many, for he was a money-making man; but I am sure he never spoke of them to his wife. His household affairs he discussed only with me, and the fact that I remained in his service until I entered yours should be taken as evidence that I gave satisfaction."

Dorris bowed respectfully to Mrs. Wedge in assent, and she proceeded,—

"Mrs. Dudley spent her time in her own room in an indolent way that was common to her, doing nothing except to look after her little girl, who was never strong. The child was four years old when I came, and the father lavished all his affection upon it. He had the reputation of being a hard, exacting man in his business, and gave but few his confidence, which I think was largely due to his unsatisfactory home; and I have heard him say that but two creatures in all the world seemed to understand him—the child, and myself. It was a part of my duty to carry the child to its father's room every night before putting it to bed; and though I usually found him at a desk surrounded with business papers, he always had time to kiss its pretty lips if asleep, or romp with it if awake.

"While the mother cheerfully turned over the household affairs to me entirely, she was jealous of the child, and constantly worried and fretted with reference to it. The father believed that his daughter was not well cared for, in spite of the mother's great affection, for she humored it to its disadvantage; and I have sometimes thought that the child was sick a great deal more than was necessary. From being shut up in a close room too much, it was tender and delicate, and when the door was open, it always went romping into the hall until brought back again, which resulted in a cold and a spell of sickness. This annoyed Mr. Dudley, and from remarks he occasionally made to me I knew he believed that if the little girl should die, the mother would be to blame.

"'It would be better if she had no mother,' he was in the habit of saying. When children are properly managed, they become a comfort; but if a foolish sentiment is indulged in, the affections of the parents are needlessly lacerated, and they become a burden. I say this with charity, and I have become convinced of it during my long life. Little Dudley was managed by the mother with so much mistaken affection that she was always a care and a burden.

- 51 -

Instead of going to bed at night, and sleeping peacefully until morning, as children should, she was always wakeful, fretful, and ill, and Mr. Dudley's rest was disturbed so much that I thought he had some excuse for his bad humor; for nothing is so certain as that all this was unnecessary. The child was under no restraint, and was constantly doing that which was not good for her, and though her mother protested, she did nothing else.

"Because the father complained of being disturbed at all hours of the night, the mother accused him of heartlessness and of a lack of affection, but he explained this to me by saying that he only protested because his child was not cared for as it should be; because that which was intended as a blessing became an irksome responsibility, and because he was in constant dread for its life.

"Whether the mother was to blame or not will perhaps never be known; but it is certain that the child died after a lingering illness, and the father was in a pitiful state from rage and grief. He did not speak to his wife during the illness, or after the death, which she must have accepted as an accusation that she was somehow responsible; for she soon took to her bed, and never left it alive except to wearily climb the stairs at twelve o'clock every night, to visit the child's deserted room,—the room next to this, and into which no one is permitted to look. Her bed was on the lower floor, in the room back of the parlor, and every night at twelve o'clock, which was the hour the child died, she wrapped the coverings about her, and went slowly up the stairs, clinging to the railing with pitiful weakness with one hand, and carrying the lamp with the other.

"I frequently tried to prevent her doing this; but she always begged so piteously that I could not resist the appeal. She imagined, poor soul, that she heard the child calling her, and she always asked me not to accompany her.

"One night she was gone such a long time that at last I followed, and found her dead, kneeling beside her child's empty crib, and the light out. Mr. Dudley was very much frightened and distressed; and I think the circumstance hastened his departure from Davy's Bend, which occurred a few weeks later. He has never been in the house since.

"It is said that once a year—on the third of May—at exactly twelve o'clock at night, a light appears in the lower room, which soon goes out, and appears in the hall. A great many people have told me that they have seen the light, and that it grows dimmer in the lower hall, and brighter in the upper, until it disappears in the room where the empty crib still stands, precisely as if it were carried by some one climbing the stair. It soon disappears from the upper room, and is seen no more until another year rolls round. I have never seen the light, but I have often heard the step. Sometimes it is silent for months together, but usually I hear it whenever I am in the main house at night. Just before there is a death in the town, or the occurrence of any serious accident, it goes up and down with unvarying persistency; but there is a long rest after the death or the accident foretold has occurred."

When Mrs. Wedge had ceased talking, there was perfect silence in the room again, and the footsteps were heard descending the stair. Occasionally there was a painful pause, but they soon went on again, and were heard no more.

"Poor Helen," Mrs. Wedge said, wiping her eyes, "how reluctantly she leaves the little crib."

Mrs. Wedge soon followed the ghost of poor Helen down the stair, carrying Betty in her arms; and as Dorris stood on the landing lighting them down, he thought, as they passed into the shadow in the lower hall, that poor Helen had found her child, and was leaving the house forever, content to remain in her grave at last.

CHAPTER VIII.

A REMARKABLE GIRL.

Annie Benton had said that she usually practised once a week in the church; and during the lonely days after his first meeting with her, Allan Dorris began to wonder when he should see her again. The sight of her, and the sound of her voice, and her magic music, had afforded him a strange pleasure, and he thought about her so much that his mind experienced relief from the thoughts that had made him restless and ill at ease. But he heard nothing of her, except from Mrs. Wedge, who was as loud in her praise as ever; though he looked for her as he rode about on his business affairs, and a few times he had walked by her father's house, after dark, and looked at its substantial exterior.

There was something about the girl which fascinated him. It may have been only the music, but certainly he longed for her appearance, and listened attentively for notice of her presence whenever he walked in his yard, which was his custom so much of late that he had worn paths under the trees; for had he secured all the business in Davy's Bend he would still have had a great deal of time on his hands.

During these weeks he sometimes accused himself of being in love with a girl he had seen but once, and laughed at the idea as absurd and preposterous; but this did not drive thoughts of Annie Benton out of his mind, for he stopped to listen at every turn for sounds of her presence. After listening during the hours of the day when he was not occupied, he usually walked in the path for a while at night, hoping it might be possible that she had changed her hours, and would come to practise after the cares and duties of the day were over. He could see from his own window that the church was dark; but he had little to do, so he took a turn in the path down by the wall to convince himself that she was not playing softly, without a light, to give her fancy free rein. But he was always disappointed; and, after finding that his watching was hopeless, he went out at the iron gate in front, and walked along the roads until he recovered from his disappointment sufficiently to enter his own home.

This was his daily experience for several weeks after his first meeting with the girl, for even the Sunday services were neglected for that length of time on account of the pastor, who was away recruiting his health; when one afternoon he heard the tones of his old friend the organ again. Climbing up on the wall, and looking at the girl through the broken window, he imagined that she was not playing with the old earnestness, and certainly she frequently looked toward the door, as if expecting someone. Jumping down from the wall, he went around to the front door, which he found open, and entered

- 54 -

the church. The girl heard his step on the threshold, and was looking toward him when he came in at the door leading from the vestibule.

"I seem to have known you a long time," he said, as he sat down near her, after exchanging the small civilities that were necessary under the circumstances, "and I have been waiting for you as anxiously as though you were my best friend. I have been very busy all my life, and I don't enjoy idleness, though I imagined when I was working hard that I would relish a season of rest. I have little to do here except to wait for you and listen to the music. Had you delayed your coming many days longer I should have called on you at your home. You are the only acquaintance I have in the town whose society I covet."

There was no mistaking that the girl had been expecting him, and that she was pleased that he came in so promptly. Her manner indicated it, and she was perfectly willing to neglect her practice for his company, which had not been the case before. She was better dressed, too; and surely she would have been disappointed had not Dorris made his appearance.

Annie Benton, like her father, improved on acquaintance. She was neither too tall nor too short, and, although he was not an expert in such matters, Dorris imagined that her figure would have been a study for a sculptor. A woman so well formed as to attract no particular comment on first acquaintance, he thought; but he remarked now, as he looked steadily at her, that there was a remarkable regularity in her features. There are women who do not bear close inspection, but Annie Benton could not be appreciated without it. Her smile surprised every one, because of its beauty; but the observer soon forgot that in admiring her pretty teeth, and both these were forgotten when she spoke, as she did now to Dorris, tiring of being looked at; for her voice was musical, and thoroughly under control:

"I have dreaded to even pass The Locks at night ever since I can remember," she said with some hesitation, not knowing exactly how to treat the frankness with which he acknowledged the pleasure her presence afforded him, "and I don't wonder that anyone living in it alone is lonely. They say there is a ghost there, and a mysterious light, and a footstep on the stair; and I am almost afraid to talk about it."

Allan Dorris had a habit of losing himself in thought when in the midst of a conversation, and though he said he had been waiting patiently to hear the music, it did not arouse him, for the girl had tired of waiting for his reply, and gone to playing.

Now that he was in her presence he did not seem to realize the pleasure he expected when he walked under the trees and waited for her. Perhaps he was thinking of the footstep on the stair, which he had become so accustomed to that he thought no more of it than the chirping of a cricket; but more likely he was thinking that what he had in his mind to say to the girl, when alone, was not at all appropriate now that he was with her.

"An overture to 'Poor Helen,'" Dorris thought, when he looked up, and heard the music, after coming out of his reverie; for it was full of whispered sadness, and the girl certainly had that unfortunate lady in her mind when she began playing, for she had spoken of her tireless step on the stair; and when he walked back to the other end of the church, he thought of the pretty girl in white, at the instrument, as a spirit come back to warn him with music to be very careful of his future.

Where had the girl learned so much art? He had never heard better music, and though there was little order in it, a mournful harmony ran through it all that occasionally caused his flesh to creep. She was not playing from notes, either, but seemed to be amusing herself by making odd combinations with the stops; and so well did she understand the secret of the minors that her playing reminded him of a great orchestra he had once heard, and which had greatly impressed him.

Where had this simple country-girl learned so much of doubt, of despair, and of anguish? Allan Dorris thought that had *his* fingers possessed the necessary skill, *his* heart might have suggested such strains as he was hearing; but that a woman of twenty, who had never been out of her poor native town, could set such tales of horror and unrest and discontent to music, puzzled him. The world was full of hearts containing sorrowful symphonies such as he was now listening to, but they were usually in older breasts, and he thought there could be but one explanation—the organist was an unusual woman; the only flower in a community of rough weeds, scrub-oaks, and thistles, wind-sown by God in His mercy; a flower which did not realize its rarity, and was therefore modest in its innocence and purity. But her weird music; she must have thought a great deal because of her motherless and lonely childhood, for such strains as her deft fingers produced could not have been found in a light heart.

"There are few players equal to you," he said, standing by her side when she finally concluded, and looked around. "A great many players I have known had the habit of drowning the expert performance of the right hand with the clumsy drumming of the left; but you seem to understand that the left hand should modestly follow and assist, not lead, as is the habit of busy people. There are many people who have devoted a lifetime to study, surrounded with every advantage, who cannot equal you. I am an admirer of the grand organ, and have taken every occasion to hear it; but there is a natural genius about your playing that is very striking."

"No one has ever told me that before," she replied, turning her face from him. "I have never been complimented except by the respectful attention of the people; and father once said I could play almost as well as my mother. Your good opinion encourages me, for you have lived outside of Davy's Bend."

Well, yes, he *had* lived outside of Davy's Bend, and this may have been the reason he now looked away from the girl and became lost to her presence. He did not do this rudely, but there was a pathetic thoughtfulness in his face which caused the girl to remain silent while he visited other scenes. Perhaps Allan Dorris is not the only man—let us imagine so, in charity—who has lived in other towns, and become thoughtful when the circumstance was mentioned.

"If there is genius in my playing, I did not know it, for it is not the result of training; it comes to me like my thoughts," the girl finally continued, when Dorris looked around. "When you were here before, you were kind enough to commend me, and say that a certain passage gave evidence of great study and practice. I am obliged to you for your good opinion, but the strains really came to me in a moment, and while they pleased me, I never studied them."

The girl said this with so much simple earnestness that Allan Dorris felt sure that his good opinion of her playing would not cause her to practise less in the future, but rather with an increased determination for improvement.

"I think that your playing would attract the attention of the best musicians," he said. "The critics could point out defects, certainly, for a great many persons listen to music not to enjoy it, but to detect what they regard as faults or inaccuracies; but the masters would cheerfully forgive the faults, remembering their own hard experience, and enjoy the genius which seems to inspire you. I only wonder where you learned it."

"Not from competent teachers," she replied, as though she regretted to make the confession. "The best music I ever heard was that of the bands which visit the place at long intervals. I have seldom attended their entertainments, but my father has listened with me when they played on the outside, and we both enjoyed it. All that I know of style and expression I learned from them. I once heard a minstrel band play in front of the hall, on a wet evening, when there was no prospect of an audience, and there was such an air of mournfulness in it that I remember it yet. It is dreadful to imitate minstrel music in a church, but you have spoken so kindly of my playing that I will try it, if you care to listen."

They were both amused at the idea, and laughed over it; and after Dorris had signified his eagerness to hear it, and reached his favorite place to listen, the back pew, he reclined easily in it, and waited until the stops were arranged.

The music began with a crash, or burst, or something of that kind, and then ran off into an air for the baritone. This was the girl's favorite style of playing, and there was really a very marked resemblance to a band. There was an occasional exercise for the supposed cornets, but the music soon ran back into the old strain, as though the players could not get rid of the prospect of an empty house, and were permitting the baritone to express their joint regrets. The accompaniment in the treble was in such odd time, and expressed in such an odd way, that Dorris could not help laughing to himself, although he enjoyed it; but finally all the instruments joined in a race to get to the end, and the music ceased. He started up the aisle to congratulate the player, and when half way she said to him:

"At another time I heard a band coming up from the river. The players seemed to be in better spirits that day"—

A distant march, and a lively one, came from the organ, and surely there were banners in front of the players. The music gradually became louder, and finally the girl said,—

"Now it turns the corner of the street."

Then came a crash of melody, and Dorris was almost tempted to look out of the window for the procession that he felt sure was passing. It was just such an air as a band-master might select to impress the people favorably on his first appearance in a town; and every member did his best until the grand finale, which exhausted the powers of the organ.

When the girl turned round, Dorris was laughing, and she joined him in it.

"It is a dreadful thing for a girl to do," she said, though her face indicated that she did not think it was so dreadful, after all, and that she enjoyed it; "but when father comes to hear me practise, he insists on hearing the band pieces; and he sometimes calls for jigs, and quadrilles, and waltzes, and imitations of the hand-organ. The hand-organs, with their crippled players, have been of great use to me, for their music is all well arranged, and father says that if I can equal them he will be very proud of me. Please don't laugh at the idea, for father never says anything that is silly, and he knows good music when he hears it. I know it is the fashion to make light of the barrel-organ; and the people talk a great deal about bribing the players to leave town; but father says a great many customs are not founded in good sense, and perhaps this is one of them. We so rarely find innocent pleasure that we should be free to enjoy it, no matter what it is, or where found, whether custom happens to look on approvingly or not."

"I am glad you said that," Dorris returned, "for I enjoy coming here to listen to your practising, and whether the world approves or not, I intend to come whenever there is opportunity, and you do not object. It is my opinion that you have never been appreciated here, and I will repay you for the music by fully and thoroughly appreciating it. Do you know that you are a remarkable girl?"

Dorris was a bold fellow, the girl thought, but there was nothing offensive in his frankness. He seemed to say whatever occurred to him, without stopping to think of its effects.

"It never occurred to me," she said.

"Really and truly?"

"Really and truly," she replied. "If there is merit in my playing, I might have lived all my life without finding it out, but for you."

"Then let me be the first to tell you of it. You are very pretty, and you have talent above those around you. I hear that your father is a very sensible man; he no doubt appreciates what I have said, but dreads to tell you of it, fearing you will become discontented, and lose much of the charm that is so precious to him. The friends of Cynthia Miller force themselves into the belief that you are no handsomer than she, and that your playing is no better than her drumming. All the other Davy's Bend maids have equally dull and enthusiastic friends; but I, who have lived in intelligent communities, and am without prejudice, tell you that I have never seen a prettier girl in my life. You have intelligence and capacity, too. Mrs. Wedge has told me the pretty story of how you became an organist, and I admire you for it. Some people I have known were content to be *willing* to do creditable things, and came to believe in time that they had accomplished all they intended, without really accomplishing anything; but I admire you because you do not know yourself how much of a woman you are; at least you make no sign of it. I am glad to be the first to do justice to a really remarkable woman."

The remarkable woman was evidently surprised to hear this; for she was very much flustered, and hung her head.

"If a girl as pretty and intelligent as you are," he continued, "should fall in love with me, I believe I should die with joy; for a girl like you could find in her heart a love worth having. I don't know what I should do under such circumstances, for I have had no experience; but I imagine I should be very enthusiastic, and express my enthusiasm in some absurd way. No one ever loved me, that I can remember; for as a child I do not believe I was welcome to the food I ate, though I was not more troublesome than other children who receive so much attention that they care nothing for it. I have been indignant at men for beating their dogs, and then envied the love the brutes displayed while the smart was yet on their bodies. It has so chanced that the dogs I have owned were well treated and ungrateful, and finally followed off some of the vagrants who were hard masters. I have thought that they despised me because they were fat and idle, believing these conditions to be uncomfortable, having never experienced poverty and hard treatment; but certainly they regarded me with indifference and suspicion. But I didn't try to force them to admire me; I rather kept out of their way; for an animal cannot be driven to love his master, and you cannot force or persuade a man to admire any one he dislikes."

"It is possible that you only imagine it," the girl said. "Such doubts as you express have often come to me, but I have comforted myself with the poor reflection that there is so little love in the world that when it is divided among the people, it does not amount to as much as they wish. I know nothing of your situation, past or present, but is it not possible that everyone has the same complaint that you have?"

"There is force in your suggestion," he replied thoughtfully, "but I do not believe that I overdraw my condition; I know too much of real wretchedness to permit myself to worry over fancied wrongs. I hope I am too sensible to weave an impossible something out of my mind, and then grieve because of a lack of it. I might long for something which does not exist, but so long as I am as well off as others, I will be as content as others; but when I have seen that which I covet, and know that I am as deserving as others who possess my prize, its lack causes me regret which I can shake off, but which, nevertheless, is always in my mind. This regret has no other effect than to make me gloomy, which no man should be; I can get it out of my actions when I try, but I cannot get it out of my mind. Happiness is not common, I believe; for I have never known a man or woman who did not in some way excite my pity on closer acquaintance, but owing to a strange peculiarity in my disposition, I have always felt the lack of honest friendship. This is my malady, and perhaps my acquaintances pity me because of it, as I pity them because of their misfortunes. It must be that I have a disagreeable way about me, and repel friendship, though I am always trying to be agreeable, and always trying to make friends. I have little ambition above this; therefore I suppose it may be said that I am no more unfortunate than others who have greater ambitions, and fail in them. I have been told that men who have great success find friends a bother and a hindrance; so it comes about that we are all disappointed, and I am no worse off than others. How old are you?"

"I shall be twenty on my next birthday; you asked me that before."

"A little too old to become my pupil," he continued, "but let me say that if you are as contented as you look, make no experiments in the future; pursue the course you have already pursued as long as you live, and never depart from it. If you are given to dreaming, pray for sound slumber; if you occasionally build castles, and occupy them, extol your plain home, and put aside everything save simplicity, honesty, and duty. There is nothing out in the great world, from which I came, which will afford the happiness you know here. I know everything about the world except the simplicity and peace of your life, and these are the jewels which I seek in Davy's Bend. The road leading from this town is the road to wretchedness, and I have heard that those who have achieved greatness would scatter their reputation to the quarters from whence it came for the quiet contentment you know. Many lives have been wrecked by day dreaming, by hope, by fancy. Pay attention only to the common realities. If you feel that there is a lack in your life, attack it as an evil, and convince yourself that it is a serious fault; an unworthy notion, and a dangerous delusion."

"Must all my pretty castles come tumbling down, then?" she said, in a tone of regret. "Can this be the sum of life, this round of dull days? This dreaming which you say is so dangerous—I have always believed it to be ambition—has been the only solace of my life. I have longed so intensely to mingle with more intelligent people than we have here, that I cannot believe it was wrong; I almost believe you are dangerous, and I will leave you."

She walked half way down the aisle, as if intending to go out, but as Dorris did not move, and continued looking at the floor, she came back again.

"That is what you ought to do—go away and never come into my presence again," he said, raising his eyes and looking into her face. "That was a good resolve; you should carry it out."

Annie Benton looked puzzled as she asked why.

"Because every honest sentiment I ever expressed seemed wrong, and against the established order. The friendship of the people does not suit me—neither does their love; and, miserable beggar though I am to feel dissatisfied with that which The King offers, I am not content with it. I wander aimlessly about, seeking—I know not what. A more insignificant man than I it would be difficult to find; but in a world of opulence, this mendicant, this Prince Myself, finds nothing that satisfies him. A beggar asking to be chooser, I reject those things that men prize, and set my heart upon that which is cheap but impossible. Sent into the world to long for an impossibility, I have fulfilled my mission so faithfully that I sometimes wonder that I am not rewarded for it. *You* must not follow a path that ends in such a place."

He pointed out of the window, and the girl thought he referred to The Locks; certainly it was not a cheerful prospect.

"For you, who are satisfied with everything around you, and who greet every new day for its fresh pleasures, I am a dangerous companion, for my discontent is infectious. And though I warn you to go away, you are a suspicion of that which I have sought so long. Your music has lulled me into the only peace I have ever known; but principle—which has always guided me into that which was distasteful—demands that I advise you to keep out of my company, though I cannot help hoping that you will not heed the advice."

"I regret that what you say—that I am contented with everything around me—is not true," the girl replied, "but though I am not, and wish I were, I do not repine as you do. You are the gloomiest man I ever knew."

"Not at all gloomy," he answered. "Listen to my laugh. I will laugh at myself."

Surely such a good-natured laugh was never heard before; and it was contagious, too, for the girl joined him in it, finally, though neither of them knew what they were laughing about.

"I seldom afflict my friends with melancholy," he said, "for I am usually gay. Gay! I am the gayest man in the world; but the organ caused me to forget. It's all over now; let's laugh some more."

And he did laugh again, as gayly as before; a genteel, hearty laugh it was, and the girl joined him, as before, though she could not have told what she was laughing about had her life depended upon it, except that it was very funny that her companion was laughing at nothing. The different objects in the church, including the organ, seemed to look at the pair in good humor because of their gayety; perhaps the organ was feeling gay itself, from recollections of the minstrel band.

"It makes me feel dreadfully gay to think you are going home presently, and that I am to return to my cheerful room in The Locks, the gayest house in the world. Bless you, there is no ghost's walk about that place, and the sunshine seems to be brighter there than anywhere else in the town. I leave it with regret, and return to it with joy; and the wind—I can't tell you what pleasing music the wind makes with the windows and shutters. But if you will let me, I will walk home with you, although I am dying with impatience to return to my usual gayety. I wish it would rain, and keep you here a while longer. I am becoming so funny of late I must break my spirit some way."

It was now dusk, and the girl having signified her willingness to accompany him, they walked out of the church, leaving the old janitor to lock the door, which he probably did with unusual cheerfulness, for Dorris had given him an amount of money that was greater than a month's wages.

"They say here that if Thompson Benton should see a gentleman with his daughter," Dorris said, as they walked along, "that he would give it to him straight. I suppose they mean, by that, that he would tell him to clear out; but I will risk it."

"They say a great many things about father that are unjust," the girl answered, "because he does not trifle. Father is the best man in the world."

"The lion is a dear old creature to the cub," he replied, "but I am anxious to meet this gentleman of whom I have heard so much, so you had better not invite me in, for I will accept. A lion's den would be a happy relief to the gayety of The Locks, where we go on—the spectres and I—in the merriest fashion imaginable."

Dorris seemed determined to be gay, and as they walked along he several times suggested another laugh, saying, "now, all together," or, "all ready; here we go," as a signal for them to commence, in such a queer way that the girl could not help joining.

"I am like the organ," he said, "gay or sad, at your pleasure. Just at present I am a circus tune, but if you prefer a symphony, you have only to say the word. I am sorry, though, that you cannot shut a lid down over me, and cause me to be oblivious to everything until you appear again. Something tells me that the stout gentleman approaching is the lion."

They were now in the vicinity of the home of the Bentons', and the girl laughingly replied that the stout gentleman was her father. By the time they reached the gate, he was waiting for them, and glaring at Dorris from under his shaggy eyebrows. Annie presented the stranger to her father, who explained who he was, and said that, having been attracted by the music in the church, he had taken the liberty of walking home with the player.

"I have the habit myself," old Thompson grunted, evidently relieved to know that Dorris was not a lover, and looking at him keenly.

He held the gate open for the girl, who walked in, and then closed it, leaving Dorris on the outside. He raised his hat, wished them good night, and walked away, and he imagined when he looked back that the girl was standing at the door looking after him.

CHAPTER IX.

THE "APRON AND PASSWORD."

The guests at the hotel, with their dull wit and small gossip, had disappeared, and the proprietor was seated at the long table in the dining-room, eating his supper, with no companion save Silas Davy, the patient man-of-all-work.

A queer case, the proprietor. Instead of being useful to the hotel, as would naturally be expected, he was a detriment to it, for he did not even come to his meals when they were ready, making a special table necessary three times a day, greatly to the disgust of Mrs. Armsby, who did about everything around the place, from tending the office to superintending the kitchen; and she succeeded so well in all these particulars that occasional strangers had been known to familiarly pat her husband on the back, and congratulate him on keeping a house which was known far and near for its fine attention to guests.

Armsby did not drink, or gamble, or anything of that kind, but he owned a gun and a hunting dog, and knew exactly when the ducks appeared in the lakes, and when the shrill piping of quail might be expected in the thickets; and he was usually there, in his grotesque hunting costume, to welcome them. In addition to this he was fond of fishing, and belonged to all the lodges; so that he had little time to attend to business, even had he been inclined that way.

Mrs. Armsby regarded the men who sold powder and fishing-tackle, and encouraged the lodges, about as many another sad-hearted woman regards the liquor-sellers; and, as she went wearily about her work, had been heard to wonder whether hunting and fishing and lodge-going were not greater evils than drinking; for she had no use for her husband whatever, although he was a great deal of trouble. He never got out of bed without being called a dozen times, but when he did get up, and was finally dressed (which occupied him at least an hour) he was such a cheerful fellow, and told of his triumph at the lodge election the night before, or of his fancy shots the day before, with such good nature that he was usually forgiven. Indeed, the people found no other fault with his idleness than to good-naturedly refer to his hotel as the "Apron and Password," probably a tribute to the English way of naming houses of public entertainment; for they argued that if Mrs. Armsby could forgive her husband's faults, it was no affair of theirs; and by this name the place was known.

But he had one good habit; he was fond of his wife—not because she made the living, and allowed him to exist in idleness, but really and truly fond of her; though everyone was fond of capable Mrs. Armsby: for though she was nearly always at work, she found time to learn enough of passing events to be a fair conversationalist, and sometimes entertained the guests in the parlor by singing, accompanying herself on the piano.

It was said that as a girl Mrs. Armsby had been the favorite of a circle of rich relatives and friends, and that she spent the earlier portion of her life in a pleasant and aristocratic home; but when she found it necessary to make her own living, and support a husband besides, she went about it with apparent good nature, and was generally regarded as a very remarkable woman. She had been Annie Benton's first teacher, in addition to her regular duties, and a pupil still came to the house occasionally, only to find her making bread in the kitchen, or beds in the upper rooms.

Armsby had been out hunting, as usual, and his wife had prepared his supper with her own hands, which he was now discussing.

"There are a great many unhappy women in the world, Davy," Armsby said, looking admiringly at the contents of the plates around him, "for the reason that most husbands are mean to their wives. I wouldn't be a woman for all the money in Thompson Benton's safe; I am thankful that I am a man, if for nothing else. It is very pretty to say that any woman is so good that she can have her pick of a husband, but it is not true, for most of them marry men who are cross to them, and unfair, and thoughtless; but Mrs. Armsby has her own way here. She has a maid and a man, and I fancy she is rather a fortunate woman. Instead of being bossed around by her husband, he keeps out of the way and gives her full charge. Pull up to the table and eat something, won't you? Help yourself to the sardines."

Davy accepted the invitation, and was helping himself when Mr. Armsby said:

"You will find them mighty good; and they ought to be good, for they cost sixty cents a box—the three you have on your plate cost a dime. But they are as free as the air you breathe. Help yourself; have some more, and make it fifteen cents."

Davy concluded not to take any sardines after this, and after browsing around among the mixed pickles and goat-cheese awhile, and being told that they ought to be good, for they cost enough, he concluded that Armsby's hospitality was intended as a means of calling attention to his rich fare; for he was very particular, and in order to please him his wife always provided something for his table which was produced at no other time. There was a bottle of olives on the table, and when Davy took one of them, Armsby explained that he had imported them himself at enormous expense, although they had been really bought at one of the stores as a job lot, the proprietor having had them on hand a number of years.

"Any guests to-night?" Armsby inquired, trying to look very much vexed that the clerk had not accepted the invitation to refresh himself.

"No," Davy answered, a little sulky because of his rebuff.

"I am sorry for that," Armsby continued. "Mrs. Armsby enjoys a lively parlor, and she has a great deal of time in which to make herself agreeable. What a wonderful woman she is to fix up! Always neat, and always pleasant; but she has little else to do. You don't take very kindly to the ladies yourself, Davy?"

The boarders frequently accused Davy of being fond of various old widows and maids in the town, whom he had really never spoken to, and gravely hinted that the streets were full of rumors of his approaching nuptials; but he paid no attention to these banters, nor did he now, except to give a little grunt of contempt for any one so foolish as to marry.

"Why, bless me, Davy," Armsby said, laying down his knife and fork in astonishment; "how bald you are becoming! Let me see the back of your head."

Silas turned his back to his employer's husband, and looked up at the ceiling.

"It's coming; you will be as bald as a plate in a year. But we must all expect it; fortune has no favorites in this respect. I know a man who does not mistreat his wife, but I never knew one who wasn't bald. You might as well quit washing your head in salt water, Davy; for it will do no good."

The facts were that Davy gave no sign of approaching baldness; but Armsby, being very bald himself, was always trying to discover that other people's hair was falling out.

"Better remain single, though," he continued, referring to matrimony again, "than to marry a woman and mistreat her. All the men are unjust to their wives, barring the honorable exception just named; therefore it has always been my policy to make Mrs. Armsby a notable exception. Is there another woman in the Bend who handles all the money, and does exactly as she pleases? You are around a good bit; do you know of another?"

Davy thought to himself that she was entitled to the privilege of handling the money, since she earned it all, besides supporting a vagrant husband; but he said nothing, for Silas was not a talkative man.

"Whatever she does is entirely satisfactory to me," continued the model husband. "I never complain; indeed, I find much to admire. There is not another woman like her in the world, and it contains an awful lot of people."

Mrs. Armsby appeared from the kitchen at this moment, and, greeting her husband pleasantly, really seemed charmed with his presence. While she was looking after his wants, he told her of his hunting that day; how he had made more double shots than any of his companions; how his dog had proved, for the hundredth time, that he was the very best in the country, as he had always contended; how tired and hungry he was, and how fortunate it was that there was no lodge that night, as in that event he would have to be present.

His wife finally disappeared into the kitchen again, to arrange for the first meal of the next day, and Armsby said to Davy,—

"Poor woman, she has so little to occupy her mind that she has gone into the kitchen to watch Jennie peel the potatoes. If business was not so dull—you say it is dull; I know nothing about it myself—I would hire a companion for her; someone to read to her, and walk about with her during the day. It's too bad."

Unfortunately for the patrons of the Apron-and-Password, Armsby had been to New York; and though he had remained but two days, since his return he had pretended to a knowledge of the metropolis which was marvellous. When a New York man was mentioned, Armsby pretended to know him intimately, telling cheerful anecdotes of how their acquaintance began and ended. Whenever a New York institution was referred to, he was familiar with it, almost to intimacy; and a few of the Davy's Bend people amused themselves by inventing fictitious names and places in New York, and inducing Armsby to profess a knowledge of them, which he did with cheerful promptness.

He never neglected an opportunity to talk about his trip, therefore when he put his chair back from the table, and engaged in quiet meditation, Silas felt sure he was about to introduce the subject in a new way; for Armsby was a very ingenious as well as a very lazy man.

"You ought to wear the apron, Silas," Mr. Armsby said, looking at Silas with the greatest condescension and pity; "but it would be dreadful if your application should be greeted with the blacks. I don't recommend that you try it, mind, for that is not allowed, and the records will show that we lodge men have so much regard for principle that it has never been done; but it is something that everyone should think about, sooner or later. Only the very best men wear this emblem of greatness. But if you have faults, I should advise you not to run the risk of being humiliated, for the members are very particular. A lazy man, or a shiftless man, or a bad man of any kind, cannot get in; and when a man belongs to a lodge, it can be depended upon that he is as near right as they make them. This is the reason we must be particular in admitting new members. Reputation is at stake; for, once you are in, the others stand by you with their lives and their sacred honor. There's nothing like it."

The landlord occupied himself a moment in pleasant thought of the lodges, in connection with their cheapness and general utility, and then continued, after smiling in a gratified way over his own importance in the lodge connection,—

"When I first went to New York I became acquainted with the very best people immediately; for every man who wears the apron has confidence in every other man who wears it; each knows that the other has been selected from the masses with care, and they trust each other to the fullest extent. One day I went over into—"

Armsby could not remember names, and he snapped his fingers now in vexation.

"It is strange I am unable to name the town," he said; "I am as familiar with it as I am with my own stable. Well, no matter; anyway it is a big suburb, and you reach it by crossing the—"

Again he stopped, and tried to recall the name of the bridge he had crossed, and the city he had visited, but to no avail; though he rapped his head soundly with his knuckles, for its bad behavior, and got up to walk up and down the room.

"If I should forget your name, or Mrs. Armsby's, it would not be more remarkable," he continued, at last, giving up in despair. "I was brought up in sight of them; but what I started out to say was, that I walked into a bank one day, and the fine-looking man who was at the counter looked at me, at first, with the greatest suspicion, thinking I was a robber, no doubt, until I gave him a certain sign. You should have seen the change in his manner! He came through a little door at the side, and shaking hands with me in a certain way, known only to those on the inside, took me into a private office in the rear, where a number of other fine-looking gentlemen were seated around a table.

"'President Judd,' he said to them, 'this gentleman wears the apron.'

"All the elegant gentlemen were delighted to see me. It was not feigned, either, for it was genuine delight; and a controversy sprang up as to which of them should give his time to my entertainment while in the city, though I protested that I was so well acquainted that I could get along very well alone. But they insisted upon it, and when they began to quarrel rather fiercely about it, I gave them a sign (which reminded them of their pledge to be brothers), whereupon they were all good-natured at once, and one of them said,—

"'Thank you for reminding us of our duty, brother; the best of us will occasionally forget. Will you do us the favor to pick out one of our number to show you about, and make your stay in the city pleasant?'"

Davy noticed that Mrs. Armsby was listening at the kitchen door, though Armsby did not know it, for his back was turned toward her; but he did not mention the circumstance.

"I liked the looks of Mr. Judd," Armsby continued, "so I said that if the other brothers would not take offence, I would like his company. The others said, 'Oh, not at all,' all of them making the sign to be brothers at the same time, and President Judd at once began arranging his business so he could go out with me, not neglecting to put a big roll of money in his pocket; and, though it was very big, the others said it wasn't half enough."

Davy believed everything the people saw fit to tell him, and vouched for the truth of it when he repeated it himself, and was very much interested in what Armsby was saying.

"Well, sir, when we went out, the sign was everything. You cannot imagine how potent it was. We made it when we wanted a carriage, and the driver regarded it as a favor to carry us for nothing; we made it when we were hungry, and it assured us the greatest attention at the hotels, which were nothing like this, but larger—very much larger."

Davy gave evidence of genuine astonishment on learning that there were hotels larger than the "Apron and Password;" but as the proprietor himself had made the statement, he presumed it must be true, though it was certainly very astonishing.

"I can't think of the name of it now, but they have a railroad in the second story of the street there, and instead of collecting fare, when the proprietors came around they put money in our outside pockets, thinking we might meet someone who was not a brother. Judd remained with me five days, taking me to his own residence at night, which was twice as big as The Locks, and when we finally parted, he loaded me down with presents, and shed tears. Next to the sign, the apron is the greatest thing in the world; I am sorry you do not wear it."

Armsby wandered leisurely out into the office soon after, probably to smoke the cigars his wife kept there in a case for sale, when Mrs. Armsby came into the dining-room, and sat down, looking mortified and distressed.

"Silas," she said, "don't believe a word Armsby has said to you, or ever will say, on this subject. Before he became a slave to this dreadful lodge habit, he was a truthful man, but you can't believe a word he says now. Do you know what they do at the lodges?"

Davy shook his head, for of course no one except a member·could know.

"Let me tell you, then. They tie cooks' aprons around their waists, put fools' caps on their heads, and quarrel as to whether the hailing sign, or the aid sign, or whatever it is, is made by holding up one finger when the right thumb is touching the right ear, or whether it is two or three or four fingers. It is all about as ridiculous as this, and my advice to you is, never join. Armsby has been talking to you a good deal about the matter lately, and I suspect he wants the fun of initiating you, which is accompanied with all sorts of tricks, which gives them opportunity to make fun of you from behind their paper masks."

Since it was impossible to believe both stories, Silas made up his mind to ask Tug's opinion,—Tug would know,—but he said nothing.

"Some of them wear swords," Mrs. Armsby went on to say; "but, bless you, they can't draw them, and even if they should succeed in getting them out, they couldn't put them back in their scabbards again. Armsby came home one night wearing his sword, and in this very room he took it out to make a show of himself, and was so awkward with it that he broke half the dishes on the dresser, besides upsetting the lamp and wounding me on the hand. To complete his disgrace, he was compelled to ask me to put it in its case again; but I fear the lesson did the misguided man little good, for he has been as bad as ever since. But while these men might be pardoned for their foolishness if they remained in their halls, they are utterly unpardonable for disgracing their wives and friends by appearing on the street, which they occasionally do, dressed in more fantastic fashion than ever. If you should join, you would be expected to do this, and after one appearance you could never look a sensible person in the face again, unless you are lost to all sense of self-respect. Besides, it is expensive; my husband keeps me poor in attending grand lodges, and most of the failures are caused by neglecting business to talk lodge. My only fear is that my misguided husband will finally consider it his duty to kill somebody for telling about the signs and grips, and then we will all be disgraced. It is your misfortune as well as mine, Silas, that Armsby is not a drunkard. Drunkards are occasionally reformed, and are of some use in their sober intervals; but a lodge man never reforms. If a lodge man engages in business, he fails, for he does not attend to it; but a drinking man admits that he is doing wrong, and sometimes succeeds in his efforts to do better; whereas a lodge man argues all the time that his foolishness is good sense, and therefore don't try to get out of the way. Compared to me, Mrs. Whittle is a very fortunate woman."

Mrs. Armsby got up at this and went out; and as Silas was preparing to follow, he heard a whistle which he recognized at once as Tug's. Whenever Tug had use for Silas early in the evening, he had a habit of whistling him out, since he never came into the hotel until his friend had possession.

Silas at once put on his hat and went down to the wagon yard, where he found Tug impatiently waiting, who started off at a rapid swinging gait toward the lower end of the town and the river as soon as Silas caught sight of him. When the pair travelled, Davy always lagged behind, as he did in this instance; for in the presence of genius like Tug's, he felt that his place was in the rear. Others might doubt the ability or even the honesty of his friend, but Silas had no doubt that Tug would some day be a wonderful man, and prove that everything said to his discredit was untrue. It was a favorite saying of his that when he "came into his own," he would move about, with the magnificence of a circus procession, on the back of an elephant, with a brass band in front and a company of trumpeters behind; and Silas was content to wait. Tug occasionally illustrated this idea now as he walked along, by swinging and flinging his body about as those who ride on elephants do, and it occurred to Silas that "his own" must have arrived by boat, and that he was going after it; for he walked rapidly toward the river without looking around.

Tug had not spoken a word since setting out, and after reaching the street which led down to the crazy collection of houses where he lived, he travelled down that way a while, and at last turned off toward the right, following the course of the river through alleys and back yards, and over fences and gaping sloughs, until at last he stopped near an old warehouse, which had been used a great many years before in storing freight arriving by the boats when the Bend was an important town. It was entirely deserted now, and as the two men stopped in its shadow, Tug gave his companion to understand that he must be very quiet and secret.

After they had blown awhile, Tug began crawling around the building on his hands and knees, followed by his companion, occasionally raising his hand as a warning when they both stopped to listen. When Tug had reached the other end of the warehouse, he motioned Davy to come up to him; and when he did so this is what he saw:—

A light skiff tied to the bank, with the oars laid across it, and a woman seated in the stern—the woman they had seen when they followed the shadow down the river, after its appearance at Allan Dorris's window. They were certain it was the same woman, because she wore a waterproof cloak, as she did on the night when they followed the shadow down the river, and she was very small. Her back was turned toward them, and she was motionless as a statue; and realizing that as her ears were covered with the waterproof she could not hear well, the two men arose to their feet after a careful inspection, and walked back to the other end of the building.

"I intend to steal her," Tug whispered into his companion's ear, at the same time reaching down into Davy's pocket and taking out a handkerchief, which he arranged in his hand like a sling ready for use.

CHAPTER X.

TUG WHITTLE'S BOOTY.

After resting a while, and looking carefully around to make sure that they were not watched, Tug and Silas crawled cautiously back to the bank which overlooked the boat and its singular occupant, and after warning his companion to remain where he was by shaking his hand at him like a club, Tug began to climb down the bank, feeling every step as he went with the cunning stealth of a tiger. Gradually he worked his way to the water's edge; so careful was he, that even Silas, watching him with breathless interest above, could not hear his step, and at last he stood on the brink of the water. The boat was in an eddy, floating easily about, and when it came within Tug's reach, he clapped the handkerchief over the woman's mouth, tied it in a knot at the back of her head, and came clambering up the bank with her on his shoulders. Without saying a word, he started to retrace his steps, only stopping once or twice to see that his booty was not smothering, when, finding the little woman all right, he went on over the fences and sloughs, and through the alleys and yards, until he entered his own door.

"Now then, sister," he said, putting the woman on her feet, and breathing heavily from his exercise, "Tell us who you are. Davy, make a light."

Silas came lagging in about this time, and did as he was told, though he was a long time about it, for the matches were damp, and the flame slow in coming up. Everything seemed to be damp in Davy's Bend, and it was no wonder that the matches were slow and sleepy, like the other inhabitants of the town; therefore they came to life with a sputtering protest against being disturbed. While Silas was rubbing them into good humor, Tug was closely watching the little woman with his great eye, and getting his breath; and when the light was fairly burning, he went over to her side, and removed the handkerchief from her mouth.

"Gentlemen!" she cried out, in a weak voice, as soon as she could. "Gentlemen! In the name of God! I appeal to you as gentlemen!"

"Don't gentleman me," Tug said, bringing the light over to look at the woman's face. "I'm not a gentleman; I'm a thief, and I've stolen a woman. Nor is *he* a gentleman," pointing to Davy, and holding his head to one side to get a bead on him. "He's the greatest scoundrel that ever lived. Look at the audacious villain now! Look at him! Did you ever see a person who looked so much like the devil? And he *is* the devil, when he gets started. He's keen to get at you now, and I'll have trouble with him if you are at all unreasonable."

Davy looked like anything but a villain as he meekly watched the pair from the other side of the room; indeed, he was thinking that Tug was carrying the matter entirely too far, and was becoming alarmed. But Tug did not share this feeling of apprehension, for he seemed desperately in earnest as he held the lamp close to the woman's face, who tried to shield it from his sight with her thin, trembling hands, and cried out in the same weak voice: "Gentlemen! In the name of God! I appeal to you as gentlemen!"

A very small woman, with shrivelled face and sharp features, was Tug's booty, and she trembled violently as she piteously held out her hands to the two men. Tug thought of her as the key to the problem he had been attempting to solve, so he stood between her and the door to prevent escape. But Silas felt sure that the woman had but lately risen from a sick bed; for she was weak and trembling, and from sitting long in the damp river air, there was a distressed and painful flush in her face.

"Come now, sister," Tug said, seating himself in front of her, and frowning like a pirate. "Tell us what you know, and be carried back to your boat. If you refuse to do it, we will take you on a journey to the Hedgepath graveyard, in the woods over the river, where we will erect a stone Sacred to the Memory of an Obstinate Woman. Which will you have? Use your tongue; which will you have?"

But the woman made no other reply than to appeal to them as gentlemen, in the name of God, and cry, and wring her hands.

"In case you ever see that foxy companion of yourn again, which is extremely doubtful, for I have a companion who murders for the love of it—(Here, now, take your hand off that knife, will you," Tug said, by way of parenthesis to Silas, looking at him sharply. Then going over to him, he pretended to take a knife out of Davy's inside coat pocket, and hide it in the cupboard). "If you ever see your friend Sneak again, say to him that I intend to get his head. He is bothering a friend of mine, and I intend to create a commotion inside of him for it."

Tug walked over to the table where the lamp stood, and, taking the package of poison from his pocket, carefully divided it into two doses; a large one for a man, and the other for a smaller person, probably a woman. He also took occasion, being near to Davy, to whisper to him that the woman reminded him of his wife's sister Sis.

"You are evidently a married woman, sister," the bold rascal said, seating himself in front of his captive, and looking at her in the dignified manner which distinguished him. "I suppose you were very handsome as a girl, and the men fell desperately in love with you, and were very miserable in consequence. But I will let you into a secret; you are bravely over your beauty now. I suppose your mother braided your hair, and did all the work, that your hands might be as pretty as your face; and certainly she believed that while the boys might possibly fail in life, *you* would be all right, and marry a prince, and repay her for her kindness. Your poor mother rented a pianow for you, too, I reckon, and hired you a teacher; and when you could drum a little, she thought you could play a great deal, and felt repaid for all her trouble, believing that you would turn out well, and make your brothers feel ashamed of themselves for being so worthless. And while I don't know it, I believe that she paid five dollars to somebody to make you a artist, and that you painted roses and holly-hocks on saucers and plates, which your poor mother, in the kindness of her heart, recognized, and greatly admired. I shall believe this as long as I live, for you *look* like a painter and a pianowist out of practice."

This train of thought amused Mr. Whittle so much that he paused as if to laugh; but he apparently thought better of it, though his scalp crawled over on his forehead,—an oddity which distinguished him when he was amused.

"Did your poor mother get to sleep peacefully at night, after working all day for you?" inquired Mr. Whittle fiercely. "You don't answer; but you know she didn't. You know she spent the night in wrangling with your father to induce him to give her money that she might buy you more ribbons and millinery and dry goods; and kid gloves, probably, although your brother Bill was out at his toes, and hadn't so much as a cotton handkercher; and how your mother went on when your husband came courting you! He wasn't good enough for you *then*, whoever he was; though I'll bet he thinks he's too good for you *now*, whoever he is; and what a time you must have had borrowing silverware and chairs for the wedding! I've been married, and I know. Your tired mother hoped that when her children grew up they would relieve her, and love her, and be good to her; but I'll bet you find fault because she didn't 'do' more for you; and that your brother Bill, who ran away because you had all the pie in the house, is taking care of her, providin' she aint dead from bother and too much work, which is likely. And after all this trouble in your behalf, look at you now!"

The little woman seemed to be paying some attention to what he was saying, for she looked at him timidly out of the corners of her black eyes a few times, and occasionally forgot to wring her hands and cry.

"Look at you now, I say! Your health has gone off after your beauty, for you seem to have neither with you, and I find you wandering around at night with a Thief. A great fall you've had, sister, providin' you ever were young and pretty, for I was never acquainted with a worse-looking woman than you are; and if you knew my wife you would be very indignant, for she has the reputation of being a Terror for looks. When I was younger I fell in love with every girl I met, and had no relief until they married; *then* I soon got over it, for you ought to know how they fade under such circumstances; but you are worse than the rest of them; you are so ugly that I feel sorry for you. Honestly, I wonder that you do not blush in my presence; and I am not handsome, God knows. I really feel sorry for you, but in connection with your friend Prowler you are annoying an amiable and a worthy gentleman, who happens to be a friend of Mr. Blood's, the party sitting opposite you; and I fear he does *not* feel sorry for you. A little less of that word 'gentlemen,' sister, if you please."

The woman was appealing to them again as before: "Gentlemen! In the name of God! I appeal to you."

"Promise to take your friend Prowler, and leave this country," Mr. Whittle continued, "and never return, and you shall go free; but if you refuse— Blood!"

Tug sprang up and glared savagely at his meek little partner, at the same time advancing toward him.

"You sha'n't satisfy that devilish disposition of yourn by shooting a woman in the back when *I'm* around, you cut-throat," he said. "Haven't I always been ready to join you in putting men out of the way, and haven't I enjoyed the pleasure of it with you? Then why do you want to take the credit of this job to yourself, and enjoy it alone? You must wait, Blood, until she speaks. We *may* forgive her, providin' she speaks up cheerful and don't attempt to deceive us."

Again Tug pretended to take a dangerous weapon from his companion, standing between Davy and the prisoner while about it; after which he regarded him for a few moments in contemptuous silence.

"It's your tongue, sister, and not your tears, as will do you good in this difficulty," Tug said, in answer to a fresh burst of grief from the woman. "I'll give you five minutes to decide between tongue and tears. At the end of that time, if it's tears, the cravings of that bad man in the corner shall be satisfied. Blood, where is the watch you took from the store? Hain't got it? My guess is that you've lost it gambling, as usual. Well, I'll count three hundred seconds, sister, since we have no watch. One, two, three; here we go."

Tug looked reverently up at the ceiling; and appeared to be engaged in counting for two or three minutes, occasionally looking at the woman and then at Silas, who thought Tug had been counting at least half an hour already.

"Two hundred and twenty-one, two hundred and twenty-two, two hundred and twenty-three," he counted aloud. "Fifth call, sister, the time is going; two hundred and twenty-four, two hundred and—"

At this moment there was a strange interruption to the proceedings. A tall man wearing a rubber coat, which reached below his knees, opened the door, and, leaving it open, stood just upon the inside, carrying a pistol in his right hand, which hung by his side.

"The shadow!" both men thought at once; and very determined and ugly looked the shadow, with his long, sallow face, and dark moustache.

"Alice," he said to the woman, "come out."

The woman quickly jumped up, and hurried outside. The shadow followed, backing out like a lion-tamer leaving a cage, and closing the door after him. But while he stood inside the door, although he was there only a moment, both men noticed a strange peculiarity. The upper part of his left ear was gone,—cut off clean, as if with a knife; and this peculiarity was so unusual that they remarked it more than his face. The circumstance gave them both an impression that the shadow was a desperate man, and that he was accustomed to fierce brawls.

Tug and Silas looked at each other in blank dismay a long time after the mysterious pair had disappeared, not venturing to look out, fearing it might be dangerous; but finally Tug said,—

"Silas, I must have a gun. Do you happen to have one?"

Silas shook his head.

"Then I must steal one, for I need a gun. The shadow looks so much like an uncle of my wife's that I am more determined than ever to kill him."

Whereupon he went over to the table, emptied the two packages of poison on to the floor, and went to bed.

CHAPTER XI.

THE WHISPERS IN THE AIR.

There is a wide and populous world outside of Davy's Bend, from which Allan Dorris recently came; let the whispers in the air, which frighten every man with their secrets, answer why he had resolved never again to see Annie Benton.

During his residence in Davy's Bend he had met the girl frequently, usually at the stone church near his house, where she came to practise; and after every meeting he became more than ever convinced, after thinking about it,—and he thought about it a great deal,—that if their acquaintance continued, there would come a time when he would find it difficult to quit her society. The pleasure he enjoyed in the company of the pretty organist was partly due to the circumstance that she was always pleased at his approach, although she tried to disguise it; but beyond this,—a long way beyond this,—there was reason why he should avoid her; for the girl's sake, not his own.

He repeated this often to himself, as though he were a desperate man ready to engage in any desperate measure; but his manner visibly softened when he thought of the pretty girl whose ways were so engaging, innocent, and frank. He knew himself so well,—the number of times he had gone over the story of his life, in his own mind, since coming to The Locks even, would have run up into the hundreds; therefore he knew himself very well indeed,—that he felt in honor bound to give up his acquaintance with her, although it cost him a keen pang of regret, this determination to hear the music no more, and never again see the player.

Avoiding even a look at the church, which was a reminder of how much pleasure he had found in Davy's Bend, and how much misery he would probably find there in the future, he passed out of the iron gate of The Locks, and set his face toward the quiet country, where he hoped to walk until his body would call for rest at night, and permit him to sleep; a blessing that had been denied him of late more than before he knew Annie Benton, and when he thought that Davy's Bend contained people only fit to be avoided.

But he was glad that he had resolved never to see the girl again,—for her sake, not his own.

He had made this resolve after a struggle with himself, thinking of the strange fatality that had made duty painful throughout his entire life; and he walked toward the country because he believed the girl was in the direction of the town; probably seated in the church at that moment, watching the door for his approach. She was a comfort to him, therefore he must avoid her; but this had always been the case—he was accustomed to being warned that he was an intruder whenever he entered a pleasant place.

There was something in store for her besides a life of hiding and fear, and an unknown grave at last, with a fictitious name on the headboard; and he would not cross a path which led toward happiness for one he so much admired.

Thus he argued to himself as he walked along; but when he remembered how dull his life would be should her smile never come into it again, he could not help shuddering.

"But I have been so considerate of others," he said aloud, as he pursued his way, "that even the worms in my path impudently expected me to go round them, and seemed to honestly believe me unworthy of living at all if I did not. Let me not show a lack of consideration now that my heart is concerned."

Above his house, and so near the river that the water rippled at its base, was a rugged bluff, separated from the town by a deep and almost impassable ravine, and for this reason it was seldom visited; Allan Dorris had found it during his first month in the town, and he resolved to visit it now, and get the full benefit of the sunshine and delightful air of the perfect summer day.

It occurred to him as he sat down to rest, after making the difficult ascent, that he would like to build a house there, and live in it, where he would never be disturbed. But did he want solitude? There seemed to be some question of this, judging from the look of doubt on his downcast face. When he first came to Davy's Bend, he believed that the rewards of life were so unsatisfactory that all within his reach that he desired was his own company; but an experience of a month had satisfied him that solitude would not do, and he confessed that he did not know what he wanted. If he knew what it was his heart craved, he believed that it was beyond him, and unobtainable; and so his old habit of thinking was resumed, though he could never tell what it was all about. Everything he desired was impossible; that within his reach was distasteful—he could make no more of the jumble in his brain, and finally sat with a vacant stare on his face, thoroughly ashamed of the vagrant thoughts which gave him a headache but no conclusions.

Even the pure air and the bright sunshine, that he thought he wanted while coming along the road, were not satisfactory now; and as he started to walk furiously up the hill, to tire himself, he met Annie Benton in the path he was following.

She had been gathering wild flowers, and, as he came upon her, she was so intent on arranging them after some sort of a plan, that she was startled when he stood beside her.

"I was thinking of you," she said hurriedly, instead of returning his greeting. "I intended sending you these."

Dorris could not help being amused that he had encountered the girl in a place where he had gone to avoid her, but there was evidence in his light laugh that he was glad of it; so he seated himself on a boulder beside the path, and asked what she had been thinking of him.

"That you were a very odd man," she answered frankly.

"That has always been a complaint against me," he said, with a tone of impatience. "I think I have never known any one who has not said, during the course of our acquaintance, that I was 'odd;' whatever is natural in me has been called 'odd' before. If I wanted bread, and was not satisfied with a stone, they called me 'odd.' The wishes of the horse that has a prejudice for being bridled on the left side are respected, but there is no consideration for a man who cannot be contented simply because it is his duty. I remember that we had a horse of this description in our family when I was a boy, and if he injured any one who failed to respect his wishes, the man was blamed, not the horse. But the people do not have equal charity for a man who is not content when circumstances seem to demand it of him, no difference what the circumstances are, or how repugnant they may be to his taste. So you were finding fault with me? I am not surprised at it, though; most people do."

The girl had seated herself near him, and was busily engaged in arranging the flowers until he inquired again,—

"So you were finding fault with me?"

"No," she answered, "unless it was finding fault to think of you as being different from any other person I have ever known. It was not a very serious charge to think of you as being different from the people in Davy's Bend."

There was something in that, for they were not the finest people in the world, by any means; nor could the town be justly held responsible for all their faults, as they pretended.

"No, it is not serious," he replied; "but I am sorry you are looking so well, for I am running away from you. It would be easier, were you less becoming. I am sorry you are not ugly."

There was a look of wonder in the girl's face that made her prettier than ever.

"Running away from *me?*"

"Yes, from you," he answered.

She began arranging the flowers again, and kept her eyes on them while he watched her face. Dorris thought of himself as a snake watching a bird, and finally looked down the river at the ferry, which happened to be moving.

"Why?" she asked at last.

"Because I am dangerous," he replied, with a flushed face. "You should run away when you see me approach, for I am not a fit companion for you. I have nothing to offer that you ought to accept; even my attentions are dangerous."

The bouquet was arranged by this time, and there was no further excuse for toying with it, so she laid it down, and looked at him.

"I suppose I should be very much frightened," she said, "but I am not. I am not at all afraid of you."

He laughed lightly to himself, and seemed amused at the answer she had made.

"I know nothing whatever about women," he said, "and I am sorry for it, for you are a puzzle to me. I know men as well as I know myself, and know what to expect of them under given circumstances; but all those of your sex I have ever known were as a sealed book. The men are always the same, but I never know what a woman will do. No two of them are alike; there is no rule by which you can judge them, except that they are always better than the men. I have never known this to fail, but beyond that I know nothing of your sex. I say to you that I am dangerous; you reply that you are not afraid of me. But you ought to be; I am sure of that."

"If you desire it," she said, "I am sorry, but I feel perfectly safe in your company."

"It's a pity," he returned, looking down the river again. "If you were afraid of me, I would not be dangerous. I am not liable to pelt you with stones, or rob you; but the danger lies in the likelihood of our becoming friends."

"Is friendship so dangerous, then?"

"It *would* be between you and me, because I am odd. Look at me."

She did as requested, with quiet confidence and dignity.

"You say you are not afraid of me; neither am I of you, and I intend to tell you what you can hardly suspect. I am in love with you to such an extent that I can think of nothing else; but I cannot offer you an honorable man's love, because I am not an honorable man, as that expression is used and accepted. I have been looking all my life for such a woman as you are, but now that I have found you, I respect you so much that I dare not attempt to win your favor; indeed, instead of that, I warn you against myself. Until I was thirty I looked into every face I met, expecting to find the one I sought; but I never found it, and finally gave up the search, forced to believe that such a one as I looked for did not exist. I have found out my mistake, but it is too late."

He jumped up from the stone on which he was seated, as if he intended to run away, and did walk a distance, but came back again, as if he had something else to say.

"I speak of this matter as I might tell a capable artist that I was infatuated with his picture, and could not resist the temptation to frequently admire it. I have no more reason to believe that there is a responsive feeling in your heart than I would have reason to believe that the picture I admired appreciated the compliment, but there is nothing wrong in what I have said to you, and it is a pleasure for me to say it; there can be no harm in telling a pretty, modest woman that you admire her—she deserves the compliment."

Annie Benton did not appear to be at all surprised at this avowal, and listened to it with the air of one who was being told of something commonplace.

"You do not make love like the lovers I have read about," she said, with an attempt at a smile, though she could not disguise the oddity of her position. "I do not know how to answer you."

"Then don't answer me at all," he replied. "I am not making love to you, for I have denied myself that privilege. I am not at liberty to make love to you, though I want to; therefore I ask the privilege of explaining why I shall avoid you in the future, and why I regret to do it. The first feeling I was ever conscious of was one of unrest; I was never satisfied with my home, or with those around me. If I thought I had a friend, I soon found him out, and was more dissatisfied than ever. Of course this was very unreasonable and foolish; anyone would say that, and say it with truth, but while it is an easy explanation, I could not help it; I was born that way, nor can I help saying that I am satisfied with you. You suit me exactly, and I was never contented in my life until I sat in the old church and looked at you."

Though the girl continued to look at him without apparent surprise, her face was very pale, and she was breathing rapidly.

"You may regard what I have said as impudent," Dorris continued, "and think that while you are satisfactory to me, I would not be to you. I am not now, but I would give a great deal to convince you that I am the man you dreamed of when you last put wedding-cake under your pillow, providing you ever did such a ridiculous thing. It is not conceit for me to say that I believe I could compel you to respect me, therefore I regret that we have ever met at all, for I am not at liberty to woo you honorably; if you want to know why, I will tell you, for I would place my life in your hands without the slightest hesitation, and feel secure; but it is enough for the present to say that nothing could happen which would surprise me. I am in trouble; though I would rather tell you of it than have you surmise what it is, for I am not ashamed of it. I can convince you—or any one with equally good sense—that I am not nearly so bad as many who live in peace. Would you like to hear my history?"

"No," she replied; "for you would soon regret telling it to me, and I fear that you will discover some time that I am not worthy of the many kind things you have said about me. I am only a woman, and when you know me better you will find that I am not the one you have been looking for so long and so patiently."

"Excuse me if I contradict you in that," he said with as much grave earnestness as though he had been talking politics, and found it necessary to take issue with her. "You *are* the one. Once there came to me in a dream a face which I have loved ever since. This was early in life, and during all the years which have brought me nothing but discontent and wretchedness, it has been my constant companion; the one little pleasure of my life. From the darkness that surrounded me, the face has always been looking at me; and whatever I have accomplished—I have accomplished nothing in Davy's Bend, but my life has been busy elsewhere—has been prompted by a desire to please this strange friend. I have never been able to dismiss my trouble—I have had no more than my share, perhaps, as you have said, but there is enough trouble in the world to render us all unhappy—except to welcome the recollection of the dream; and although I have often admitted to myself that this communion with the unreal was absurd, and unworthy of a sensible man, it has afforded me a contentment that I failed to find in anything else; therefore the fancy made a strong impression on my mind, and it grew stronger as I grew older, causing me many a heartache because there was nothing in life like it. Most men have dreams of greatness, but my only wish was to find the face that always came out of the shadows at my bidding."

He paused for a moment, looking into the empty air, where his dream seemed to realize before him, for he looked intently at it, and went on to describe it.

"It was not an angel's face, but a woman's, and there was no expression in it that was not human; expressions of love, and pity, and forgiveness—you have them in your face now, and I believe they are not uncommon. I have never expected unreal or impossible things, and as I grew older, and better understood the unsatisfactory nature of life, I became more than ever convinced that I would feel entirely satisfied could my dream come true. At last I came to believe that it was impossible; that I was as unreasonable as the man who pined because his tears were not diamonds; but I could not give up the recollection of the face, to which I was always so true and devoted, and comforted myself with brooding over it, and regretting my misfortune. Instead of greatness or grandeur, I longed for the face, and it was the only one I ever loved."

Again he was gazing intently at nothing; at his fancy, but this time he seemed to be dismissing it forever, after a careful inspection to convince himself that the counterpart he had found on earth was exactly like it.

"Until I met you," he said, looking at Annie Benton again, "this sweetheart of my fancy lived in Heaven, Maid of Air. When you turned upon me that afternoon in the church, I almost exclaimed aloud: 'The face! My vision has come true!' Not a feature was missing, and your actions and your smile were precisely what I had seen so often in my fancy. Therefore you are not a stranger to me; I have loved you all my life, and instead of worshipping a vision in the future I shall worship you. Why don't you speak to me?"

"I don't dare to," she answered, looking him full in the face, and without the slightest hesitation. "I am afraid I would say something I ought not to."

He looked at her curiously for a moment, trying to divine her meaning, and concluded that if she should speak more freely, he would hear something surprising; either she would denounce him for his boldness, or profess a love for him which would compel him to give up his resolution of never seeing her again.

"That was an unfortunate expression," he said. "I am sorry you said that, for it has pleased my odd fancy; indeed, it is precisely what I was hoping you would say, but there is all the more reason now for my repeating to you that I am dangerous. I know how desperate my affairs are; how desperate I am, and how unfortunate it would be if you should become involved. Therefore I say to you, as a condemned prisoner might shut out the single ray of light which brightened his existence, so that he might meet his inevitable fate bravely, that you must avoid me, and walk another way when you see me approaching."

A hoarse whistle came to them from the ferry in the river, and Dorris thought of it as an angry warning from a monster, in whose keeping he was, to come away from a presence which afforded him pleasure.

"May I speak a word?" the girl inquired, turning abruptly toward him.

"Yes; a dozen, or a thousand, though I would advise you not to."

"Is what you have said to me exactly true?"

"Upon my honor; exactly true," he answered.

"Is there no morbid selfishness in it; no foolish fancy?"

"Upon my honor, none!"

"Do you believe I am your dream come true with the same matter-of-fact belief which convinces you that there is a ferry in the river?"

She pointed out the boat as it moved lazily through the water, and as he looked at it he seemed to resolve the matter carefully in his mind.

"Yes," he answered, "I am as certain that you are the woman I have loved devotedly all my life, as I am certain that there is a river at the foot of the hill. What I have said to you is generally regarded as sentimental nonsense except when it is protected by the charity of a sweetheart or a wife; but it is in every man's heart, though it is sometimes never expressed, and my idle life here has made me bold enough to state that it is true. I have been seeking contentment with so much eagerness, and know so well that it is hard to find, that I have come to believe that there is but one more chance, and that I would find what I lack in the love of a woman like you. Even if I should discover by experience that I am mistaken in this belief, I would feel better off than I ever did before; for I would then conclude that my fancies were wrong, and that I was as well off as any man; but this feeling will always be denied me, for I am denied the privilege of happiness now that it is within my reach. My lonely life here has wrung a confession from me which I should have kept to myself, but it is every word true; you can depend on that."

Annie Benton seemed satisfied with the answers he had made, and there was another long silence between them.

"And your music—you play like one possessed," he said finally, talking to the wind, probably, for he was not looking at the girl. "Every sentiment my heart has ever known you have expressed in chords. Had I not known differently, I should have thought you were familiar with my history and permitted the organ to tell it whenever we met. What a voice the old box has, and what versatility; for its power in representing angels is only equalled by its power to represent devils. There is a song with which I have become familiar from hearing you play the air; it is a sermon which appealed to me as nothing ever did before. Before I knew the words, I felt sure that they were promises of mercy and forgiveness; and when I found them, I thought I must have been familiar with them all my life; they were exactly what I had imagined. To look at your cold, passionless face now, no one would suspect your wonderful genius. You look innocent enough, but I do not wonder that you are regarded as a greater attraction than the minister. I have been told that you can kill the sermon, when you want to, by freezing the audience before it commences, and I believe it. I have no doubt that you take pride in controlling with your deft fingers the poor folks who worship under the steeple which mounts up below us. I only wonder that you do not cause them to cheer, and swing their hats, for they say that you can move them to tears at will."

"I never feel like cheering myself," she answered, "and I suppose that is why the organ never does. But I very often feel sad, because I am so commonplace, and because there is so little in the future for me. If I play so coldly at times that even the minister is affected, it is because I am indifferent, and forget, and not because I intend it."

"If you are commonplace," Allan Dorris replied, "you have abundant company; for the world is full of common people. We are all creatures of such common mould that I wonder we do not tire of our ugly forms. Out of every hundred thousand there is a genius, who neglects all the virtues of the common folks, and is hateful save as a genius. For his one good quality he has a hundred bad ones; but he is not held to strict account, like the rest of us, for genius is so rare that we encourage it, no matter what the cost. But I have heard that these great people are monstrosities, and thoroughly wretched. I would rather be a king in one honest heart, than a sight for thousands. But this is not running away from you, as I promised, and if I remain here longer I shall lose the power. My path is down the hill; yours is up."

He lifted his hat to her, and walked away; but she called to him,—

"I am going down the hill, too, and I will accompany you."

He waited until she came up, and they walked away together.

The girl had said that she was going down the hill, too, and would accompany him; but Dorris knew that she meant the hill on which they were standing, not the one he referred to. He referred to a hill as famous as wickedness, and known in every house because of its open doors to welcome back some straggler from the noisy crowd travelling down the famous hill; but he thought that should a woman like Annie Benton consent to undertake the journey with him, he would change his course, and travel the other way, in spite of everything.

"Did I do wrong in asking you to wait for me?" she inquired, after they had walked awhile in silence.

"Yes," he answered, "because it pleased me. Be very careful to do nothing which pleases me, for I am not accustomed to it, and the novelty may cause me to forget the vow I have made. A man long accustomed to darkness is very fond of the light. What do you think of me, anyway?"

"What a strange question!" the girl said, turning to look at him.

"Be as frank with me as I was with you. What do you think of me?"

The girl thought the matter over for a while, and replied,—

"If I should answer you frankly, I should please you; and you have warned me against that."

Dorris was amused at the reply, and laughed awhile to himself.

"I didn't think of that," he said, though he probably had thought of it, and hoped that her reply would be what it was. "I am glad to hear that I am not repugnant to you, though. It will be a comfort to me to know, now that my dream has come true, that the subject of it does not regard me with distrust or aversion. I am glad, too, that after dreaming of the sunshine so long, it is not a disappointment. In my loneliness hereafter that circumstance will be a satisfaction, and it will be a pleasure to believe that the sunshine was brighter because of my brief stay in it. I can forget some of the darkness around me in future, in thinking of these two circumstances."

They had reached Thompson Benton's gate by this time, and, the invitation having been extended, Dorris walked into the house. The master was not due for an hour, so Dorris remained until he came, excusing himself by the reflection that he would never see the girl again, and that he was entitled to this pleasure because of the sacrifice he had resolved to make.

It was the same old story over again; Allan Dorris was desperately in love with Annie Benton, but she must not be in love with him, for he was dangerous, and whether this was true or not, his companion did not believe it. He told in a hundred ways, though in language which might have meant any one of a hundred things, that she was his dream come true, and of the necessity which existed for him to avoid her. Occasionally he would forget to be grave, and make sport of himself, and laugh at what he had been saying; and at these times Annie Benton was convinced more than ever that he was not a dangerous man, as he said, for there was an honest gentility in his manner, and a gentle respect for her womanhood in everything he did; therefore she listened attentively to what he said, saying but little herself, as he requested. Although he made love to her in many ingenious ways, and moved Annie Benton as she had never been moved before, he did not so intend it. Could his motives have been impartially judged, that must have been the verdict; but while he knew that his love was out of place in the keeping of the girl, he could not resist the temptation of giving it to her, and then asking her to refuse it.

Several times Annie Benton attempted to speak, but he held up his hand as a warning.

"Don't say anything that you will regret," he said. "Let me do that; I am famous for it. I never talked ten minutes in my life that I didn't say something that caused me regret for a year. But I will never regret anything I have said to you, for I have only made a confession which has been at my tongue's end for years. I have known you all my life; you know nothing of me, and care less, therefore let it be as I suggest."

"But just a word," the girl insisted. "You do not understand what I would say—"

"I don't know what you would say, but I can imagine what a lady like you *should* say under such circumstances, and I beg the favor of your silence. Let me imagine what I please, since that can be of little consequence to you."

There was a noise at the front door, and old Thompson came in. Dorris bowed himself out, followed by a scowl, and as he walked along toward his own house he thought that his resolution to see Annie Benton no more would at least save him from a quarrel with her father.

CHAPTER XII.

RUINED BY KINDNESS.

John Bill, editor of the Davy's Bend *Triumph*, was ruined by a railroad pass. When he taught school over in the bottoms, on the other side of the river, and was compelled to pay his fare when he travelled, he seldom travelled, and therefore put his money carefully away, but when he invested his savings in the *Triumph*, and the railroad company sent him an annual pass, he made up for lost time, and travelled up and down the road almost constantly, all his earnings being required to pay his expenses.

A day seldom passed that John Bill did not get off or on a train at the Davy's Bend station, carrying an important looking satchel in his right hand, and an umbrella in his left, and though he imagined that this coming and going gave the people an idea of his importance, he was mistaken, for they knew he had no business out of the town, and very little in it: therefore they made fun of him, as they did of everything else, for the Davy's Bend people could appreciate the ridiculous in spite of their many misfortunes. They knew enough, else they could not have been such shrewd fault-finders, and they had rather extensive knowledge of everything worldly except a knowledge of the ways of Capital, which was always avoiding them; but this was not astonishing, since Capital had never lived among them and been subject to their keen scrutiny.

When an event was advertised to take place on the line of road over which his pass was accepted, John Bill was sure to be present, for he argued that, in order to report the news correctly, he must be on the ground in person; but usually he remained away so long, and gave the subject in hand such thorough attention, that he concluded on his return that the people had heard of the proceedings, and did not write them up, though he frequently asserted with much earnestness that no editor in that country gave the news as much personal attention as he did.

Still, John Bill claimed to be worth a good deal of money. There was no question at all, he frequently argued, that his business and goodwill were worth fifteen thousand dollars—any man would be willing to pay that for the *Triumph* and its goodwill, providing he had the money; therefore, deducting his debts, which amounted to a trifle of eleven hundred dollars on his material, in the shape of an encumbrance, and a floating indebtedness of half as much more, he was still worth a little more than thirteen thousand dollars. The people said that everything in his office was not worth half the amount of the encumbrance, and that his goodwill could not be very valuable, since his business did not pay its expenses; but John Bill could prove that the people had never treated him justly, therefore they were likely to misrepresent the facts in his case.

There was a mortgage, as any one who cared to examine the records might convince himself, but it was a very respectable mortgage, and had been extended from time to time, as the office changed hands, for fifteen years past. It had been owned by all the best men in the neighborhood; but while a great many transfers were noted thereon, no credits appeared, so John Bill was no worse than the rest of them. The former parties of the first part had intended paying off the trifling amount in a few weeks, and thereby become free to act as they pleased; John Bill had the same intention concerning the document, therefore it was no great matter after all.

Besides, there were the accounts. He had a book full of them, and was always showing it to those who bothered him for money. The accounts were all against good men; a little slow, perhaps, but good, nevertheless, and the accounts should be figured in an estimate of John Bill's affairs, which would add a few thousands more to the total.

It was a little curious, though, that most of the men whose names appeared on John Bill's ledger had accounts against John Bill, and while he frequently turned to their page and showed their balances, they also turned to John Bill's page in *their* ledgers, and remarked that there was no getting anything out of him. Thompson Benton had been heard to say that each of these men were afraid to present their bills first, fearing that the others would create a larger one; so the accounts ran on from year to year. But whoever was in the right, it is certain that the accounts were a great comfort to John Bill, for he frequently looked them over as a miser might count his money.

John Bill was certain the people of Davy's Bend were ungrateful. He had helped them and their town in a thousand ways, and spent his time (or that part of it not devoted to using his pass) in befriending them; but did they appreciate him? They did not; this may be set down as certain, for if the editor had put them in the way of making money, they were thoroughly ungrateful. Indeed, the people went so far as to declare that John Bill was the ungrateful one, nor were they backward in saying so. They had taken his paper, and helped him in every way possible, but he did not appreciate it; so they accused each other, and a very uncomfortable time they had of it. But though John Bill claimed to be always helping the people, and though the people claimed that they had done a great deal for John Bill, the facts were that neither John Bill nor the people gave substantial evidence of any very great exertions in each other's behalf, so there must have been a dreadful mistake out somewhere. Likewise, they quarrelled as to which had tried to bring the greater number of institutions to the town; but as to the institutions actually secured, there were none to quarrel over, so there was peace in this direction.

John Bill frequently came to the conclusion that his wrongs must be righted; that he must call names, and dot his i's and cross his t's, even to pointing out to the world wherein he had been wronged. He could stand systematic persecution no longer, he said, so he would fill his ink-bottle, and secure a fresh supply of paper, with a view of holding up to public scorn those who had trampled him in the dust of the street. But it was a bold undertaking; a stouter heart than John Bill's would have shrunk from attacking a people with a defence as sound as the Davy's Bend folks could have made, so he usually compromised by writing paid locals about the men he had intended to accuse of ingratitude, referring to them as generous, warm-hearted men, who were creditable to humanity, all of which he added to the accounts at the rate of eight cents per line of seven words.

John Bill was so situated that he did little else than write paid locals, though he usually found time once a week to write imaginary descriptions of the rapid increase in circulation his paper was experiencing. He had discovered somehow that men who would pay for nothing else would pay for being referred to as citizens of rare accomplishments, and as gentlemen whose business ability was such that their competitors were constantly howling in rage; and it became necessary to use this knowledge to obtain the bare necessities of life. The very men who declared that John Bill could have no more goods at their stores until old scores were squared would soften under the influence of the puff, and honor his "orders" when in the hands of either of the two young men who did his work.

Perhaps this was one reason the *Triumph* was on all sides of every question. Whoever saw fit to write for it had his communication printed as original editorial; for the editor was seldom at home, and when he was, he found his time taken up in earning his bread by writing palatable falsehoods; therefore all the contributions went in, and as correspondents seldom agree, the *Triumph* was a remarkable publication. Whenever a citizen had a grievance, he aired it in the *Triumph*, his contribution appearing as the opinion of the editor. The person attacked replied in like manner; hence John Bill was usually in the attitude of fiercely declaring *No* one week, and *Yes* with equal determination the next. It was so on all subjects; politics, religion, local matters—everything. The Republican who aired his views one week in John Bill's remarkable editorial columns was sure to find himself confronted by a Democrat who was handy with a pen in the next issue; the man who wrote that This, or That, or the Other, was a disgrace, would soon find out that This, or That, or the Other, were very creditable; for John Bill's printers must have copy, and John Bill was too busy travelling and lying to furnish it himself.

Having returned home on the night train, John Bill climbed the stairway at the head of which his office was situated, and was engaged in preparing for his next issue. Although he felt sure that a large amount of important mail matter had arrived during his absence, it could not be found; and therefore the editor was in rather bad humor, as he produced a list of paid notices to be written, and made lazy preparation for writing them. The editor was always expecting important mail matter, and because it never came he almost concluded that the postmaster was in the intrigue against him. While thinking that he would include that official in the exposé he felt it his duty to write at some time in the future, a knock came at the door. He had heard no step ascending the stair, therefore he concluded it must be one of his young men; probably the pale one, who was wasting his life in chewing plug tobacco, and squirting it around in puddles, in order that he might realize on a joke which he had perpetrated by printing a sign in huge letters, requesting visitors not to spit on the floor.

In response to his invitation a tall gentleman came in,—a stranger, dressed in a suit of black material that gave him the appearance of being much on the road, for it was untidy and unkempt. He looked a good deal like a genteel man who had been lately engaged in rough work, and John Bill noticed that he kept his left side turned from him. The stranger's hair, as well as his moustache and goatee, were bushy, and sprinkled with gray; and he had a rather peculiar pair of eyes, which he used to such an advantage that he seemed to remark everything in the room at a single glance. An odd man, John Bill thought; a man who might turn out to be anything surprising; so he looked at him curiously quite a long time.

"You are Mr. Bill?" the stranger asked, after the two men had looked each other over to their joint satisfaction.

The editor acknowledged his name by an inclination of the head, at the same time offering a chair.

"I came in on the night train," the tall man said, seating himself with the left side of his face toward the door at which he had entered; "therefore I call upon you at this unseasonable hour to make a few inquiries with reference to your place. It is not probable that I shall become an advertiser, or a patron of any kind; but I think you may depend on it that I will shortly furnish you with an item of news. I have read your editorial paragraphs with a good deal of interest, and concluded that you could give me the information desired."

John Bill expressed a wish to himself that the stranger would never find out that he did not write the editorials he professed to admire; but there was a possibility that his visitor was not sincere. He had said that he came to the town on the night train. John Bill knew this to be untrue, for he had been a passenger on that train himself, and no one else got off when he did. He was glad, however, that the determined-looking visitor did not bring a folded copy of the *Triumph* with him for convenience in referring to an objectionable paragraph; for John Bill felt sure that such a man as the stranger looked to be would not go away without satisfaction of some kind. He was bothered a good deal in this way, by reason of his rather peculiar way of conducting the *Triumph*; but questions with reference to Davy's Bend,—he could answer them easy enough.

But he did not contradict the statement of his visitor concerning the time he arrived in town, for he did not look like a man who would take kindly to a thing of that sort; so the editor meekly said he would be pleased to give him any information in his power.

"I will inquire first about the man calling himself—Allan Dorris," the stranger continued, consulting a book which he took from his pocket, and pausing a little before pronouncing the name, "and I ask that this conversation be in confidence. How long has this fellow been here?"

The tall stranger put up his book, and looked at the responsible head of the *Triumph*, as though he would intimate that his displeasure would be serious should his instructions be neglected.

"This is October," Mr. Bill replied, counting on his fingers. "He came in the spring, some time; probably six months ago. I do not know him personally. He is a doctor, and lives in a place called 'The Locks,' on the edge of the town, in this direction," pointing his finger toward the stone church, and the house in which Allan Dorris lived. "That's about all I know of him."

The peculiar pair of eyes owned by the odd man followed the direction pointed out for a moment, and then settled on John Bill again.

"I have heard that he has a love affair with a young woman named—Annie Benton," the visitor said with business precision, once more consulting his book, and pausing before pronouncing the name, as he had done before. "What do you know about that?"

"I have heard something of it," the editor replied, "but nothing in particular; only that he is with her a great deal, and that he meets her usually in a church near his house. The people talk about it, but I am too busy to pay much attention to such matters."

John Bill was trying to create the impression that he was kept busy in writing the sparkling editorials which the stranger had pretended to admire, but thinking at the last moment that his travelling was his credit, he added, with a modest cough: "Besides, I travel a good deal." But this was not the first time John Bill had tried to create a wrong impression. He foolishly imagined that, being an editor, he was expected to know more than other people; but as he did not, he frequently filled his mind with old dates, and names, and events, by reading of them, and then talked of the subject to others, pretending that it had just occurred to him, and usually adding a word or two concerning the popular ignorance. If he encountered a word which he did not know the meaning of, he looked it up, and used it a great deal after that, usually in connection with arguments to prove that the average man did not understand the commonest words in his language. Nor was this all; John Bill was a deceiver in another particular. He frequently intimated in the *Triumph* that if he were a rich man he would spend his money liberally in "helping the town;" that is, in mending the streets and sidewalks, and in building manufactures which would give employment to "labor." John Bill was certainly a deceiver in this, for there never was a poor man who did not find fault with the well-to-do for taking care of their means. The men who have no money of their own claim to know exactly how money should be invested, but somehow the men who have money entertain entirely different ideas on the subject.

Upon invitation the editor told of old Thompson Benton and his disposition; of the beauty of his daughter, and of her talent as a musician; of Allan Dorris's disposition, which seemed to be sour one day, and sweet the next, and so on; all of which the stranger noted in his book, occasionally making an inquiry as the narrative of the town's gossip progressed. When this was concluded, the book in which the notes were made was carefully put away, and the stranger backed toward the door, still keeping his left side in the shadow, first leaving a ten-dollar note on the editorial table.

"I shall need your services soon," he said, "and I make a small payment in advance to bind the bargain. When the time comes you will know it. Your business then will be to forget this interview. You are also to say nothing about it until you receive the warning to forget. I bid you good-night."

So saying the stranger was gone, retreating down the stairway so lightly that his footsteps could not be heard.

A rather remarkable circumstance, the editor thought; a visit at such an hour from a mysterious man who inquired minutely about a citizen who was almost as much of a mystery as the visitor himself; and when he heard a step on the stair again, he concluded that the stranger had forgotten something, and was coming back, so he opened the door, only to meet Mrs. Whittle, the milliner, who carried a sealed envelope in her hand.

John Bill did not like Mrs. Whittle, the milliner, very well; for she had a habit of saying that "her work" was all the advertising she needed, referring to the circumstance that she had become the town busybody in her attempts to reform the people; but he received her politely, and thought to himself that when his sensation finally appeared it would refer to this party as fluffy, fat, and beardy.

Mrs. Whittle had a good deal to say concerning the careless, good-natured wickedness of the people, and the people had a good deal to say about Mrs. Whittle. One thing they said was, that while she was always coaxing those who were doing very well to become better, she was shamefully neglecting her own blood in the person of little Ben Whittle, her only child, who was being worked to death by the farmer named Quade, in whose employ he was. This unfortunate child had not seen his mother for years, and was really sick, distressed, ragged, and dirty; but while Mrs. Whittle imagined that he was doing very well, and felt quite easy concerning him, she could not sleep at night from worrying over the fear that other children, blessed with indulgent parents and good homes, were growing up in wickedness. Her husband was a drunkard and a loafer, but Mrs. Whittle had no time to bother about him; there were men in the town so thoroughly debased as to remain at home, and rest on Sunday, instead of going to church, and to this unfortunate class she devoted her life. She frequently took credit to herself that the best citizens of Davy's Bend were not in jail, and believed that they would finally acknowledge their debt to her; but of her unfortunate son and her vagrant husband she never thought at all; so John Bill could not very well be blamed for disliking her.

"I heard you would return to-night," the good woman said, panting from her exertion in climbing the stairs, "and I wanted to deliver this with my own hands, which is my excuse for coming at this late hour, though I don't suppose that any one would doubt that I came on a good errand, even if they had seen me coming up. Bless me, what a hard stair you have!"

John Bill took the envelope, and, after tearing it open, hung the note it contained on an empty hook within reach of his hand, without looking at it. Meanwhile Mrs. Whittle continued to pant, and look good.

"It refers to Allan Dorris's affair with Annie Benton," she said, recovering her breath at last. "Something should be done, and I don't know who else is to do it. The people all mean well enough, and they are good enough people as a rule; but when there is good to be accomplished, I usually find it is *not* accomplished unless I take an interest in it. No one knows better than John Bill that I do not suspect people, and am always inclined to believe good of them, but there is something wrong about this Allan Dorris. Mr. Ponsonboy and Mr. Wilton say so, and you know they are very careful of what they say."

John Bill had heard that statement questioned, and he mentally added their names to his black list. Two greater talking old women never wore pants, John Bill had heard said, than Messrs. Ponsonboy and Wilton, and when he got at it he would skin them with the others.

"Better men than Mr. Ponsonboy and Mr. Wilton never lived," Mrs. Whittle said, "and I have concluded to write a hint which Annie Benton as well as Allan Dorris will understand. If nothing comes of it, I will try something else. I am not easily discouraged, Mr. Bill; I would have given up long ago if I were."

Mrs. Whittle found it necessary to pause for another rest, and the editor took opportunity to make mental note of the fact (for use in the coming exposure) that she was dressed in the most execrable taste; that her clothes seemed to have been thrown at her from a miscellaneous assortment, without regard to color, material, or shape, and that she had not taken the trouble to arrange them. John Bill felt certain that when the people were buying copies of his paper to burn, they would read that Mrs. Whittle was in need of the refining influences of a dress-maker.

"You are a good man at heart, Mr. Bill," Mrs. Whittle said again, which was an expression the editor had heard before, for he was always being told that he was a better man than he appeared to be, though he knew a great many people who were not better than they appeared to be. "I know you are, and that you do not mean all the bad things you say sometimes. I know you will help me in doing good, for it is so important that good *should* be done. When I think of the wickedness around me, and the work that is to be done, I almost faint at the prospect, but I only hope that my strength may enable me to hold out to the end. I pray that I may be spared until this is a better world."

Mr. Bill promised to find a place in his crowded columns for the good woman's contribution, and she went away, with a sigh for the general wickedness.

"The world will be better off for that sigh," John Bill said, as he settled down in his chair, and heard Mrs. Whittle step off the stair into the street. "What we need is more sighing and less work. There is no lack of workers; in fact, the country is too full of them for comfort, but there is a painful lack of good people to sigh. The first one who called to-night on Allan Dorris business looked like a worker; a worker-off, I may say. This Dorris is becoming important of late. I must make his acquaintance. Hello! Another!"

The owner of the legs that were climbing the stairway this time turned out to be Silas Davy, who came in and handed John Bill a piece of paper. It proved to be a brief note, which read,—

> "TO JOHN BILL,—If the party who has just left your office
> left a communication concerning Allan Dorris, I speak for
> the privilege of answering it.
>
> "TUG WHITTLE."

John Bill read the note several times over after Silas had disappeared, and finally getting up from his chair, said,—

"I'll write no more to-night; there may be interesting developments in the morning."

CHAPTER XIII.

THE REBELLION OF THE BARITONE.

During the summer and winter following the arrival of Allan Dorris in Davy's Bend, he met Annie Benton at intervals after their strange meeting out on the hills, in spite of his resolution to keep out of her way, and though he was convinced more than ever after each meeting that their acquaintance was dangerous, he candidly admitted to himself that he was powerless to resist the temptation to see her when opportunity offered, for the girl waited as anxiously for his appearance as he did for hers; she was as deeply concerned as he was, and while this circumstance afforded him a kind of pleasure, it was also painful, for he felt certain that no good could come of it.

Usually he attended the services in the church once a week, and watched the organist so closely that she always divined his presence, and looked timidly toward where he sat when opportunity offered. Dorris believed that he could cause the girl to think of him by looking at her, and though he changed his position at every service, he had the satisfaction of finally seeing her pick him out, and she never made a mistake, always looking directly at him when she turned her head.

After the people were dismissed, he occasionally met her at the door, and walked home with her behind her glowering father, who received the attentions of Dorris with little favor. A few times he remained in the church with her a few minutes after the congregation had passed out, but after each meeting he felt more dissatisfied than ever, and chafed under the restraint which held him back. A few times, also, he went into the house, after accompanying her home, which pleased Annie Benton as much as it displeased old Thompson, but somehow he did not enjoy her company there as he did when she was alone in the church, for the Ancient Maiden, as well as the Ancient Gentleman, seemed to regard him with suspicion and distrust; therefore in spite of his vows to let her alone, which he had made with honesty and sincerity, he called on her at the church nearly every week.

He believed that he was entitled to some credit because he only saw the girl occasionally, for he longed to be with her continually; and there were times, when he heard the organ, that he overcame the temptation and did not enter the church. On these occasions he turned his face doggedly toward The Locks, and paced up and down in his own room until he knew the temptation was removed; when he would go out into the yard again, hoping that some good fortune had detained the player longer than usual, and that he would meet her unexpectedly.

This same spirit caused him to haunt the road which she frequented on her visits to and from the town, and quite often he had occasion to appear surprised at her approach when he was not, when he would walk with her one way or the other until it seemed necessary for them to separate. It was not a deep *ruse*—nor did it deceive himself, for he often laughed at its absurdity—but it afforded occupation to a man who was idle more than half his time, and Allan Dorris was like other men in the particular that he wanted to do right, but found it very difficult when inclination led in the other direction. When they met in this manner, each usually had time to say only enough to excite the curiosity of the other, and to cause them to long for another meeting, and thus the winter was passed, and the early spring came on; the season of quarreling between frost and sunshine.

On a certain wild March evening, after a day of idleness and longing to see the girl, Dorris put on his heavy coat and walked in the yard, up and down the old path under the trees, which gave evidences of his restless footsteps even in the snows of winter. As soon as he came out he heard the music, and between his strong desire to see the player, and his conviction that he should never enter her presence, he resolved to leave Davy's Bend and never return. He could better restrain his love for her in some distant town than in Davy's Bend, therefore he would go away, and try to forget. This gave him an excuse to enter the church, though he only intended to bid her good-by; and so impatient was he that he scaled the wall, and jumped down on the outside, instead of passing out at the gate.

Annie Benton was watching for him when he stepped into her presence from the vestibule, and as he walked up the aisle he saw so much pleasure in her face that he regretted to make the announcement of his departure; but he knew it was the best thing to do, and did not hesitate. He even thought of the prospect that she might regret his determination, and say so, which would greatly please him.

"I have concluded to leave Davy's Bend," he said, as he took the hand she offered him, "and have called to say good-by. As soon as I can dispose of my effects I will leave this forbidden ground, and travel so far that I will forget the way back. The more I see of you, the more I love you; and if I continue to live in sight of your house, I will finally forget everything except that I love you, and do you a great harm. It will not take me long to settle up my affairs, and within a few days, at the farthest, I shall be gone."

The smile on Annie Benton's pretty face vanished at once, as she turned her head and looked from him, at the same time trying to run her fingers over the keys; but they had lost their cunning, and her hands soon lay idly on the keyboards. When Dorris finally caught her head gently, and turned it toward him, he saw that tears were in her eyes. She did not attempt to hide this, and quietly submitted when he brushed them away.

"It pains me to know that you regret this announcement," Dorris said, after looking at her a moment, "though it would pain me more to believe that you did not. It seems to be always so; there is sorrow in everything for me. I have cursed myself a thousand times for this quality, and thought ill of a nature which had no peace or content in it. I have hated myself for years because of the belief that nothing would satisfy me; that I would tire of everything I coveted, and that I was born a misanthrope and an embodied unrest. When I have envied others their content, I have always concluded afterwards that there was something in my nature opposed to peace, and that I was doomed to a restless life, always seeking that which could not be found. I have always believed that my acquaintances have had this opinion of me, and that for this reason they did not grant me the charity I felt the need of. But now that I am going away, and will never see you again, I hope you will pardon my saying that your absence has been the cause of the unrest which has always beset me. Long before I knew you existed I was looking for you; and I know now that all my discontent would have vanished had I been free to make honorable love to you when we first met. In our weakness we are permitted to know a few things; I know this to be true."

"Since you have always wished me to take no interest in this acquaintance of ours," Annie Benton replied, in a tone which might have been only sullen, but it sounded very much like the voice of an earnest woman expressing vexation and regret, "let me at least express in words what I have often expressed in my actions—that I would have long ago shown you that your affection was returned; that you are not more concerned than I am. I have always been in doubt as to what my course should be; but let me say this, in justice to my intelligence, though it be a discredit to my womanhood, you can never love me more than I do you. Nor do you more sincerely regret the necessity which you say exists for your going away."

"I hope I do not take undue credit to myself," he replied, "when I say that I have known this ever since our acquaintance began, and I only asked you to remain silent because I could not have controlled myself with declarations of love from your lips ringing in my ears. You trusted my judgment fully, and refused to hear the reasons why I said our acquaintance was dangerous; and I will deserve that confidence by going away, for I know that is the best thing to do. Sometimes there is a little pleasure in a great sorrow. I have known mothers to find pleasure in talking of their dead children, and I find a fascination in talking to you about a love which can never be realized. Heretofore I have been a man shut up in a dungeon, craving sunlight, hating myself because I came to believe that there was no sunlight; now I realize that sunlight was a natural necessity for my well-being, for I have found it, and it is all I hoped. But I must go back into the dungeon, and the necessity is more disagreeable than I can tell you. I am an average man in every respect save that I feel that I have never had an average man's chance in this matter of love, and fret because of it. That which I crave may be a mistake of the fancy, but I am not convinced of it; therefore I am not as philanthropic as those who have outgrown in experience an infatuation such as I feel for you. I have tried everything else, and have learned to be indifferent, with all my idols broken and dishonored at my feet; but there is a possibility in love which I can never know anything about."

While the girl was listening, there were times when Dorris thought she would interrupt him, and make the declaration which he had forbidden; but she controlled herself, and looked steadily away from him.

"It may occur to you as strange—it *is* strange—that while I declare my love for you, I run away from it. In explanation I could only repeat what I have said before; that it is for your good that I have adopted this course. Had you listened to my brief story, you would now understand why my going away seems to be necessary; since you preferred not to, I can only say in general terms that nothing could happen, except good fortune, which would surprise me. I am surrounded by danger, and while my life has been one long regret, the greatest regret of all is that which I experience in leaving you. Were I to consult my own bent, I would deny all that I have intimated to my discredit, and make such love to you that you could not resist it; but I love you, and this course would not prove it. We are doing now what millions of people have done before us; making a sacrifice for the right against strong inclinations, and we should meet it bravely. There is no hesitation in my manner, I hope."

Annie Benton turned and looked at him, and saw that he was trembling and very much agitated.

"Then why are you trembling?" she asked.

"Because of the chill in the air, I presume," he answered, "for I am very determined to carry out my resolution. I might tremble with excitement in resolving to rescue a friend from danger, though it would not indicate a lack of courage. You are willing for me to go?"

"Since you say it is for the best," she replied, "yes."

Believing that he had said all that was necessary, Allan Dorris hesitated between going away and remaining. Walking over to the window, and looking out, he saw that the light he had been talking about was fading away from the earth, as it was fading away from him, and that the old night was coming back. A hill-top he saw in the distance he likened to himself; resisting until the last moment, but without avail, for the darkness was gradually climbing up its sides, and would soon cover it.

"You will no doubt think that I should have kept away from you when I saw that my presence was not objectionable, and that our acquaintance would finally result in this," he said, coming back to the girl, and standing by her side, "but I could not; let me acknowledge my fault, and say that I am sorry for it. I could not resist the temptation to enter the only presence which has ever afforded me pleasure, try hard as I could, so I kept it up until I am now forced to run away from it. Do I make my meaning clear?"

"Perfectly," she replied, without looking around.

"Life is so unsatisfactory that it affords nothing of permanent value except the love and respect of a worthy, intelligent, and agreeable woman. It is the favor I have sought, and found too late. It is fortunate that you are not as reckless as I am; otherwise no restraint would keep us apart. But for the respect I have for your good name, I would steal you, and teach you to love me in some far-away place."

"You have taught me already," the girl timidly replied, still looking away.

"Don't say that," Dorris said in alarm. "That pleases me, for it is depravity, and everything depraved seems to suit me. You must say nothing which pleases me, else I will fail in my resolve. Say everything you can to hurt my feelings, but nothing to please me."

"I cannot help saying it," she replied, rising from her seat at the organ, and facing him. "If it is depravity to love you, I like depravity, too."

"Annie," Dorris said, touching her arm, "be careful of what you say."

"I must say it," she returned, with a flushed face; "I am only a woman, and you don't know how much weakness that implies. I am flesh and blood, like yourself; but you have made love to me as though I were an unconscious picture. I fear that you do not understand womankind, and that you have made an idol of me; an idol which will fall, and break at your feet. My love for you has come to me as naturally as my years, and I want you to know when you go away that my heart will be in your keeping. Why may not I avow my love as well as you? Why may not I, too, express regret that you are going away?"

The girl asked the question with a candor which surprised him; there was the innocence of a child in her manner, and the enthusiasm of a woman thoroughly in earnest.

"For the reason that when I am gone it will be in the nature of things for you to forget me," he replied. "You are young, and do not know your heart as well as I know mine. In course of time you will probably form an honorable alliance; *then* you will regret having said this to me."

"It will always be a pleasure for me to remember how ardently I have loved you," she replied, trembling and faltering, as though not quite certain that the course she was pursuing was right. "I will never feel ashamed of it, no matter if I should live forever. It may not be womanly for me to say so; but I can never forget you. Your attentions to me have been so delicate, and so well calculated to win a woman's affection, that I want you to know that, but for this hindrance you speak of, your dream might be realized. If I am the Maid of Air, the Maid of Air returns your affection. Surely my regard for you may excuse my saying this, now that you are going away, for you may think of it with pleasure in your future loneliness. I appreciate your love so much that I must tell you that it is returned."

They were standing close together on the little platform in front of the organ, and the girl leaned against him in such a manner that he put his left arm around her shoulders to support her. Her head rested on his arm, and she was looking full into his face. The excitement under which she seemed to labor lent such a charm to her face that Allan Dorris thought that surely it must be the handsomest in the world.

"Kiss me," she said suddenly.

The suggestion frightened the great brawny fellow, who might have picked up his companion and ran away with her without the slightest inconvenience; for he looked around the room in alarm.

"I don't know whether I will or not," he replied, looking steadily at her. "Were you ever kissed before?"

"By my father; by no one else."

"Then I think I will refuse," he said, "though I would give twenty years of my life to grant your request. What a request it is! It appeals to me with such force that I feel a weakness in my eyes because of the warmth in my heart, and the hot blood never ran races through my veins before as it is doing now. You have complete possession of my heart, and I am a better man than I was before, for you are pure and good; if I have a soul, it has forgotten its immortality in loving this earthy being in my arms. But it is the proudest boast of a loyal wife that no lips save those of her husband ever touched hers, and my regard for you is such that I do not wish to detract from the peace of your future. If I have made an idol of you, let me go away without discovering my mistake; grant me the privilege of remembering you as the realization of all my dreaming. In a year from now you will only remember me to thank me for this refusal of your request."

"In a year from now I will feel just as I do now. I will never change. I will have only this to remember you by, and my acquaintance with you has been the only event in my life worth remembering. *Please* kiss me."

He hurriedly pressed her lips to his own, and looked around as though he half expected to be struck dead for the sacrilege, but nothing serious resulted, and the girl continued to talk without changing her position.

"I have never regretted the restraint which is expected of women until I knew you, for why should I not express my preferences as well as you? In my lonely, dreamy childhood, I had few acquaintances and fewer friends, and you have supplied a want which I hardly knew existed before. Ever since I can remember, I have longed so much to know the people in the great world from which you came that I accepted you as a messenger from them, and you interested and pleased me even more than I expected. My life has always been lonely, though not unhappy, and the people I read of in books I accepted as the people who lived outside of Davy's Bend, in the cities by the lakes and seas, where there is culture as well as plenty. I have been familiar with their songs, and played them on the organ when I should have been practising; everything I have read of them I have put to music, and played it over and over. Once I read of a great man who died, and who was buried from a church filled with distinguished mourners. The paper said that when the people were all in their seats, the voice of a great singer broke the stillness, in a song of hope, and I have imitated the voice on the organ, and imagined that I was playing a requiem over distinguished dust; but in future I shall think only of you when I play the funeral march. Since I have known you, I have thought of little else, and I shall mourn your departure as though you had always been a part of me. If I dared, I would ask you on my knees to remain."

"I have heard you play the songs to which you refer," Dorris replied musingly, "and I have thought that you played them with so much expression that, could their authors have listened to the performance, they would have discovered new beauties in them. I never knew a player before who could render the words of a song as well as the music. You do it, and with so much genius that I wonder that you have nothing but the cold, passionless notes to guide you. One dark afternoon you played 'I Dreamt I Dwelt in Marble Halls,' and a savage could have told what the words were. The entire strength of the organ seemed to be united in the mournful air, and the timid accompaniment was peopled with the other characters in the play from which the song is taken. That represented you; but you have had me before the organ, telling all I knew, a hundred times. Although you have refused to hear my story, you seem to know it; for you have told it on the organ as many times as I have thought of it."

"If I have told your story on the organ," the girl said, "there must have been declarations in it that you were a brave, an honorable, and an unfortunate man, for I have always thought that of you. In spite of all you have said to me against yourself, I have never doubted this for a moment, and I would trust you to any extent."

"If I expect to carry out my resolution," Allan Dorris replied, as though in anger, though it was really an unspoken protest against doing a disagreeable thing, "I must hear no more of this; a very little more of what you have said, and retreat will be impossible. But before I leave you, let me say this: You once said I was an odd man; I will tell you why. I seem to be an odd man because you have heard every sentiment there is in my heart; I have kept nothing back. The men you have known were close-mouthed and suspicious, knowing that whatever they said was likely to be repeated, and this made them cautious. Place other men in my situation as to loneliness and misfortune, and I would not seem so unusual. There are plenty of staid business men who are as 'odd' as I am, but they have never been moved to tell their secrets, as I have done to you. Even were your honorable father to express the love he feels for your dead mother, it would sound sentimental and foolish, and surprise his acquaintances; but rest assured that every man will turn out a strange creature when you get his confidence. I say this in justice to myself, but it is the truth. When you know any man thoroughly, you either think more or less of him."

"I don't dare to tell you what is in my mind," Annie Benton said, as she stood beside him, his arm still around her. "It would startle you, and perhaps cause you to change the good opinion you have expressed of me; but there can be no harm in my saying this—every day of our acquaintance has brought me more respect and love for you. Let me pay you the poor compliment of saying that the more I know of you, the more I respect and honor you."

"I believe I deserve that," he replied. "I have more than my share of faults, but it has always been a comfort for me to know that my best friends are those who know most of me. But though I have faults, I am not the less sensitive. I believe that should I kill a man, I would as keenly feel the slights of my fellows as would one whose hands were clean. Should I become so offensive to mankind as to merit banishment, my wickedness would not cause me to forget my loneliness. My mistakes have been as trifling in their nature, and as innocent, as neglect to lock a door in a community of thieves; but I have been punished as severely as though I had murdered a town. The thieves have pursued and beaten me because I carelessly permitted them to steal my substance; and the privilege of touching a pure woman's lips with my own, and folding her in my arms, becomes a serious wrong, though it has only brought me a joy which other men have known, and no harm came of it."

"I do not wish to do anything that is wrong," the girl said, with some alarm, stepping away from him, as if frightened at her situation; "but on the score of friendship, I may say that I shall be very lonely when you are gone. Davy's Bend was never an agreeable place, but I was content with it until you came and filled me with ambition. I wanted to become worthy of the many kind things you said of me; I hoped that I might distinguish myself in some way, and cause you to rejoice that you had predicted well of me, but now that you are going away, you will never know of it even if I succeed. I may regret your departure on this account, if nothing else. I *do* regret it for another reason, but you reprimand me for saying it."

The dogged look which distinguished him when thinking came into his face again, and though he seemed to be paying no attention, he was listening with keen interest.

"Regret seems to be the common inheritance," he said, after a protracted silence between them. "Your regret makes me stronger; it convinces me that I am not its only victim. Duty is a master we must all obey, though I wonder that so many heed its demands, since it seldom leads us in the direction we would travel. The busy world is full of people who are making sacrifices for duty as great as yours and mine; let us not fail in doing ours. In the name of the only woman I ever loved, I ask you to bid me good-by with indifference. For the good of the best woman in the world, play a joyful march while I leave your presence, never to return."

Without another word, the girl sprang to her seat at the organ, and Allan Dorris having awakened the sleeping janitor, the music commenced; a march of joy, to the time of which he left the church without once looking back.

But on reaching the outside he could not resist the temptation to look once more at Annie Benton; so he climbed up to his old position on the wall, and looked at her through the broken pane.

He saw her look around, as if to convince herself that he was gone, when the music changed from joy to regret while her face was yet turned toward the door at which he had departed. She was thinking, and expressing her thoughts with the pipes, and Allan Dorris knew what she was thinking as well as if she were speaking the words. There were occasional passages in the music so fierce and wild that he knew the girl was struggling with desperate thoughts; nor could she easily get rid of them, for the reckless tones seemed to be fighting for mastery over the gentler ones. The old baritone air again; but strong and courageous now, instead of mournful, and it seemed to be muttering that it had ceased to be forbearing, and had no respect for customs, or usages, or matters of conscience; indeed, there was a certain reckless abandon in it which caused the listener to compare it to the roaring song of a man reeling home to squalor and poverty—a sort of declaration that he liked squalor and poverty better than anything else. The mild notes of the accompaniment with the right hand—how like entreating human voices they sounded—a chord of self-respect, of love of home, of duty, in all their persuasive changes, urging the enraged baritone air to be reasonable, and return to the pacific state which it had honored so long; but the baritone air continued to threaten to break over all restraint, and become as wild and fierce as it sounded. Occasionally the chord of self respect, of love of home, and of duty, seemed to gain the mastery, but the wicked baritone broke away again, though it was growing more mild and tractable, and Allan Dorris thought that it must finally succumb to the eloquent appeal in the treble. "I have been mild and gentle all my life"—it seemed to be grumbling the words, as an apology for giving in, instead of declaring them as an excuse for breaking over all restraint—"and what good has it done me? Am I happier than those who have mingled joys with their regrets? My mild sacrifices have resulted in nothing, and I am tempted to try what a little spirit will do."

But the unruly spirit was pacified at last, and the music resolved itself into a lullaby of the kind which mothers sing to their children; it may have been a recollection of the player's own childhood, for it soon caused her to bow her head on the keyboard, and burst into tears.

CHAPTER XIV.

THE ANCIENT MAIDEN.

Jane Benton, old Thompson's maiden sister, was as good as anybody, though no one urged the point as steadily as she did herself. Had the President walked into Jane Benton's presence, she would have believed that he had heard of her (although there was no reason that she should entertain that opinion) and had called to pay his respects; and instead of being timid in so great a presence, she would have expected him to be timid in hers.

There were people who cared to distinguish themselves: very well, let them do it; but Jane Benton did not have that ambition, though she had the ability, and could have easily made a name for herself which would have gone thundering down the ages. Let other people distinguish themselves and pay the price; Jane Benton was distinguished naturally—effort was not necessary in her case. If the people did not acknowledge it, it was their loss, not hers.

The Ancient Maiden was a book-worm, and devoured everything she heard of; but only with a determination to tear it to pieces, for of course no one could hope to amuse or instruct a lady of forty-five, who not only knew everything worth knowing already, but who had taught school in her younger days on the strength of a certificate ranging from ninety-eight to ninety-nine. This certificate had been issued by three learned men, each one of whom knew absolutely everything; and it was agreed by them that Jane Benton should have had an even hundred but for the circumstance that her "hand write" was a little crooked. This fault had since been remedied, and the Ancient Maiden still retained the certificate, and the recollection of the conclusion by the three learned men, as an evidence that, so far as education was concerned, she lacked nothing whatever.

When she consented to favor a book by looking through it, there was unutterable disgust on her features as she possessed herself of the contents, since she felt nothing but contempt for the upstarts who attempted to amuse or instruct so great a woman as Jane Benton. And her patience was usually rewarded.

Thompson! Annie! Ring the bells, and run here! The ignorant pretender has been found out! A turned letter in the book! A that for a which! A will for a shall! A would for a should! Hurrah! Announce it to the people! Another pretender found out! Lock the book up! It is worthless! Jane Benton's greatness, so long in doubt, is vindicated!

But while there is not a perfect book in existence now, there is likely to be one, providing Jane Benton lives three or four hundred years longer, for the thought has often occurred to her that she ought to do something for the race, although it does not deserve such a kindness, as a pattern for all future writers. She has done nothing in forty-five years; but she has been busy during that time, no doubt, in preparing for a book which will not only astonish the living, but cause the dead to crawl out of their graves, and feel ashamed of themselves. Let the people go on in their mad ignorance; Jane Benton is preparing to point out their errors, and in the course of the present century—certainly not later than toward the close of the next one—a new prophet will appear in such robes of splendid perfection that even the earth will acknowledge its imperfections, and creep off into oblivion.

But notwithstanding her rather remarkable conceit, Jane Benton was a useful woman. For fifteen years she had "pottered around," as old Thompson said, and made her brother's home a pleasant one. Since she could not set the world on fire, she said she did not want to, and at least knew her own home perfectly, and had it under thorough control. When old Thompson needed anything, and ransacked the house until he concluded that it had been burned up, his sister Jane could put her hand on the article immediately; and perhaps Jane Benton's genius, in which she had so much confidence, was a genius for attempting only what she could do well; for whatever her intentions were, she had certainly accomplished nothing, except to distinguish her brother's house as the neatest and cleanest in Davy's Bend.

Notwithstanding her lofty ambitions, and her marvellous capacity in higher walks, she was jealous of what she had really accomplished; and the servant girl who promised to be industrious and generally satisfactory around old Thompson's house was soon presented with her walking papers, for Jane Benton believed that she was the only woman alive who knew the secret of handling dishes without breaking them, or of sweeping a carpet without ruining it; therefore a servant who threatened to become a rival was soon sent away, and a less thrifty one procured, who afforded the mistress opportunity of regretting that the girls of recent years knew nothing, and stubbornly refused to learn. Old Thompson had been heard to say once, after his sister had ordered the cook to leave in an hour, that he would finally be called upon to send his daughter Annie away, for no other reason than that she was useful, and careful, and industrious, and sensible; but the Ancient Maiden had good sense, in spite of her eccentricities, and dearly loved her pretty niece; and it is probable that old Thompson only made the remark in fun.

Thompson Benton was too sensible a man to go hungry in anticipation of improbable feasts in the future; therefore his sister Jane and his daughter Annie were well provided for; and were seated in a rather elegant room in a rather elegant house, on a certain wet afternoon in the spring of the year, busy with their work. The girl had been quiet and thoughtful all day, but finally she startled her aunt by inquiring,—

"Aunt Jane, were you ever in love?"

The Ancient Maiden dropped her work, and looked at the girl in indignation and astonishment.

"Annie," she sharply said, "what do you mean by asking me such a question as that?"

The Ancient Maiden was particularly severe on the men who attempted to write books, but the sex in general was her abomination. Every man who paid court to a young woman, in Jane Benton's opinion, was a married man, with a large family of children; and though it sometimes turned out that those she accused of this offence were only twenty years old, or such a matter, she said that made no difference; they had married young, probably, and investigation would reveal that they had ten or twelve ragged children and a pale wife somewhere in poverty. Therefore the presumption of the girl in asking such a question caused her to repeat again, and with more indignation than before:—

"What do you mean by asking me such a question as that?"

Annie Benton was like her father in another particular; she was not afraid of Jane, for they both loved her; therefore she was not frightened at her indignation, but laughingly insisted on the question.

"But *were* you ever in love?"

"Annie," her aunt replied, this time with an air of insulted dignity, "I shall speak to your father about this when he comes home to-night. The idea of a chit of a girl like you asking me if I have ever been in love! You have known me all your life; have I ever *acted* as though I were in love?"

"The question is easy to answer," the girl persisted. "Yes or no."

Seeing that the girl was not to be put off, Jane Benton pulled a needle out of her knitting—for Thompson Benton wore knit socks to keep peace in the family, since his sister believed that should he go down town wearing a pair of the flimsy kind he kept for sale, he would return in the evening only to fall dead in her arms—and picked her teeth with it while she reflected. And while about it, her manner softened so much that, when she went out of the room soon after, Annie believed there was a suspicion of tears in her eyes. She remained away such a length of time that the girl feared she had really offended the worthy woman, and was preparing to go out and look for her, when she came back wiping her eyes with her apron, and carrying a great packet of letters, which she threw down on the table in front of Annie.

"There!" she said pettishly. "Since you are so curious, read them."

The girl was very much amused at the turn affairs had taken, and, after breaking the string which held the letters together, looked over several of them. They were dated in the year Annie was born, and one seemed to have been written on her birthday. They all referred to her aunt in the most loving and extravagant terms possible; and while thinking how funny it was that her wrinkled aunt should be referred to as dear little angel, the Ancient Maiden said,—

"In love! I was crazy! And I can't laugh about it yet, though it seems to be so amusing to you."

"It only amuses me because I know now that you are like other women," the girl replied quietly. "I think more of you than ever, now that I know you have been in love."

"Well, you ought to think a good deal of me, then," the Ancient Maiden said, "for I was so crazy after the writer of those letters that I couldn't sleep. Love him! I thought he was different from any other man who ever lived, and I worshipped him; I made a god of him, and would have followed him to the end of the earth."

There was more animation in Aunt Jane's voice than Annie had ever noticed before, and she waved the knitting needle at her niece as though she were to blame for getting her into a love mess.

"He knew every string leading to my heart," the excited maid continued, "and he had more control over me than I ever had over myself. It was a fortunate thing that he was an honorable man. Now you know it all, and I feel ashamed of myself."

Miss Jane applied herself to knitting again, though she missed a great many stitches because of her excitement.

"But why didn't he marry you, since he loved you?" Annie inquired.

"Well, since you *must* know, he found a girl who suited him better," the Ancient Maiden replied. "But before that girl came in the way, he *thought* he loved me, and I was so well satisfied with his mistaken notion that I worshipped him. And if his old fat wife should die now, I'd marry him were he to ask me to. After you have lived as long as I have, you'll find out that fickleness is not such a great fault, after all. Why, sometimes it bothers me to have your father around, and a man can as easily tire of his wife or sweetheart as that!"

She snapped her fingers in such a manner that it sounded like the report of a toy pistol, and the girl looked at her in surprise.

"We're all fickle; you and I as well as the rest of them," she continued. "Had the wives of this country pleasant homes to go back to; were their fathers all rich men, for example, who would be glad to receive them, half of them—more than that, two thirds of them—would leave their husbands, as they ought to do; but a wife usually has no other home than that her husband has made for her, and she gets along the best she can. The men are no worse than the women; we are all fickle, fickle, fickle. As sure as we are all selfish, we are all fickle. If I were married to a rich man who treated me well, I would be more apt to love him than one who was poor, and who treated me badly; sometimes we forget our own fickleness in our selfishness. Look at the widowers; how gay they are! Look at the widows; how gay *they* are! I have known men and women so long that I feel like saying fiddlesticks when I think of it."

"But father is a widower, Aunt Jane," the girl said, "and he is not gay."

"Well, he had to run away with his wife, to get her," the Ancient Maiden replied, after some hesitation. "There seems to be a good deal in love, after all, in cases where people make a sacrifice for it. These runaway matches, if the parties to it are sensible, somehow turn out well."

"Did father ever think any less of my mother because she ran away with him?" the girl asked.

"No," her aunt replied. "He thought more of her for it, I suppose. Anyway, I never knew another man to be as fond of his wife as he was."

Annie Benton and the Ancient Maiden pursued their work in silence for a while, when the girl said,—

"I want to make a confession to you, too, Aunt Jane. I am in love with Allan Dorris."

"Don't hope to surprise me by telling me that," her aunt returned quickly, and looking at the girl as if in vexation. "I have known it for six months. But it won't do you any good, for he is going away on the early train to-morrow morning. Your father told me so this morning, and he seemed glad of it. You haven't kept your secret from him, either."

To avoid showing her chagrin at this reply, the girl walked over to the window, and looked out. Allan Dorris was passing in the road, and she felt sure that he was walking that way hoping to catch a glimpse of her; perhaps he was only taking a farewell look at the house in which she lived. But she did not show herself, although he watched the house closely until he passed out of sight.

"I supposed everyone knew it," the girl said, returning to her chair again. "I have always thought that any girl who is desperately in love cannot hide it;

but I wanted to talk to you about it, and I am glad you told me what you did, for I can talk more freely after having heard it. I have no one else to make a confidant of, and I am very much concerned about it. The matter is so serious with me that I am scared."

"Don't be scared, for pity's sake," the Ancient Maiden replied, with a show of her old spirit. "They all feel that way, but they soon get over it. When I was in love I wondered that the sun came up in the morning, but everything went on just as usual. I thought the people were watching me in alarm, fearing I would do something desperate, but those who knew about it paid little attention, and I *had* to get over it, whether I wanted to or not. You will feel differently after he has been gone a week."

"The certainty that I will not is the reason I have spoken to you," Annie continued gravely. "Allan Dorris loves me as the writer of the letters you have shown me loved you before the other girl came in his way; and I love him as you have loved the writer of the letters all these years. You have never forgotten your lover; then why should you say that I will forget mine within a week? What would you advise me to do?"

"Ask me anything but that," the aunt replied, folding up her work with an unsteady hand. "No matter how I should advise you, I should finally come to believe that I had advised you wrong, love is so uncertain. It is usually a matter of impulse, and some of the most unpromising lovers turn out the best. I cannot advise you, Annie; I do not know."

Jane Benton imagined that Dorris was going away because Annie would not marry him; but the reverse was really the case,—he was going away for fear she would become his wife.

"My greatest fear is," the girl continued again, "that I do not feel as a woman should with reference to it. I would not dare to tell you how much concerned I am; I am almost afraid to admit it to myself. I am thoroughly convinced that his going away will blight my life, and that I shall always feel toward him as I do now; yet there are grave reasons why I should not become his wife. Do you think the women are better than the men?"

The Ancient Maiden leaned back in her chair to think about it, and picked her teeth with the knitting-needle again.

"What is your honest opinion?" the girl insisted.

"Sometimes I think they are, and sometimes I think they are not," the aunt replied, bending over her work again. "When I hear a man's opinion of a woman, I laugh to myself, for they know nothing of them. The women all seem to be better than they really are, and the men all seem to be worse than they really are; I have often thought that. Women have so many *little* mean ways, in their conduct toward one another, and are so innocent about it; but when a man is mean, he is mean all over, and perfectly indifferent to what is thought about him. A lot of women get together, and gabble away for hours about nothing, but the men are either up to pronounced mischief or they are at work."

"If you were in love with a man, would you have as much confidence in his honesty as you had in your own?" the girl asked.

"Certainly," her aunt replied promptly.

"Then won't you advise me? Please do; for I have as much confidence in Allan Dorris as I have in myself."

"If you will see that all the doors are fastened," Jane Benton replied excitedly, "I will. Quick! Before I change my mind."

The girl did as she was directed, and hurried back to her aunt's side.

"Since there is no possibility of anyone hearing," Jane Benton continued, "I will tell you the best thing to do in my judgment; but whatever comes of it, do not hold me responsible. Think over the matter carefully, and then do whatever you yourself think best. No one can advise you like yourself. You are a sensible girl, and a good girl, and I would trust your judgment fully, and so would your father, though he would hardly say so. There; that's enough on *that* subject. But you can depend on one thing: there is a grand difference between a lover and a husband; and very few men are as fond of their wives as they were of their sweethearts. All the men do not improve on acquaintance like your father, and I have known girls who were pretty and engaging one year who were old women the next; matrimony has that effect on most of them, and you should know it. The women do the best they can, I suppose, but you can't very well blame a man sometimes. In 1883 he falls in love with a fresh and pretty girl, and marries her; in 1884 she has lost her beauty and her freshness, and although he feels very meanly over it, somehow his feelings have changed toward her. Of course he loves her a little, but he is not the man he was before they were married—not a bit of it. A good many husbands and wives spend the first years of their marriage in thinking of the divorce courts, but after they find out that they should have known better than to expect complete happiness from matrimony, and that they are not different from other people, they get on better. Since you have locked the door to hear the truth, I hope you are satisfied with it."

"But is it *necessary* for girls to become old so soon?" Annie inquired.

"Well, I don't suppose that it is," her aunt replied, "but the men had better expect it; and the women had better expect that since there never was yet an angel in pants, there never will be one. The trouble is, not the men and women, but the false notions each entertain toward the other. Now run and open the doors, or I'll faint."

Annie Benton, after opening the doors and watching her aunt revive, did not seem at all impressed by what she had heard; indeed, she acted as though she did not believe it, so the Ancient Maiden gave her another dose.

"I imagine I have been rather satisfactory to your father," she said, "but had I been his wife I doubt if we would have got along so well. A man who is rather a good fellow is often very mean to his wife; and it seems to be natural, too, for he does not admit it to himself, and thinks he has justification for his course. I don't know what the trouble is, but I know that the most bitter hatreds in the world are those between married people who do not get along. Since you are so curious about matrimony, I'll try and give you enough of it. Even a man who loves his wife will do unjust things toward her which he would not do to a sister he was fond of; and there is something about marriage which affects men and women as nothing else will. There are thousands of good husbands, but if you could see way down to the bottom of men's wicked hearts not one in ten would say he was glad he had married. That's a mean enough thing to say about the women, I hope, and if you do not understand what my real preferences in your case are, you must be blind."

Thompson Benton came in soon after, and they spent a very quiet evening together. Annie retired to her own room early, and when she came to bid her father good-night, tears started in her eyes.

"What is the matter with the girl?" he asked his sister after Annie had disappeared.

Jane Benton did not reply for a long time, keeping her eyes on the pages of a book she held in her hand, but at last she said,—

"I don't know."

Thompson Benton must have noticed that his sister was nervous, and had he followed her up the stairs when she retired for the night, he must have marvelled that she went into Annie's room, and kissed her over and over, and then went hurriedly away.

CHAPTER XV.

A SHOT AT THE SHADOW.

The regular patronage of the "Apron and Password," like the attendance at a theatre when reported by a friendly critic, was small, but exceedingly respectable.

A gentleman of uncertain age who answered to the name of Ponsonboy, and who professed to be a lawyer, usually occupied the head of the one long table which staggered on its feet in the dingy dining-room, and when his place was taken by a stranger, which happened innocently enough occasionally, Ponsonboy frowned so desperately that his companions were oppressed with the fear that they would be called upon to testify against him in court for violence.

The minister, who occupied the seat next to Ponsonboy, and who was of uncertain age himself, could demonstrate to a certainty that the legal boarder was at least forty-five, but the legal boarder nevertheless had a great deal to say about the necessity which seemed to exist for the young men to take hold, and rescue Davy's Bend from the reign of "the fossils," a term which was applied to most of the citizens of the town after the other epithets had been exhausted, and as but few of them knew what a fossil was, they hoped it was very bad, and used it a great deal.

Ponsonboy was such a particular man that he could only be pleased in two ways—by accusing him of an intention to marry any stylish girl of twenty, or of an intention to remove to Ben's City, which he was always threatening to do.

"It would be useless for me to deny that I have had flattering offers," it was his custom to reply, when asked if there was anything new with reference to his contemplated change of residence. "But I am deuced timid. I came here a poor boy, with a law-book in one hand and an extra shirt in the other, and I don't want to make a change until I fully consider it."

It was a matter of such grave importance that Ponsonboy had already considered it fifteen years, and regularly once a year during that time he had arranged to go, making a formal announcement to that effect to the small but select circle around the table, the members of which either expressed their regrets, or agreed to be with him in a few months. But always at the last moment Ponsonboy discovered that the gentleman who had been making the flattering offers wanted to put too much responsibility on him, or something of that kind, whereupon the good lady on his left, and the good gentleman on his right, were happy again.

It was true that the legal boarder came to Davy's Bend a poor boy, if a stout man of thirty without money or friends may be so referred to; it was also true that he was poor still, though he was no longer a boy; but Ponsonboy rid himself of this disagreeable truth, so far as his friends were concerned, by laying his misfortunes at the door of the town, as they all did. He was property poor, he said, and values had decreased so much of late years, that he was barely able to pay his taxes, although he really possessed nothing in the way of property except a tumble-down rookery on which there was a mortgage. But Ponsonboy, whose first name was Albert, appeared to be quite content with his genteel poverty, so long as he succeeded in creating an impression that he would be rich and distinguished but for the wrong done him by that miserable impostor, Davy's Bend.

The good man on his right, the Rev. Walter Wilton, and pastor of the old stone church where Annie Benton was organist, was a bachelor, like Ponsonboy; but, like Ponsonboy again, he did not regard himself as a bachelor, but as a young man who had not yet had time to pick out a lady worthy of his affections.

Close observers remarked that age was breaking out on good Mr. Wilton in spots, like the measles in its earlier stages; short gray hairs peeped out at the observer from his face, and seemed to be waving their arms to attract attention, but he kept them subdued by various arts so long that it was certain that some time he would become old in a night. He walked well enough, *now*, and looked well enough; but when he forgets his pretence of youth, then he will walk slowly down to breakfast some fine morning with a crook in his back and a palsy in his hand.

When it was said of Rev. Walter Wilton that he was pious, the subject was exhausted; there was nothing more to say, unless you chose to elaborate on piety in general. He knew something of books, and read in them a great deal, but old Thompson Benton was in the habit of saying that if he ever had an original idea in his head, it was before he came to the Bend as a mild menace to those whose affairs did not permit of so much indolent deference to the proprieties.

The Reverend Wilton did not gossip himself, but he induced others to, by being quietly shocked at what they said, and regularly three times a day Ponsonboy and his assistant on the left laid a morsel before him, which he inquired into minutely—but with the air of a man who intended to speak to the erring parties; not as a gossip. Reverend Wilton never spoke a bad word against anyone, nor was he ever known to speak a good one, but he always gave those around him to understand by his critical indifference to whatever was in hand that, were he at liberty to desert his post, and allow the people to fall headlong into the abyss out of which he kept them with the greatest difficulty, he would certainly show them how the affairs of men should be properly conducted.

Too good for this world, but not good enough for the next, Reverend Wilton only existed, giving every sort of evidence that, were it not unclerical, he would swear at his salary (which was less than that of a good bricklayer), denounce his congregation for good and sufficient reasons, cheat his boarding-place, and hate his companions; but his trade being of an amiable nature, he was a polite nothing, with a great deal of time on his hands in which to criticise busy people, which he did without saying a word against them.

Mrs. Whittle, the milliner, sat on Ponsonboy's left; a tall and solidly built lady of forty-five, who was so very good as to be disagreeable. The people dreaded to see her come near them, for her mission was certain to be one of charity, and Mrs. Whittle's heart was always bleeding for somebody. Summer and winter alike, she annoyed the people by telling them of "duties" which were not duties at all; and finally she was generally accepted as the town nuisance, although Mrs. Whittle herself believed that she was quite popular because of the good she intended to accomplish, but which seemed to be impossible because of the selfishness of the people. Thompson Benton had given it out flat that if she ever came bothering around him, he would give her the real facts in the case, instead of putting his name on her subscription paper, but for some reason she kept away from him, and never heard the real facts, whatever they were. She regarded old Thompson, however, as a mean man, and moaned about him a great deal, which he either never heard of or cared nothing about.

Old Thompson was seldom seen at church on Sunday evening, therefore Mrs. Whittle felt quite sure that he was prowling around with a view of safe-blowing, or something of that kind, and she never referred to him except to intimate that he was up to mischief of the most pronounced sort. A man who was not at church on Sunday evening, in the opinion of Mrs. Whittle, must be drunk in a saloon, or robbing somebody, for where else could he be? Mrs. Whittle only recognized two classes of men; those who were in the churches, and those who were in the saloons; and in her head, which was entirely too small for the size of her body, there was no suspicion of a middle ground. Those who craved the attention of Mrs. Whittle found it necessary to be conspicuous either as a saint or a sinner.

Theoretically Mrs. Whittle was a splendid woman, and certainly a bad woman in no particular except that she carried her virtues to such an extent that the people disliked her, and felt ashamed of themselves for it, not feeling quite certain that they had a right to find fault with one who neglected not only her affairs, but her person, to teach others neatness, and thrift, and the virtues generally.

If she accomplished no good, as old Thompson Benton stoutly asserted, it was certain she did some harm, for the people finally came to neglect affairs in which they would otherwise have taken a moderate interest because of their dislike of Mrs. Whittle. A great many others who were inclined to attend to their own affairs (which are always sufficient to occupy one's time, heaven knows) were badgered to such an extent by Mrs. Whittle that they joined her in various enterprises that resulted in nothing but to make their good intentions ridiculous, and finally there was a general and a sincere hope that blunt Thompson Benton would find opportunity to come to the rescue of the people.

Three times a day this trio met, and three times each day it was satisfied with itself, and dissatisfied with Davy's Bend, as well as everything in it, including Allan Dorris. The new occupant of The Locks was generally popular with the people, but the hotel trio made the absurd mistake of supposing that they were the people, therefore they talked of Dorris as though he were generally hated and despised. They were indignant, to begin with, because he did not covet the acquaintance of the only circle in the town worth cultivating, and as time wore on, and he still made no effort to know them, they could come to only one conclusion; that he was deserving of their severest denunciation.

Could Thompson Benton have known of the pious conclusions to which they came concerning his child, and which she no more deserved than hundreds of other worthy women deserve the gossip to which they are always subjected, he would have walked in upon them, and given the two men broken heads, and the woman the real facts in her case which he had been promising; but there is a destiny which protects us from an evil which is as common as sunshine, and Thompson Benton was not an exception to the rule.

It was the custom of the hotel trio to come late to supper and remain late, greatly to the disgust of the cook and the man-of-all-work, and, surrounding the table in easy positions, they gossipped to their heart's content, at last wandering away to their respective homes, very well satisfied with one another, if with nothing else.

It was after nine o'clock when they got away on the evening with which we have to do, and by the time Davy had eaten his own supper and put the room in order for the morning, it was ten. Hurriedly putting up a package of whatever was at hand for Tug, he was about starting out at the kitchen door when he met Mr. Whittle on the steps. He had somehow come into possession of a long and wicked-looking musket, which he brought in with him, and put down near the door connecting the kitchen with the dining-room. Seeing Davy's look of surprise, he seated himself in Ponsonboy's place, and explained.

"Poison has its advantages, for it does not bark when it bites, but it lacks range, and henceforth I carry a gun. How was Uncle Albert to-night?"

Silas placed a plate of cold meat before his friend, and replied that Mr. Ponsonboy would be in a fine rage if he should hear himself referred to as Uncle Albert.

"Oh, would he?" Tug inquired, sighting at his companion precisely as he might have sighted along the barrel of his musket. "That man is fifty years old if he is a day, and don't let him attempt any of his giddy tricks with me. I wouldn't stand it; I know too much about him. I have known Uncle Albert ever since he was old enough to marry, and I know enough to hang him, the old kicker. I've known him to abuse the postmaster for not giving him a letter with money in it, although he didn't expect one, and accuse him of stealing it, and whenever he spells a word wrong, and gets caught at it, he goes around telling that he has found a typographical error in the dictionary. What did he say about me to-night?"

"He said—I hope you won't believe that I think so,"—Davy apologized in advance—"that you robbed the only client you ever had of a thousand dollars."

"*Did* he, though?" Tug impudently inquired. "Well, I'll give him half if he'll prove it, for I need the money. Uncle Albert hears what is said about me, and I hear what is said about him. If he'll make a date with me, I'll exchange stories with him; and he won't have any of the best of it, either. The people sometimes talk about as good a man as I am, and even were I without faults, there are plenty of liars to invent stories, so you can imagine that they give it to Uncle Albert tolerable lively."

Tug did not mingle with the people a great deal, but he knew about what they were saying, and when talking to Silas he did not hesitate to quote them to substantiate any position he saw fit to take. He had a habit of putting on his hat on these occasions, and inviting Silas to accompany him out in the town to see the principal people, in order that they might own to what Tug had credited them with saying. But Silas always refused to go, not doubting that his friend's inventions were true, so it happened that Tug made out rather strong cases against his enemies.

"I can stand up with the most of them," he said, with an ill humor to which hunger lent a zest; "and them that beat me, I can disgrace with their poor relations. Show me the man that can't be beat if you go at him right, and you may hang me with a thread. Them that are well-behaved have shiftless relations, and I'll get them drunk, and cause them to hurrah for 'Uncle Bill,' or 'Aunt Samantha,' or whoever it may be, in front of their fine houses. I pride myself on my meanness, and I'll not be tromped on. Let him that is without sin cast the first stone, and I'll not be stoned. You can bet on that, if you want to."

Tug proceeded with his meal in silence until Silas said to him that Reverend Wilton was a good man. Silas had a habit of inducing Tug to abuse his enemies by praising them, and the ruse never failed.

"Well, don't he get paid for being good?" Tug replied, waving a kitchen fork in the air like a dagger. "Ain't that his business? It's no more to his credit to say that he is good, than to say that Silas Davy is a hotel Handy Andy. If you say that he knows a good deal about books, I will say, so does Hearty Hampton know a good deal about mending shoes, for it's his trade. Shut Hearty up in a room, and pay him to post himself regarding certain old characters he cares nothing about, and pay him well, and in the course of years he will be able to speak of people, events, and words which you, having been busy all the time, will know nothing about. He ought to be good; it's his business. I always know what a preacher is going to say when he opens his mouth, for don't I know what he's hired to say? I don't like good men, any way, but a man who is paid to be good, and expects me to admire him for it, will find—well, I'll not do it, that's all. How's the old lady?"

There was a faint evidence that Tug was about to laugh at the thought of his divorced wife, and his cheeks puffed out as a preliminary, but he changed his mind at the last moment, and carefully sighted at Silas, as if intending to wing his reply, like a bird from a trap.

"She is uncommonly well, for her," Silas said, looking meekly at his companion. "She is almost gay."

"Oh, the young thing; *is* she," Tug retorted. "Do you know what she reminds me of? An old man in a dress trying to imitate a girl."

There was unutterable meanness in Mr. Whittle's last remark, and when he looked around the room with fierce dignity, he seemed to be wondering why any one should continue to live in the face of his displeasure.

"I heard her say to-night, when I brought in a third lot of cakes, that you were the bane of her life," Silas said, timidly, and dodging his head to one side, as if expecting Tug Whittle to jump at him for repeating the scandalous story. "Although she says she is heart-broken, I notice she eats mighty well; for her."

"And I suppose Reverend Good and Uncle Alfred encouraged her," Tug replied. "What good husbands bachelors imagine they would be, and what miserable old growlers they turn out. Before a man is married he takes a great deal of comfort to himself in thinking what a kind, indulgent husband and father he would be, and how different from other men, but they soon fall with a dull sickening thud to the level of the rest of us. It's easy enough to be a good husband in theory, and it's easy enough to be brave in theory, but when the theorists come down to actual business, they are like the rest of us. It's like an actor in a show. He wants to find a villain, and punish him, and the villain appears about that time, and makes no resistance, and is beaten to great applause, finally shrinking away while the other fellow looks ferociously at him, but it is not that way in real life. The villain fights in real life, and usually whips. If I knew that the men I dislike would stand it peaceable, like the villains in a show, I'd beat 'm all to death; but as it is, I am a coward, like Ponsonboy, and you, and Armsby, and all the rest of them; except Allan Dorris—there's a man who'd fight. When I read in books about brave men, it makes me feel ashamed, until I remember that the men in actual life are not like those in the books. What did Her Ladyship say about Hector?"

Mrs. Whittle's first husband had been a certain Hector Harlam, with whose history Silas was very familiar from his association with Tug, so he answered,—

"She wiped away a tear, and regretted his death. She seemed greatly affected,—for her."

"She can't possibly regret his death more than I do," Tug said. "He appreciated her; I never did, and I am sorry she does not join Hector in glory, or wherever he is, for she is no earthly good in Davy's Bend. She told me once that he always called her his baby."

There was no keeping it in now; the thought of his wife being called a "baby" was so absurd to Tug that he was about to laugh. His cheeks swelled out as though the laugh came up from below somewhere, and he found it necessary to swallow it, after which there was a faint smile on his face, and a gurgle in his throat. When Mr. Whittle smiled, it was such an unusual proceeding that his scalp had a habit of crawling over towards his face, to take a look, which it did in this instance, and then went back to its old position at the top of his head. It was a dreadful laugh, but Silas was used to it, and was not alarmed.

"That woman wants to be a man the worst way," the old scoundrel went on to say. "I hope it accounts for the circumstance that she never looks like a woman should. A white dress on a woman—a *real* woman, understand; not an imitation one—looks handsome; and I never see a girl dressed in white that I do not fall in love with her, but when the old lady puts it on, with a frill at her neck, or any such trifling thing, I want to find a woodpile and an axe to cut off my feet. I don't know why anyone should want to be a man; I know what a man is, and I wonder at this strange ambition of the old lady. I never see a man that I don't want to spit on him. Ugh!"

He shrugged his shoulders in unutterable disgust, but soon modified his manner, as Davy began talking of another matter.

"Barney Russell, of Ben's City, was here to-day," the little man said. "He used to live in Davy's Bend; I suppose you remember him."

"There's another feller I don't like," Mr. Whittle replied, with a snort. "He comes up here regularly once a month to crow over us, and tell around that he has two overcoats; one for winter, and another for spring. Some say he has seven canes, a different one for every day in the week; but he ain't half the man Dorris is, although he carries silk handkerchiefs with a red 'R' in the corner. If I should leave Davy's Bend, I'd never come back, as he does; for I have done so many contemptible things here that I wouldn't want to be reminded of them by seeing the place again. I don't blame Barney, though, for having two overcoats," Tug continued thoughtfully. "Next to two pairs of shoes, it's the greatest luxury a rich man can afford—I'd own two overcoats myself if I had the money. A man who has two overcoats and two pairs of shoes, and uses a knife to cut his tobacco, instead of biting it off like a pig, is ready to die; there will be little left in the world for him to regret after he's gone,—but to return to the serious business of life: it is usually on a Wednesday when the shadow appears. This is his night, and I'm looking for him."

He turned his big eye toward the corner where he had left the musket, and, seeing it was safe, resumed,—

"I have never been of any use to a single human being in all my life, but I intend to make myself useful to Allan Dorris by shooting the shadow. Give me that gun."

Silas went over to where the gun was standing, and returned with it in his hand. Placing his finger about half way up the barrel, and following it with his great eye, Tug said,—

"It is loaded to there. Thompson Benton trusted me for the ammunition, though he said he knew he would never get the money. I have a notion to pay him now, for contrariness. Have you fifty cents about you?"

Silas carefully went through his pockets, as if he were not quite sure about it, but after a long examination replied that he hadn't a cent.

"Well, it's no great matter, though you ought to keep money about you; I am liable to need it. But, if let alone by the shadow, Allan Dorris will marry Annie Benton, and become a happy man, which he has never been before. I don't know what he has been up to before he came here, and I don't care, for I like him, and I am going out now to get a shot at his enemy."

Without further words he walked out, followed by Silas, who carefully locked the kitchen door and put the key in his pocket. Viewed at a distance, the pair looked like a man and a boy out hunting; the boy lagging behind to carry the game.

It was a bad night, for which the Bend was famous, and though it was not raining, there was so much moisture in the air from a recent rain, that it occurred to Silas, as he went limping along towards The Locks, for they walked in that direction, that if Tug should find the shadow, and fire his gun at it, the discharge would precipitate another shower; for the prop under the water in the sky seemed to be very unsubstantial and shaky that night.

It had been raining at intervals all day, and the two men floundered along in the mud until they reached the church which stood near Allan Dorris's house, where Tug stopped awhile to consider. Coming to a conclusion after some deliberation, he pulled two long boards up from the church steps, and, giving the gun to Silas to hold, he carried them to the middle gable of the building, on the side looking towards The Locks. Climbing up on the window-sill, he placed one end of each board on the wall which surrounded The Locks, and which was only a few feet from the church, and the other on the window-sash, pulling the upper one down to aid the lower one in holding his weight, and allowing one end of each board to protrude into the church. Then climbing up, and straddling one of the boards, he took his gun, and motioned his companion to follow.

When Davy seated himself by the side of his friend, he found that the low gable would protect them from the rain, should it come on, and that from where they sat they commanded a view of Dorris's window; the one above the porch where they had once seen the shadow appear, and in which a light now appeared. Silas felt certain that it was Tug's intention to wait there all night for a shot, and he made himself as comfortable as possible.

Occasionally he fell into a light doze, but on coming out of it, by losing his balance, he saw that Tug was still intently watching the window, with the musket in his hands ready for use.

Two hours passed in this manner, when the patience of Silas was rewarded by seeing Tug crane his neck, and look intently through the trees. Silas looked himself, and saw a man's head slowly rising to the porch roof from below. It came up in full view, and then a part of the body was seen as the shadow climbed over the low railing. As near as Silas could make out, the man wormed himself around, and finally stood upon the porch railing to look in at the top of the window; so that only a part of his head and none of his body could be seen from where the men were.

Although he heard Tug cock the gun when the head first appeared, he seemed to be waiting for a larger mark to shoot at; for there was nothing to be seen except a part of a hat. Occasionally this would be withdrawn, but it would soon appear again, and remain motionless a long time, as though the wearer was intently gazing at something transpiring in the room which greatly interested him. Tug did not seem at all excited, as Silas was, but sat watching the shadow, as motionless as a stone.

After a longer disappearance than usual, during which time Tug became very nervous, the hat came in view again, and Silas said softly,—

"Suppose it should disappear, and never come back?"

Apparently Tug had not thought of this possibility, for he hurriedly threw the gun to his shoulder, aimed a moment, and fired. The report was tremendous, and seemed to frighten Tug himself; for he hurriedly jumped down, and softly raised the sash into position, replaced the boards on the steps, and set out toward the town. Reaching the vicinity of the hotel, he waited until Silas came up, and said,—

"Sleep in your own bed to-night; we must not be found together."

So saying he disappeared, and Silas crept to his lonely room to wonder what Allan Dorris would find when he went out to investigate the shooting.

CHAPTER XVI.

THE STEP ON THE STAIR.

There had been two days of rain already, and Allan Dorris sat in his lonely room at ten o'clock at night, listening to its ceaseless patter at the windows, and on the roof, and its dripping from the eaves, thinking that when the sun came out again he would go away and leave it, and remove to a place which would always be in the shadow. Davy's Bend was noted for its murky weather, and the nights were surely darker there than elsewhere; but he felt that after his departure he would think of the sun as always shining brightly around The Locks, and through the dirty town, even lighting up the dark woods across the river, which seemed to collect a little more darkness every night than the succeeding day could drive out; for Annie Benton would remain, and surely the sun could not resist the temptation to smile upon her pretty face.

Davy's Bend, with all its faults, would always remain a pleasant memory with Allan Dorris, and he envied those who were to remain, for they might hope to see Annie Benton occasionally pass on her way to church, and be better for it.

He loved Annie Benton to such an extent that he would rather be thousands of miles away from her than within sight of the house in which she lived, since he had sworn not to ask her to share his life; and the next morning before daylight he intended to go to some far-away place,—he did not know where,—and get rid of the dark nights, and the rain, and the step on the stair, and the organ, and the player who had exerted such an influence over him.

He had not been able to sell The Locks at the price he paid, although the people had been grumbling because they were not offered the bargain originally; so he intended to turn it over to Mrs. Wedge, and poor Helen, and the noises and spectres which were always protesting against his living there at all, and become a wanderer over the face of the earth. Perhaps his lonely life of a year in The Locks would cause another ghost to take up its residence in the place, and join poor Helen in moaning and walking through the rooms.

Mrs. Wedge had disappeared an hour before, her eyes red from weeping, but she was coming back at three o'clock in the morning, at which time Dorris intended to leave for the railroad station; so Dorris settled himself in his chair to wait until the hour for his departure arrived.

How distinct the step on the stair to-night! A hundred times it had passed up and down since Allan Dorris sat down a few hours before; and the dripping rain at the windows made him think of sitting up with a body packed in ice. Drip; drip; drip; and the ghostly step so distinct that he thought the body he was watching must have tired of lying in one position so long, and was walking about for exercise.

The light burned low under its shade, and the other side of the room was in deep shadow. He thought of it as a map of his life; for it was entirely dark and blank, except the one ray in the corner, which represented Davy's Bend and Annie Benton. Yet he had determined to go back into the shadow again, and leave the light forever; to exist once more in toil and discontent, hoping to tire himself by excitement and exertion into forgetfulness, and sleep, and death.

Death! Is it so dreadful, after all? Dorris argued the question with himself, and came to the conclusion that if it meant rest and forgetfulness he would welcome it. There had been a great deal of hope in his life, but he was convinced now that he was foolish for entertaining it at all, since nothing ever came of it. Perhaps his experience had been that of other men; he gave up one hope only to entertain another, but experience had taught him that hope was nothing more than a solace for a wretched race. The old hope that they will be better to-morrow, when they will get on with less difficulty and weary labor; but to-morrow they die, and their children hope after them, and are disappointed, and hope again.

Should Death open the door, and walk in to claim him, Dorris believed he would be ready, since there was nothing in the future for him more pleasant than the past had offered. He did not believe he was a morbid man, or one given to exaggerating the distress of his own condition, but he would give up life as he might give up anything else which was not satisfactory, and which gave no promise of improvement.

How distinctly the step is climbing the stair! He had never heard it so plainly before, but the faltering and hesitation were painfully natural; he had heard it almost every night since coming to the house, but there was a distinctness now which he had never remarked before. A long pause on the landing; poor Helen dreading to go into the baby's room, he thought, whither she was drawn so often from her grave. But it advanced to the door of the room in which Dorris sat, and stopped again; he drew his breath in gasps—perhaps it was coming in!

A timid knock at the door!

The face of the listener turned as pale as death, and he trembled violently when he stood upon his feet. Should he open the door or lock it! Going up to the fire, he stirred the smouldering coals until there was a flood of light in the room, and turned up the lamp to increase the illumination. Still he hesitated. Suppose he should open the door, and find poor Helen standing there in her grave-clothes! Suppose she should drop on her knees, and ask for her child, holding out her fleshless fingers to him in supplication, and stare at him with her sightless sockets?

After hesitating a long time, he went to the door and threw it wide open, at the same time springing back from it in quick alarm.

Annie Benton!

He had firmly expected to see the ghost of poor Helen; instead he saw a fresh and beautiful girl, but so excited that she could scarcely speak. There was a look of reckless determination in her face which made Allan Dorris fear for the moment that she had gone mad, and, strolling about the town, had concluded, in her wild fancy, to murder him for some imagined wrong.

"How you frightened me!" he said, coming close to her. "Just before you rapped, the ghost of poor Helen had been running up and down the stair, as if celebrating my resolution to leave The Locks, and give it over to her for night walking. You have been out in the storm, and are wet and cold. Come in to the fire."

The girl crossed the threshold, and entered the room, but did not go near the fire. She seemed to be trying to induce her hot brain to explain her presence there, for she turned her back to him, as if in embarrassment.

"I can no longer control myself," Annie Benton said, facing Dorris with quivering lips, "and I have come to give myself to you, body and soul. I am lost to restraint and reason, and I place myself in the hands of him who has brought this about, for I am no longer capable of taking care of myself. Do what you please with me; I love you so much that I will be satisfied, though disgrace comes of it. I will never leave you again, and if you go away, I will go with you. I have loved you against my reason ever since I knew you, for you always told me I must not, and I restrained myself as best I could. But I cannot permit you to go away unless you take me with you. O, Allan, promise me that you will not go away," she said, falling on her knees before him. "Do this, and I will return home, to regret this rashness forever. If you do not, I will remain, let the consequences be what they may."

Dorris looked at the girl in wonder and pity, for there was touching evidence in her last words that she was greatly distressed; but he could only say, "Annie! what are you doing!"

"You have taught me such lessons in love that I have gone mad in studying them," she continued, standing beside him again, "and there is nothing in this world, or the world to come, that I would not give to possess you. I relinquish my father, and my home, and my hope of heaven, that I may be with you, if these sacrifices are necessary to pacify my rebellion. If you have been playing upon my feelings during our acquaintance, and were not sincere, you have captured me so completely that I am your slave. But if you were in earnest, I shall always be glad that I took this step, and never feel regret, no matter what comes of it. Did you think I was made of stone, not to be moved by your appeals to me? I am a woman, and every sentiment you have given utterance to during our acquaintance has found response in my heart. It may be that you did not know differently, for there is too much sentiment in the world about women, and not enough knowledge. But I did not deserve all the good you said about me; it made me blush to realize that much that you have said in my praise was not true, though I loved you for what you said. But I show my weakness now. I could not resist the temptation to come here, and, as you have often told me, when anyone starts to travel the wrong road, the doors and gates are all open. *Yours* were all open to-night, and I came here without resistance."

Dorris was too much frustrated to attempt to explain how his front gate and door came open, which was, perhaps, the result of carelessness; but he seemed as much alarmed as though a ghost, instead of his sweetheart, had come in at them. Without knowing exactly what he did, he attempted to take her wet wrap, but she stepped back from him excitedly.

"Don't touch me!" she said excitedly. "Speak to me!"

"Sit down, and take off your wet wrap," he answered, "and I will."

She unfastened a hook at her throat, and the garment fell to the floor. Her dress had been soiled by the walk through the rain, and her hair was dishevelled; but she never looked so handsome before as she did when she stood in front of Dorris, radiant with excitement. But instead of speaking to her, as he had promised, Dorris sat motionless for a long time, looking at the floor. The girl watched him narrowly, and thought he trembled; indeed he was agitated so much that he walked over to the window, and stood looking out for a long time.

"You say you could not resist the temptation to love me, though you *said* it was wrong," the excited girl continued. "Nor could I help loving you when you asked me to, though you said I should not. You never spoke to me in your life that you did not ask me to love you. Everything you said seemed so sincere and honest, that I forgot my own existence in my desire to be with you in your loneliness, whatever the penalty of the step I am taking may be. I have so much confidence in you, and so much love for you, that I cannot help thinking that I am doing right, and that I never will regret it. Speak to me, and say that, no difference what the world may say, you are pleased; I care only for that."

A picture, unrolled from the heavens, has appeared on the outside, and Allan Dorris is looking at it through the window. A long road, through a rough country, and disappearing in misty distance; travellers coming into it from by-ways, some of whom disappear, while others trudge wearily along. There are difficulties in the way which seem insurmountable, and these difficulties are more numerous as the travellers fade into the distance; and likewise the number of travellers decreases as the journey is lengthened. At length only one traveller is to be seen, a mere speck along the high place where the difficult road winds. He tries to climb a hill, beyond which he will be lost to view; but he fails until another traveller comes up, when they help each other, and go over the hill together, waving encouragement to those who are below; into the mist, beyond which no human eye can look.

"During our entire acquaintance," Dorris said finally, coming over to her, "you have said or done nothing which did not meet my approbation, and cause me to love you more and more. You did not force yourself to do these things; they were natural, and that was the reason I told you to keep away from me, for I saw that our acquaintance was becoming dangerous; why, I have offered to tell you before. But what you have done this night pleases me most of all. I have been praying that you would do it for months, though I did not believe you would, and, much as I loved you, I intended going away in the morning for your good. I was afraid to ask you to share my life, fearing you would accept, for I am a coward when you are in danger; but now that you have offered to do it, and relieved me of the fear I had of enticing you into it, I am happier than I can express."

Annie Benton's face brightened, and she put her hands in his.

"Please say that my face is not cold and passionless," she said. "Once you told me that when we were out on the hills, and it has pained me ever since. Say that there is hot blood and passion in my veins now."

"When I said that," he answered, "I was provoked because you had so much control. I had none at all, and declared my passion within a few weeks after I knew you, but when I did it, you only looked at me in meek surprise. But I understand it all now, and I want to say that although you may regard what you have done to-night as an impropriety, it is the surest road to my heart. If it is depravity, I will make you proud of depravity, for I will be so good to you in the future that you will bless the day you lost your womanly control. The fact that you have trusted me completely caused me to resolve to make you a happy woman, and I believe I can do it. I love you because you have blood in your veins instead of water, and I will make you a queen. I am more of a man than you give me credit for; I am not the gloomy misanthrope you take me to be, for you have rescued me from that, and I will make the people of Davy's Bend say that Annie Benton was wiser than the best of them!"

He struck the table a resounding blow with his fist, and had the enemies of the man been able to look at his face then, they would have been afraid of him.

"May I sit on your knee, and put my arms around your neck while you talk?" she asked.

"Yes," he answered, picking her up with the ease of a giant, and kissing her on the cheek. "You may ride on my back all your life if you will only remain with me. I have never felt like a man until this moment, and those who have fault to find with my course had better keep out of the way. There is a reason why you and I should not be married—as we will be before the sun shows itself again, for I intend to send for the minister to come to the church when I am through telling you how much I love you, and you shall play our wedding march while I pump the organ—but I am in the right. I have endured misery long enough to accommodate others; let them expect it no longer! And now that you know what I intend to do, listen while I tell you who I am, where I came from, and why I forced you to your present novel position."

"I prefer not to hear it," the girl said, without looking up. "I did not know you before you came to Davy's Bend: I am not concerned in your history beyond that time, and as a mark of confidence in you I shall reserve the telling of it until our married life has been tested: until I am so useful to you (as I am certain you will be to me) that, no difference what your secret is, we will consider it a blessing for bringing us together. But for the disagreeable part of your life we would never have met; we should think of that."

"Another time, then, or never, as you prefer," he replied. "I would have told you long ago, had you encouraged me to. Anyway, it is a story of devotion to others, and of principle practised with the hatred and contempt and cowardly timidity which should only characterize villains, and villainous actions; of principle carried to such an extent as to become a wrong; but from this hour I shall act from a right motive, in which my heart sympathizes; which affords me a return for effort, and which will aid in making me a better man. I shall live to accommodate myself henceforth, instead of as a favor to others. But what will the people say of our strange marriage?"

"I fear it is a sad depravity," the girl answered, "but I don't care."

"Nor do I; how lucky! If it satisfies you and me, let every tongue in the world wag, if it will afford them enjoyment. I have neither time nor inclination to hunt down the idle rumors that may find their way into circulation concerning my affairs, for what does it matter whether old Miss Maid or old Mr. Bach thinks good or ill of me? I never cared about such trifles; I care less now that I have you."

Had Dorris looked at the upper sash of the window over the porch, instead of at the girl, he would have seen a malicious face looking in at him, but he was too much occupied for that, and the face was soon withdrawn.

"I have never expected anything that was unreasonable," Dorris said, probably recollecting that his actions had been such as to give rise to a suspicion that he was a fickle man, and could not be satisfied with anything. "I know all that it is possible for a woman to be, and I have hoped for nothing beyond that. I ask no more than a companion of whom I will never tire, and who will never tire of me—some one who will keep me agreeable company during my life, and regret me when I am dead. There are people, and many of them, who fret because they long for that which is impossible. I have passed that time of life, and will be content with what life affords,—with you. I am not a boy, but a man of experience, and I know I will never tire of you. I have thought of the ways in which you can be disagreeable, but your good qualities outweigh them all. I know you are not an angel; you have faults, but it gives me pleasure to forgive them in advance. If you will be equally charitable with me, we will be very happy."

"I have no occasion to be charitable with you," she answered.

"Then you never will have," was his reply. "Marriage is the greatest inheritance of man, but it is either a feast or a famine. The contrast between a man who is happily married, and one who is not, is as great as the contrast between light and darkness, but there are many more of the first class than of the latter. It may be a false social system, but very often those who ought not to marry hurry into it in the greatest haste. I have thought that the qualities which attract young people to each other are the very ones which result in misery: and that love should commence in sincere and frank friendship; not charity or sentimentality. I do not believe in affinities, but I do believe that there is only one person in the world exactly suited to be my wife, and I intend to kiss her now."

He did kiss her, but with the tenderness a rough man might display in kissing a tiny baby.

"Although you say you love me, and I *know* you do," the girl said thoughtfully, "you have always acted as though you were afraid of me. You never kissed me but once before in your life, and then I asked you to."

"Afraid of you!" There was a merry good humor in Allan Dorris's voice which would have made anyone his friend. "Afraid of you! Am I afraid of the sunshine, or of a fresh breath of air! I am afraid of nothing. I had the same fear of you that I have of heaven—a fear that you were beyond my reach, therefore I did not care to contaminate you with my touch. But if ever I get to heaven, I will not be afraid of it. I intend to make love to you all my life, though I shall be careful not to make myself tiresome. We will reverse the rule, and become lovers after we are married. You once said that I was queer; I cannot forget that charge, somehow. I *am* queer; in this respect: I was born a bull with a hatred for red flags, which have been waved in my face ever since I can remember. I may have been mistaken, but I have always believed that I never had a friend in my life, although I craved one more than anything else. But you have changed all this; I am contented now, and ready to give peace for peace. Of the millions of people in the world, am I not entitled to you?"

He held her up in his arms, as if he would exhibit her, and ask if that small bundle was an unreasonable request, since he asked no more, and promised to be entirely satisfied.

The loud report of a gun on the outside, followed by a crash in the glass in the upper pane of the window as a bullet came in to imbed itself in the wall above their heads, startled them. The girl sprang up in alarm, while Dorris hurriedly ran down stairs and into the yard.

"A careless hunter has allowed his gun to explode in the road," he said, when he returned after a long absence. But this explanation did not seem to satisfy even himself, for he soon went down to the lower end of the hall, and aroused Mrs. Wedge, by throwing the window-prop on the roof of her house. On the appearance of that worthy woman, who came in with her eyes almost closed from the sleepiness which still clung to her, but who opened them very wide at sight of Annie Benton, he said,—

"Will you two please talk about the weather, and nothing else, until I return? I will return in a few minutes, and make the necessary explanations. If there is anything wrong here, I will make it right."

He left the house hurriedly, and they heard the big iron gate in front bang after him, but when his footsteps could no longer be heard, and they no longer had excuse for listening to them, the two women sat in perfect silence. Occasionally Mrs. Wedge looked cautiously around at Annie Benton, but, meeting her eyes, they both looked away again, and tried to appear at their ease, which they found impossible. Fortunately Dorris was not gone long, and when he came back he put the girl's cloak on, as if they were going out.

"We will return in a little while," he explained to Mrs. Wedge, who looked up curiously as he walked out with Annie Benton on his arm. "If you care to wait, we will tell you a secret when we come back, as a reward for not speaking while I was out of the room."

Down the stairs they went, out at the front gate, and toward the town, until they reached the church door, which they entered. On the inside they found Reverend Wilton waiting for them at the chancel rail, and although he tried to appear very much put out because he was disturbed at that unseasonable hour, and yawned indifferently, he was really interested. Perhaps he was thinking of the rare story he would have to tell at breakfast.

Dorris had evidently given instructions as to what was expected of him, for as soon as they stood before him he read the marriage service, and pronounced them man and wife; after which he congratulated them and left the church, which was probably in accordance with his instructions, too.

A single light burned in the building, which barely extended to the vaulted ceiling, and which did not prevent the pews and the pulpit from looking like live objects surprised at being disturbed at such an hour; and leading his wife up to the organ, Dorris said: "We will have the wedding march, if you please," whereupon he disappeared behind the instrument to work the bellows.

And such a wedding march was never heard before. The girl put all the joy of her heart into melody, and made chords which caused Allan Dorris to regret that he could not leave the bellows and go round in front to wave his hat and cheer. He was seated on a box in the dusty little corner, working away industriously; and when he heard how eloquently the girl was telling the story of her love for him, tears of thankfulness came into his eyes and surprised them, for they had never been there before. Your cheek and mine have been wet with tears wrung from the heart by sorrow, but all of us have not been as happy as Allan Dorris was on his wedding night.

But there was more than joy in the music; it changed so suddenly into the plaintive strain of the minstrel baritone as to cause Allan Dorris to start. It may have been because the player was executing with the left hand, and without a light; but certainly it was difficult, like a life. But when the chords were formed, they were very sweet and tender, as we might say with a sigh that flowers on a weary man's grave were appropriate.

At last the music ceased, dying away like the memory of sobs and cheers and whispers, and taking his wife's arm through his own, Allan Dorris walked back to The Locks.

Mrs. Wedge was informed of the marriage, and could do nothing but cry from happiness; and after she left them Allan Dorris and his wife had so much to say to each other that daylight came to congratulate them while they were still seated in their chairs.

But what is this which comes into the mind of Annie Dorris and causes her to start up in alarm? It is the recollection of Thompson Benton, her plain-spoken father.

"O Allan!" she said. "What will father say?"

"I will go over and hear what he says," Dorris replied promptly, putting on his hat. "You can go along if you like."

What a bold fellow he was! And how tenderly he adjusted the wraps around his wife, after she had signified her desire to accompany him, when they stepped out into the frosty morning air!

It was about Thompson Benton's time to start down town, and as they paused before his front door, not without misgivings, he opened it wide and stood before them. Evidently the girl had not been missed from the house, for there was genuine astonishment in the father's face as he looked from one to the other.

"What does this mean?" he said, looking at Dorris sharply from under his shaggy eyebrows.

"That we were married this morning," Dorris replied, not in the least frustrated, though his wife trembled like a leaf.

He gave no evidence of the surprise which this announcement must have caused him, but looked sullenly at Dorris for several moments, as though he had a mind to try his strength with him; but when his eyes fell on his child, his manner changed for the better. Motioning them to follow him, they closed the door, and all sat down in the pleasant family room where the girl's recollection began, and where her father spent his little leisure in the evening. Here old Thompson looked hard at the floor until he had thought the matter over, when he said,—

"I have never found fault with the girl in my life; I have never had occasion to, and if she can justify what she has done I am content. Are you sure you are right, Annie?"

He looked up at her with such a softened manner, and there was so much tenderness in his words, that the girl forgot the fear which his hard look had inspired when they met him at the door, and going over to him she put her arm around his neck, and softly stroked his gray hair as she replied,—

"That which I have done has made me very happy. If that is justification, I am entirely justified."

"I require no other explanation," old Thompson answered. "From a little child you have been dutiful, sensible, and capable, and though my selfishness rebels because I am to lose you, a father's love is stronger than selfishness, and I am glad you have found a husband you regard as worthy of your affection. You have drawn a prize, sir."

He looked at Dorris as a defeated man might look at his rival when he thought it necessary to hide his mortification, and offer congratulations which he did not feel.

"There is no doubt of it," Dorris promptly answered.

"She is very much like her mother," old Thompson continued, "and her mother was the best woman in ten thousand. If I gave her a task to perform, she did it in a manner which pleased me, and she was always a pleasant surprise. *This* is a surprise, but I find no fault; I cannot regret that Annie knows the happiness of a young wife. I am a rough man, but I made her mother a very happy woman, and in remembrance of that I am glad the daughter has found a husband she can honor. I have so much confidence in the girl's good sense that I do not question her judgment, and I wish you joy with all my heart."

He took both their hands in his for a moment, and hurried away, Dorris and his wife watching him until he disappeared in a bend of the street, when they went into the house to make their peace with the Ancient Maiden.

As Thompson Benton hurried along toward his store, swinging the respectable-looking iron key in his hand, who can know the regret he felt to lose his child? His practical mind would not help him now, and he must have felt that the only creature in all the world he cared for had deserted him, for the old forget the enthusiasm of the young.

It was a fortunate circumstance that the day was bad and customers few, for they would not have been treated well had they appeared.

CHAPTER XVII.

THE PURSUING SHADOW.

Allan Dorris and his wife had been up in the hills watching the sunset, and at dusk were returning leisurely home. They were very fond of the unfrequented locality where he had first declared his passion, and when the weather was fine they frequently visited it to imagine themselves lovers again, which was easy enough, for as man and wife they got along amazingly well. And now, when they were returning at nightfall, a shadow crept after them; from bush to rock, and from tree to shrub, crawling and stealing along like a beast watching its prey.

Pretty Annie Dorris, prettier than ever before, was expressing a fear in her winning way that their happiness was too great to last, and that something dreadful would happen to them. But she had no suspicion of the lurking, creeping shadow which had hurried forward, and now stood almost within arm's length, as her husband replied,—

"I have been so discontented all my life, and am so contented now, that I believe the Fates will guard me from it in pity. It is not much that I ask; a country girl to be my wife, and love me—nothing more. And it will always be my endeavor to be so useful to the country girl that she will be happy, too, so that the simple boon of peace is not too much to ask when it will make two people entirely happy. I cheerfully give up my place in the strife for greatness and riches in which men seem to be always engaged, and will be content with the good health and plenty which my simple life here will bring me. As for a living, I can make that easy enough; I am making more even now than we can possibly spend. I hope your fears are not substantial."

The country girl had her arm through her husband's, and she looked up into his face with such a troubled expression that he stopped in the road.

"It may be that I am fearful only because I love you so much," she said. "It almost kills me when I think that any harm might happen to you."

"I am glad to hear you say that," he replied, "but you are always saying something which pleases me. You look handsome to-night; you look prettier now than before you were married, and I think more of you. You don't fade out, and I love you for that; you are as fresh and as girlish as you ever were before we were married. I think it an evidence of good blood."

"Now you are pleasing me," his wife said laughingly. "I have feared very often that you would not like me so well when you knew me better, and that you would finally tire of me."

"But I don't," Dorris replied. "The more I know of you the better I like you. It's not usual, but I am more in love after marriage than I was before."

"I have mingled so little with women," the wife said seriously, "that I sometimes fear that I am not like others of my sex in manners and dress and inclination. Did you ever notice it?"

"I think I have," he said.

She turned upon him with mock fierceness, and pretended to be very indignant.

"Because you are not like other women, who act by rule, and are nearly all alike, is the reason I have no greater ambition than to be tied to your apron-strings," he said. "I think your freshness and originality are your greatest charms."

"Long before I ever thought of becoming a wife myself," she said, seriously again, "I noticed that most men seemed to lack a knowledge of women; that they regarded them as angels while they were girls, and were disappointed because they turned out to be women as wives. I am not unjust, but I have thought the women were partly responsible for this, since many of them exhibit themselves like dolls, and pretend to be more than they are. This is the reason why I am pleased that you are not disappointed in me."

"As to your being an angel," he laughingly replied, "I know you are not one, and I am glad of it. I have an idea that an angel would soon tire of me, and fly away in disgust, to warn its companions that men were not worth saving. There are some women so amiable that no matter to what extent their affairs go wrong, they cannot muster up enough energetic regret to cause them to supply a remedy. I am not so fond of amiability as to desire it at that price. Whenever you find capacity you will find temper, and I imagine that it would be dangerous to stir you up, for you are as capable a woman as ever I knew. *Haven't* you temper?"

"Plenty of it; too much," she answered.

They both laughed at this frank confession, and Dorris took occasion to say that there was not a spark of it in his nature, though there was temper written in every line of his countenance, and that he would have been an ugly man when once fully aroused was certain.

They walked on again, and the shadow followed, as if anxious to hear what they were saying.

"I can't account for it myself," Dorris continued, "but I enjoy your company as much now as I did before we were married. It does me as much good to talk love to you; I suppose it must be because you deserve it. The fact that you are as careful to look well as you ever did may have something to do with it, but it is certainly the case. I have heard men abused a great deal for neglecting their wives after marriage, but it never occurs to me to neglect you. I don't want to neglect you; I think too much of you. If I should fail to be as considerate of you as you are of me, I know that I would no longer receive the full measure of your confidence and love, which is such a comfort to me, therefore it is my first ambition to be just and honest with you in everything. The ambition affords me a great deal of pleasure, too, for I am never so well satisfied as when in your company. With you by my side, there is nothing else that I crave in this world or the next."

"O Allan! Nothing in the next?"

They had seated themselves on a rough seat in a sort of park on the hillside, and Dorris considered the matter.

"Well, if you go to heaven, I want to go. Of course you will go, for you are good enough, therefore I intend to do the best I can, so that, when we come to be judged, the Master will realize how much we love each other, and conclude not to separate us. But I depend on you; He will let me in to please you—not because I deserve it."

"I know you do not think as I do about it," she answered, "but it is possible that you have not investigated as I have. I am not a foolish girl, but a serious woman, and have studied and thought a great deal, and I am certain there is something more than this life. I have never mentioned the subject to you before, because I know that a great many come to dislike religion because they hear so much of it from persons no better than themselves, but everything teaches us that we shall live again, and it worries me a great deal because you think lightly about a matter which seems so dreadfully serious. My mother's faith convinces me of it, though I cannot tell you why. I am not prepared, as she was, by a long life of purity to receive the evidence; but promise me that you will think about it, and not combat your own judgment."

"I have never thought about it much, and investigated but little," he answered. "It has always been natural for me to think of the grave as the end of everything, so far as I am concerned. But I have confidence in your intelligence and judgment; if you have investigated, and believe, that is enough for me; *I* believe. Please do not worry about it any more; I will try very hard to remain with you."

He said it lightly, yet there was enough seriousness in his manner to convince her that his love for her was honest, even if his religion was not.

"Religion is not natural with me: I feel no necessity for it or lack of it," he said again. "But I have no objection to it; on the contrary, I have always liked the idea, but I lack the necessary faith. It would be pleasant for me to believe that, in the next country, a day's journey removed, good gifts might be found; but if I could not believe it, I could not be reasonably blamed for my refusal to attempt the journey. I might even regret that the accounts were not true; but I would not insist that they *were* true against my honest convictions, because I *hoped* they were. I am religious enough in sentiment, but my brain is an inexorable skeptic. Nothing is more pleasing to me than the promise of your faith. What a blessed hope it is, that after death you will live in a land of perpetual summer; and exist forever with your friends where there is only peace and content! I am sure I can never see as much of you as I want to in this life, and I cannot tell you how much I hope we will be reunited beyond the grave, and live forever to love each other, even as we do now. I am willing to make any sacrifice necessary to ensure this future; it would be a pleasure for me to make greater sacrifices than are required, according to common rumor, for they are not at all exacting, except in the particular of faith; but that I lack, to a most alarming extent, though I cannot help it. You cannot have faith because it is your duty any more than you can love because it is your duty. I only regret that I cannot be religious as naturally as I love you, but I cannot, though I try because you want me to. I want to believe that men do not grow old and become a burden to themselves and those around them; but I know differently, and while I hope that there will be a resurrection, I know that those who have gone away on the journey which begins with death send back no messenger, and that nothing is known of heaven except the declaration of pious people that they believe in it. I love to hear the laughter of children, but it does not convince me that all the world is in a laughing mood, and that there are no tears. No one can find fault with your religion except that they cannot believe in it. Everything in nature teaches us that we will return to dust, and that we will be resurrected only as dust by the idle winds. You don't mind that I speak freely?"

"No."

"I have tried all my life to convince myself that I possessed the spark of immortality, but my stubborn brain resists the attempt. All my reasoning convinces me that I live for the same reason that my horse exists. I am superior to the faithful animal only in intelligence, for in physical organization I am only an animal. When an animal dies, I see its body dwindle away until there is nothing left; it becomes dust again. I *hope* that I may share a different fate, but I *believe* that I shall pass away in precisely the same manner. Understand me; I want to be religious, but I cannot be. There are some people—I suppose there are a great many, though I never knew but one personally—who ought to live forever; they are too rare to die. You are one of them, but I fear you will be lost to the world in the course of nature. You ought to be preserved for the good you can accomplish by playing the organ. I never believe in heaven so much as when I am in the back pews listening to your music. There is more religion in the old organ when you are at the keyboard than in all the people who listen to it put together; and I sometimes think that those who write the music and the songs are inspired, though when you know them, their personal characters do not encourage that impression."

She put her hand to his mouth as if to stop him, but he pushed it away with a laugh, and continued,—

"Let me finish, that you may know what I really am, and then I will never mention the subject again. But don't think me worse than other men for my unbelief; they nearly all think as I do, though only the bad ones say so. All good men rejoice that there is a pleasing hope in religion, and encourage it all they can, but only a few of them have your faith."

"All be well yet, Allan," the wife answered. "You have promised to try and get rid of your unbelief, and I know that you will be honest in it. The Master whom I serve next to you—I fear I am becoming very wicked myself, for you are more to me than everything else—"

"There it is again," Dorris said, looking at her, half laughing. "That expression wasn't studied, I know, but it pleases me greatly. You are always at it, though you have a right to now."

"He is more considerate than any of us imagine, and if He knows you did not believe, He will also know that you could not, and did not intend any disrespect."

"There is something in that," he answered. "I loved you before I knew you, though I did not believe you existed."

"But you *did* find me. Is it not possible that you will find Him, though you do not believe He exists?"

"That is worth thinking about. The next time I take a long ride into the country I will think it over, if I can get you out of my mind long enough. One thing, however, is certain; I want to follow you, wherever that leads me. Let me add, too, that in what I have said I intend no disrespect. It would be impudent in me, a single pebble in the sands surrounding the shores of eternity, to speak ill of a faith which is held by so many thousands of intelligent and worthy people. I speak freely to you, as my wife, my confidant, that you may know what I am."

"But you are leading, Allan, and I am following," she said. "You are kind enough to believe that my future is assured, but it is not unless you are saved. You can save both of us by saving yourself. If we were at the judgment now, and you should be cast out, I would follow you. I might be of some use to you even there."

"That's horrible to think about," he replied, rising to his feet; "but it pleases me. Anyway, little woman, we get along delightfully here; I hope we will always be as well off as we are now. If the next world affords me as much pleasure as this one has during the past three months, I shall be more than satisfied. It is said that a man is very happy when he is in love, and I am growing more in love with my wife every day. I suppose it is because I never was in love before. I have had extensive experience in everything else; I know a little of everything else. This may be the reason why my honeymoon lasts so long."

"When I met you that afternoon, out in the hills," she answered, "you were such an expert at love-making that I was at first afraid of you. If ever man made a desperate, cunning love to a woman, you made it to me; but I soon got over my timidity, and knew you were only desperately in earnest, which made me love you until I went mad. I had nothing to give you but myself, and that I gave so readily that I sometimes fear—when you are away from me; I never think of it at any other time—that you accuse me for it."

"It so happened," he answered, "that you did exactly what I wanted you to do, though I am not surprised at it now, since discovering how naturally you do a hundred things a day to please me. Accuse you?"

He laughed good-naturedly at the thought.

"Instead of that, it is the boast of my life that my sweetheart, my vision which came true, had so much confidence in me that she placed herself in my keeping without conditions or promises. You are the hope I have had all my life; you are the heaven I have coveted; and don't suppose that I find fault because the realization is better than the dream. When you go to heaven, and find that it is a better place than you imagined, you will not accuse the Master of a lack of propriety because he is more forgiving of your faults than you expected; nor do I. Dismiss that thought forever, to oblige me, and believe, instead, that your single fault turned out to be my greatest blessing. If I made desperate love to you up in the hills, it was natural, for I had no previous experience. I cannot remember that I ever was a young man; I was first a child, and then a man with grave responsibilities. But the fancy I told you about—the Maid of Air—I always loved it until I found you."

Putting her arm through his, they walked toward the town, and the shadow emerged from a clump of bushes within a few feet of where they had been sitting. The married lovers walked on, unconscious of the presence; and occasionally the laugh of Mrs. Dorris came to the shadow on the wind, which caused it to listen anxiously, and creep on after them again.

In turning out of the path that led up into the hills, and coming into the road, Dorris and his wife met Tug and Silas, who were loitering about, as usual; Tug in front, carrying the gun, and Silas lagging behind.

"What now?" Dorris said good-naturedly, on coming up with them. "What are you up to to-night?"

"On a Wednesday night," Tug replied, putting the stock of the gun on the ground, and turning his head to one side to get a square sight at the woman, "the woods are full of rabbits. We are out looking for them."

"Why on Wednesday night?"

Tug removed his gaze from Mrs. Dorris to Silas.

"When do we find our game?" he inquired.

"On Wednesday; at night," the little man answered meekly.

"I don't know how it is, myself," Tug continued, this time taking a shot at Dorris; "but Wednesday it is. You are both looking mighty well."

They thanked him for his politeness, and added that they were feeling well.

"They didn't think much of you when you came," he said, pointing a finger at Dorris, which looked like a pistol, "but they have changed their minds. Even Reverend Wilton says you will do; it's the first kind word he ever said of anybody. It came out—Silas, how did it come out?"

"Like a tooth," Silas answered, who had been standing by with his hands in his pockets.

"Like a *back* tooth, you told me. Come now, didn't you say a back tooth?"

Silas muttered something which was accepted as an acknowledgment, and Tug went on,—

"Why didn't you say so, then? Why do you want to put it on me in the presence of the lady? But Reverend Wilton never said anything bad about you, or anybody else; he's too lazy for that. I only wonder that he didn't drop over from exhaustion when he said you'd do. Well, I should say you *would* do; eh, pretty girl?"

Annie Dorris made no other answer than to cling closer to her husband, and Tug regarded them with apparent pleasure.

"And there's Uncle Ponsonboy. Silas, what does Uncle Ponsonboy say?"

"He says that Mr. Dorris is a man of promise," Davy answered.

"Oh, *does* he? Well, he's not the kind of a man of promise, Uncle Ponsonboy is, who has been promising to distinguish himself for forty years. Old Albert reminds me of a nephew of my wife's. I supported him four years in idleness, but he was always boasting that he was able to take care of himself, and that *he* asked favors of nobody. He used to fill up on my bread and meat, and lounge in front of my fire, and declare that he never knew solid content until he began to make his own living, although he did nothing except to write to his folks, and say that they needn't worry about him,—*he* was able to take care of himself. But the old lady holds out against you."

Tug swallowed a laugh with a great effort, apparently locking it up with a spring lock, for there was a click in his throat as he took aim at Dorris again and continued, but not before his scalp had returned to its place after crawling over on his forehead to look at the smile,—

"I am glad of that, though. The old lady and I never agree on anything. I like the devil because she hates him. I shall be quite content in purg if she fails to like it."

Allan Dorris looked puzzled for a moment.

"Oh, purgatory," he said, finishing the abbreviation, and turning to his wife, who laughed at the idea, "we were talking about that just before you came up."

"Neither of you need worry about *that*," Tug said. "*You* are all right. I am the devil's partner, and I know. But if you *should* happen down there by any mischance, I will give you the best accommodations the place affords. If there is an ice-box there, you shall have a room in it; but no ice-water for the old lady. I insist on that condition."

They were very much amused at his odd talk, and promised that his instructions should be obeyed in case they became his guests.

"But why are you the devil's partner?" Dorris asked.

"He must have assistants, of course," Tug replied, "and I shall make application to enter his service as soon as I arrive. I want to get even with Uncle Ponsonboy."

Tug locked up a laugh again with a sharp click of the lock, and his scalp hurried back to its place on learning that it was a false alarm.

"I want to get a note from him to this effect: 'Dear Tug: For the sake of old acquaintance, send me a drop of water.' Whereupon I will take my iron pen in hand, and reply: 'Uncle Ponsonboy: Drink your tears.' Then I will instruct one of my devilish assistants to lock him up, and never let him see the cheerful light of the fires again. As the door closes, I will say to him, as I now say to you,—Good-night."

Tug and Silas walked toward the hills, and Dorris and his wife toward the town, but the shadow no longer followed them; it had disappeared.

In case the shadow came back that night to prowl around The Locks, and peer in at the windows, it found a determined-looking man on guard, carrying a wicked-looking gun.

Had the eyes of the shadow followed the feet of the man, it would have noted that they walked around the stone wall at regular intervals, and that they stopped occasionally, as if listening; it would have seen them strolling leisurely away at the first approach of dawn, carrying the gun and Tug's burly body with them.

CHAPTER XVIII.

THE RISE IN THE RIVER.

The rain had been falling at intervals for weeks, and the sluggish river, which usually crawled at the foot of the town in quiet submission, had become a dangerous torrent. Long since out of its banks, its waters poured through the bottoms with an angry roar, and at night those who gathered on the brink in the town to mark its steady rising could hear cries of distress from the heavy timber, the firing of guns, and other alarms.

For two days parties had been out with boats of every description, rescuing those who believed that the waters would soon go down, and remained until escape was impossible, imprisoned in the upper rooms of their houses; and each returning party brought the most distressing news yet heard of the havoc wrought by the flood. Reaching from hill to hill, the angry waters ploughed up fair fields like heavy shot fired in battle, and crept into pretty homes to destroy in a night the work of years, wresting treasures from their fastenings with remorseless fury, and hurrying away with them like living thieves.

The citizens of Davy's Bend feared that the sun had been drowned by the flood in the heavens, as the people were being drowned by the flood in the bottoms, for its kindly face had not appeared in two weeks. The roads and lanes in the country, highways no longer, were abandoned to the rain and the mist, for no travellers ventured upon them, and if the town had been dull before, it was now doubly so, giving the people abundance of time in which to recount their miseries. Men who ventured out in wagons told wonderful tales, on their return, of the reign of the waters, for insignificant streams which had long been regarded with familiar contempt had become dangerous rivers, roaring and crashing through fruitful fields in mad haste to join the floods. Great lakes occupied the low places for so many days that the people feared the land itself had floated away, leaving caverns in the place of their fields, and there was distress in the country as well as in the town. Rude boats to ply upon the newly arrived waters were hastily constructed by men who did not know how to use them, never having lived near a navigable stream, but there seemed a chance for them to learn, for the waters increased steadily every hour.

As they lay in their beds at night, if they wakened and found that the rain had ceased, the people of the town hoped that the end had come at last, and that the waters would soon subside, but before they had framed their congratulations, the gentle patter of the rain was heard on their roofs once more, which continued through the long night, ceasing only occasionally, that the cries of distress and the alarms from the bottom might be heard, whereupon the rain commenced again with joyful vigor, sure that its fury was not without result.

The rocky hills above and below the town were oozy and wet; and those who roamed about heard great splashes in the water, and knew that portions of the bluff were tumbling into the river, as if tired of being steady and reliable while everything else was failing, and anxious to join the tide and aid in the general destruction, as well as to get away from a place which seemed so unfortunate.

The mild river, patient and uncomplaining so long, was master now, and it roared like a monster proud of its conquest, and declaring its intention to be wicked and fierce forever. The observers could not understand, so great was the awful flood, how the waters could ever subside, for surely all the lower country must have been flooded days before, and even those who lived in the hills were filled with grave apprehensions.

Every morning the simple registers, which the people put up along the creeks and sloughs, showed an alarming rise, and they feared that if the rain continued the earth itself would become liquid at last, and resolve itself into a vast sea without shores.

No one knew how the news came, but there seemed to be whispers in the air that in the upper country the flood was even worse than at Davy's Bend, which added to the general apprehension, and many believed that the rainbow was about to prove faithless at last. Houses of a pattern barely familiar to the people occasionally floated past the town in the current, and in one of them rode a man who refused to leave his property when the relief boats put off to him; for he said that he came from hundreds of miles above, and that since the world seemed to be turning into water, he preferred his strange craft to the crumbling hills. As he floated away, stark mad from excitement, fear, and hunger, he called back to the men to follow if they valued their lives; for a wave twenty feet high was coming down the river, carrying the towns along the bluffs with it.

Bridges which had been built across gullies in the highlands were seen hurrying by every hour, and it seemed that the hill on which Davy's Bend was built would shortly tremble, and start slowly down the river, at last gratifying the ambition of the people to get away.

Among those distressed by the unfortunate condition of those living in the bottoms were Allan Dorris and his wife, safe in their home above the town. The people seemed so fearful that the rain would never cease that they neglected to get sick, and Dr. Dorris would have greatly enjoyed the uninterrupted days he was permitted to spend with his pretty wife but for the distress around him.

The dripping from the eaves of The Locks at night—he thought of it again—reminded him of the dripping from the coffin of a body packed in ice, which he was commissioned to watch, and long before day he left his bed and walked the floor. His wife soon joined him, and they looked out of the window at the blank darkness.

"How it reminds me of the first night I came here," he said. "But what a different man I am! Then I cursed my existence, and was so disturbed in mind that night was a season of terror. I dreaded its approach as heartily then as I now hail it as a season of repose, and every day I have new reason to rejoice that I am alive. What a fortunate fellow I am! I can sleep nine hours out of every night, and arise every morning entirely refreshed, not a day older. I am content now to lie down at night, and let the world wag, or quarrel, or do whatever it likes, for the only part of it I care for is beside me. Sometimes I waken, and forget you for a moment, when I wonder how I ever induced such sound sleep to come to my eyes; but when I remember it all, I feel like cheering, and go off into dreamland again with the comfort of a healthy child. It is a wonderful change, and you are responsible for it all; you have made one man entirely happy, if you have accomplished nothing else."

As they stood by the window, he had his arms around her, and when she looked up at him he kissed her tenderly on the forehead.

"Our marriage has brought no more happiness to you than it has to me," she answered. "Since you became my husband, I have known only content and gladness, except when I become childish and fear you are surrounded by some grave danger. If I could charge you with a wish I could think of nothing to ask."

"Who would harm me? Who would dare?" he asked.

His wife thought to herself, as she looked at him, that it would be a dangerous undertaking to attempt to do him an injury. There were few men his equal in physical strength, and he could hold her out at arm's length.

"Danger is a game that two can play at," he said, and there was a frown on his face so fierce as to indicate that some one who was his enemy had come into his mind. "I have seen the day when I would have allowed almost any one the privilege of taking my life, if it would have afforded them pleasure, but let them keep out of my way now! The tiger fighting for her whelps would not be fiercer than I, if attacked. I have more to live for than any other man in the world, and I would fight, not only with desperation, but with skill and wickedness. If any one wants my life, let him see that he does not lose his own in attempting to take it."

Allan Dorris had been oppressed with a vague fear ever since his marriage that his long period of rest meant a calamity at last, though he had always tried to argue the notion out of his wife's mind. He had often felt that he was watched, though he had seen nothing, heard nothing, to warrant this belief. He could not explain it to himself; but frequently while walking about the town he turned his head in quick alarm, and looked about as if expecting an attack. Once he felt so ill at ease at night, so thoroughly convinced that something was wrong, that he left his wife quietly sleeping, and crawled under the trees in The Locks' yard for an hour, with a loaded pistol in his hand. But he had seen nothing, heard nothing, and his own actions were so much like the presence he half expected to find, that he was ashamed of them, and laughed at his fears.

But the dark night and the cheerless rain brought the old dread into his mind, and he said to his wife,—

"We are all surrounded by danger, though I am as exempt from it as other men, but if I should meet with an accident some time—I take many long rides at night, and I have often been in places when a single misstep of my horse would have resulted in death—I want you to know that your husband was an honorable man. I have my faults, and I have regrets; but as the world goes I am an honest man. Your love for me, which is as pure and good as it can be, has had as much warrant as other wives have for their love. It was never intended that a perfect man or woman should exist on this earth, as a reproach to all the other inhabitants, and I have my faults; but I have as clear a conscience as it was intended that the average man should have."

"I am sure of that," his wife answered. "You always impress me as being a fair man, and this was one reason why I forget myself in loving you. I did not believe you would be unjust to anyone; surely not to one you loved."

"I believe I am entitled to the compliment you pay me," he replied. "I know myself so well that a compliment which I do not deserve does not please me; but I deserve the good opinion you have just expressed. I have known people whose inclinations were usually right; but mine were usually wrong—either that, or I have been so situated that, by reason of hasty conclusions, duty has always been a task; but notwithstanding this I have always tried to be honest and fair in everything. It sometimes happens that a man is so situated that if he would be just to himself he must be unjust to others. I may have been in that situation, and there may be those who believe that I have wronged them; but I am sure that an honest judge would acquit me of blame. I have often wanted to tell you my brief and unimportant history; but you have preferred not to hear it. While I admire you for this exhibition of trust in me, I have often wondered that your woman's curiosity did not covet the secret."

"It is not a secret since you offer to tell it to me," she replied. "But I prefer not to know it now. You once said to me that every life has its sorrow; mine is the belief that I know what your history is; but I prefer to hope that I am wrong rather than know my conjecture is right."

He looked at her with incredulity, and was about to inquire what she knew, when she continued:

"You never speak to me that I do not get a scrap of your past history; I read you as easily as I read a book. But I knew it when I became your wife, and I think less of it now than ever; you are so kind to me that I think I shall forget it altogether in time. It is scarcely a sorrow; rather a regret, as I regret during my present happy life that I am growing old. Sometimes I think I love you all the more because of your misfortune, though I never think of it when I am with you; it is only when I am alone that it occupies my mind."

"You are sure that you have not made it worse than it is?"

"Quite sure."

"Who was in the right?"

"You were."

"That much is true, anyway," he answered, looking out at the torrent in the river, which the approaching daylight now made visible. "I formerly had a habit of talking in my sleep; you may have learned something in that way."

"A great deal," she replied. "I learned your name."

For the first time since she had known him he seemed confused, and there was a flush of mortification in his face. He picked up a scrap of paper and pencil which were lying on a table near them, and handing them to her, said,—

"Write it."

Without the slightest hesitation, she wrote quickly on the paper, and handed it back to him. He looked at it with a queer smile, tore up the scrap, and said,—

"That would have come out in the story you refused to hear. I have never deceived you in anything."

"Except in this," she answered, putting her arms around him. "You are a much better man than I believed you were when we were first acquainted; you have deceived me in that. My married life could not be happier than it is."

"I do not take much credit to myself that we are content as husband and wife," he replied. "I think the fact that we are mated has a great deal to do with it. There are a great many worthy people—for the world is full of good women, if not of good men—who live in the greatest wretchedness; who are as unhappy in their married relations as we are happy. I have known excellent men married to excellent wives, who are wretched, as I have known two excellent men to fail as partners in business. You and I were fortunate in our alliance. It often occurs to me that Mrs. Armsby should have had a better husband, poor woman. How many brave, capable men there are in the world who would rejoice in the possession of such a wife; worthy, honest men who made a mistake only in marrying the wrong woman, and who will die believing there is nothing in the world worth living for, as I believed before I met you. Everyone who is out in the world a great deal knows such men, and pities them, as I do; for when I contrast my past with my present, I regret that others, more deserving than I, cannot enjoy the contentment which love brings. You and I are not phenomenal people in any respect, but we are man and wife in the fullest sense of the term; and others might enjoy the peace we enjoy were they equally fortunate in their love affairs. It is a grand old world for you and I, and those like us, but it is a hell for those who have been coaxed into unsuitable marriages by the devil."

"There is as much bitterness in your voice now as there was when you said to me in the church that you were going away never to come back," his wife said, looking at him with keen apprehension.

"I am a different man now to what I was then," he replied, with his old good-nature. "Have you never remarked it?"

"Often; every time I hear you speak."

"I find that there are splendid people even in Davy's Bend, and I imagine that when the mind is not tortured they may be found anywhere. In my visits to the homes of Davy's Bend, I hear it said in every quarter that surely the neighbors are the best people in the world, and their kindness in sickness and death cause me to believe that as a rule the people are very good, unless you chain two antagonistic spirits together, and demand that they be content. I know so much of the weakness of my race—because it happens to be my business—that I wonder they are as industrious and honorable as I find them. This never occurred to me before, and I think it is evidence that I am a changed man; that I am more charitable than I ever was before, and better."

They both looked out the window in silence again. A misty morning, threatening rain, and the river before them like a sea.

"I must do something to help those who are imprisoned in their homes by the flood," Allan Dorris said, as if a sight of the river had suggested it to him. "I will go down where boats are to be had presently, and row over into the timber. Do you see that line of trees?"

Below the town, in the river bend, a long line of trees made out into the channel, which were on dry land in ordinary times, but the point was covered now, for the flood occupied the bottom from bluff to bluff. He pointed this out, and when his wife saw the place he referred to, she nodded her head.

"My boat will be carried down the stream by the strong current, and I will probably enter the timber there. I will wave my good-by to you from that point."

He went out soon after to prepare for the trip, and during his absence his wife hurriedly prepared his breakfast; and when he came back he wore coat and boots of rubber.

"What a wonderful housekeeper you are," he said, as he sat down to the table. "No difference what I crave, you supply it before I have time to worry because of the lack of it. But it is so in everything; I never want to do a thing but that I find you are of the same mind. It is very easy to spoil a boy, but I think the girls are naturally so good that they turn out well without much attention. You had no mother to teach you, but you took charge of my house with as much good grace and ease as though you had been driven to it all your life. I think a great deal more of your sex because of my acquaintance with you. If my wife is not the most wonderful woman in the world, I shall never know it."

"I am almost ashamed to say it after your kind remark," his wife replied, "but I am afraid I do not want you to go over into the bottoms. The thought of it fills me with dread, though I know you ought to go."

"And why not?" he said cheerfully. "I may be able to rescue some unfortunate over there, and there is nothing dangerous in the journey. I shall return before the night comes on,—no fear of that; but before I go I want to tell you again how much my marriage with you has done for me. I want you to keep it in your mind while I am away, that you may understand why I am glad to return. Until I came here and met you, I was as discontented as a man could possibly be, and I am very grateful to you. A life of toil and misery was my lot until you came to my rescue, and I thank you for your kindness to me. It occurred to me while I was out of the room just now, that the shadow under the trees is very much like the shadow I intended to penetrate when you came to me that dark night and blessed me. Once you came into the room where I was lying down, after returning from the country, though I was not asleep as you supposed. The gentle manner in which you touched my forehead with your lips; that was love—I have thought about it a thousand times since, and been thankful. The human body I despise, because of my familiarity with it; but such a love as yours is divine. I only regret that it is not more general. Love is the only thing in life worth having; if a man who lacks it is not discontented, he is like an idiot who is always laughing, not realizing his condition. Some people I have known suggested depravity by their general appearance; you think of your own faults from looking at them, and feel ashamed; but it makes me ambitious to look at you, and every day since I have known you I have been a better man than I was the day before."

He had finished his repast by this time, and they walked out to the front door together, arm in arm, like lovers.

"I have heard it said," he continued, as he tied up his rubber boots and made final preparations for starting, "that if a wife is too good to her husband, he will finally come to dislike her. *You* are too good to me, I suppose, but it never occurs to me to dislike you for it; on the contrary, it causes me to resolve to be worthy of your thoughtfulness. It will do me good to go into the shadow for a day; I will appreciate the sunshine all the more when I return. But if I should not return—if an accident should happen to me, which is always possible anywhere—my last thought would be thankfulness for the happiness of the past three months."

"But you do not anticipate danger?" she said, grasping his arm, as if to lead him back into the house.

"There is no danger," he replied. "Even if my boat should fail me, I could swim back to you from the farthest point, for I love you so much. You have never seen my reserve strength in action; if a possibility of being separated from you should present itself, I imagine I should greatly surprise my enemies. Never fear; I shall come back in good time. I believe that should I get killed, my body would float against the current and hug the bank at the point nearest The Locks."

He kissed her quickly and hurried away, and his form was soon lost in the bend of the street.

How dark it was under the trees! The increasing dull daylight brightened everything save the darkness under the trees; nothing could relieve that. What if he should go into it never to return, as he had intended the night they were married! No, no, no; she wrung her hands at that thought, and ran towards the door, as if intending to pursue him and bring him back before he could enter it. But Allan was strong and trusty, and he would come back to laugh at her childish fears as she took his dripping garments at the close of the day, and listened to an account of his adventures,—no fear of that.

A half hour later she saw a boat with a single rower put out from the town, and make slow headway against the strong current to the other shore. Was he going alone? It was not dangerous; she persuaded herself of that, but she thought it must be very lonesome rowing about in such a flood; and he should not go out again, for he would do anything she wished, and she would ask it as a favor.

Why had she neglected to think of this, and ask him to go with others? But it was too late now, for the rower soon reached the line of trees he had pointed out to her from the window, waved his white handkerchief, which looked like a signal of danger, and disappeared into the shadow.

CHAPTER XIX.

MR. WHITTLE MAKES A CONFESSION.

The first rays of the bad morning, as it looked in at Mr. Whittle's window, found that worthy busily engaged in cleaning and scouring his gun. It was not yet his bedtime, for of late he spent all of every night, instead of part of it, in prowling about—bent on mischief, *he* said, but Silas Davy knew that Tug had a fierce desire to protect Allan Dorris, for whom he had taken such a strange fancy, from harm; and that night after night, whether the weather was good or bad, his friend kept watch around The Locks, carrying his gun in readiness for instant use. Silas usually kept him company until he became sleepy, and knew that he must return in order to keep awake and attend to his work the next day; but Tug, who slept during the day, seldom deserted his post. He may have left his beat occasionally for an hour or two, but only to creep carefully up into the hills back of the house, where he crouched and listened beside the paths, and then crept back again.

A good many times he walked down to the hotel, always choosing an hour when he knew Silas would be alone in the kitchen, on which occasions he never failed to take a shot with his eyes up the alleys, and into all the dark places; but he did not remain long, so that almost every night, when Silas went to bed, he had the satisfaction of knowing that if the shadow should attempt to harm Allan Dorris, there would be an explosion loud enough to alarm the town.

Silas, who had been out on the bottoms the day before, came in late in the evening, and, throwing himself on the bed, he slept so soundly that when Tug appeared, late in the morning, from one of his vagrant tramps, he was not aroused. And there he lay now, in his clothes, sound asleep, his face as innocent as a child's, as his mind was.

As Tug scoured away on the gun, rubbing off the rust and dirt, he occasionally looked at Silas, and the thought no doubt occurred to him, that if there ever was a thoroughly unselfish, incapable, kind-hearted fellow, there he was, on the bed, asleep, and resting well.

"He'll soon be awake, though," Tug said aloud, looking up at the window, and noting the increasing light. "He can't sleep when it's light enough for him to work. He has been driven to it by his hard masters until he knows nothing else, and he has a habit of getting up at daylight which he can never overcome. Silas was ruined by too much work; I was ruined by too little of it, I suppose. Anyway, I'm ruined; nobody disputes that. I am so ornery that I am becoming ashamed of myself."

Mr. Whittle meditated a moment, and then putting down his gun he walked over to a piece of looking-glass, which was tacked against the wall, and took a long look at himself. The inspection was apparently unsatisfactory, for he shook his fist at the reflection, made a face at it, and muttered ill-humoredly as he walked back to his chair.

"If Davy didn't forget so easy," Mr. Whittle said aloud again, rubbing away on the gun-barrel, "what a fine man he would be! If he could make money as easily as he is good-natured, he would be a fine fellow; but they say he works to no purpose, and must have somebody to watch him, though he means well,—everybody says that. If Davy should be told to turn a crank, he would do it better than anybody, and keep at it longer; but the men who make money not only work hard, but use judgment, and Davy lacks judgment, poor fellow; they all say that. If the hotel should ketch afire he wouldn't put it out unless somebody told him to; he wouldn't think of it. But he means as well as any man in America; I can cheerfully say that for him. An ordinary man never opens his mouth without saying something mean; but if ever I heard Davy say a mean thing, or knew him to do a mean thing, may I become a preacher. Well, the talents must be divided, I suppose; for no person seems to combine any two of them. *I* know enough, but somebody else has the honesty, the industry, the decency, etc., which I lack. Unfortunately, it does not follow that a sensible man is a square man or a good man. I'd rather trust a fool for honesty than a man with a big head, any day. The worst crimes I have ever heard of were the work of men cursed with more brains than conscience. I thought he couldn't sleep long after the sun was up."

Looking over at his sleeping partner, he saw that he was becoming uneasy, and soon he sat up on the edge of the bed, and looked around in bewilderment as he rubbed his eyes.

"Well, rogue, how do you feel?" Tug inquired, stopping his scouring.

"What time is it?" Davy inquired, with a show of excitement, and getting on his feet without answering the question.

"I should say it was five o'clock, Wednesday morning," Tug replied, looking out at the window, and then back at his companion, as if wondering at his nervousness. "Why?"

"I meant to remain awake to tell you of it last night," Silas replied hurriedly; "but I was so tired, from rowing all day, that I dropped off to sleep soon after I came in. I have seen the shadow!"

Tug sprang up from the low chair in which he had been sitting, and began to nervously fumble through his pockets, as if looking for ammunition.

"I was out in the bottoms with Armsby, yesterday," Davy continued, "and twice we passed a man rowing about alone. We were not very close to him, but I am sure it was the shadow, and that he meant mischief. Each time when we encountered him he rowed away rapidly, and when Armsby hailed him he paid no attention."

Tug was much concerned over this news, for, after finding his ammunition, he went to loading his gun with great vigor.

"Could you see his short ear?" he stopped to inquire, after ramming down a great quantity of powder.

"No, his left side was from me, but I am sure it was the same man. And I am sure that the boat in which he rowed was the same one you took the little woman out of. I hurried here as fast as I could to tell you, but when I lay down on the bed to wait for you, I fell asleep. Armsby made me row all day while he kept a look-out for ducks. I am sorry I fell asleep."

Silas rubbed his sore arms, and looked very meek, but Tug was too busy making arrangements to go out to notice him.

"The impudence of the scoundrel," he said, as he poured in the shot. "I never thought to look for him in daylight. Which way did he go?"

Tug peered into the tube of the gun with his big eye, before capping it, as if expecting to find his enemy crouching down in the powder, but finding that the powder primed, he put on a cap, and stood ready to go out.

"Into the woods," Silas answered. "When we first met him, he was rowing toward town, but on seeing us he turned the other way. That was about noon, and just before night we saw him again, coming toward town as before, but he pulled off to the right when he met us, and disappeared under the trees. I expected you in every moment when I fell asleep, or I would have gone up to The Locks, and told Allan Dorris. We ought to tell him about this man, Tug. His appearance here so regularly means trouble. Within a year we have seen him a dozen times, and each time he has been lurking around Allan Dorris. We really ought to do something."

In the emergency Silas did what he had done a hundred times in other emergencies—he said that something should be done, and folded his hands.

"Ain't I *trying* to do something?" his companion answered testily. "Haven't I tried my best to shoot him? What more can I do? But he has only been here seven times. Here is the record."

He handed the gun over to Silas, who saw for the first time that there were seven notches cut in the stock, the particularly long one representing the time that Tug had shot at the shadow, and missed.

The men had talked of warning Dorris a great many times before, but Tug had always argued that it was unnecessary; that it would only render him nervous and suspicious, whereas he was now contented, and very useful to the townspeople and his young wife. Silas had always been in favor of putting his friend on his guard against an enemy who seemed to come and go with the night, but Tug had stubbornly held out against it, and perhaps this was the reason he guarded The Locks so faithfully. Sometimes he would only hear a noise in the underbrush; at other times he saw a crouching figure, but before deciding to fire at it, it would disappear, but there was always something to convince him that his old enemy was still occasionally lurking about the town. A few times he had seen him openly, as has been narrated, but there was always something in the way of the accomplishment of the purpose nearest his heart; the only purpose of his life. He did not know himself why he had taken such an interest in Dorris, nor had he ever attempted to explain it to Silas, but he admired the man, and the only ambition he had ever acknowledged was connected with the safety of the person he admired, according to his own confession, next to Rum and Devilishness, for not even Davy out-ranked the owner of The Locks in Tug's callous heart. And Dorris himself was not more pleased when his wife was praised than was the rusty old lawyer, and at her suggestion he had worked whenever he could get it to do during the winter which had just passed; at copying, drawing legal papers, and at keeping books, for he was competent at any of these occupations. It is probable that had she asked him to go to work as a day laborer he would have consented, for she was kind to him in a great many ways, and often invited him to visit The Locks, when he appeared looking very much like a scarecrow, the result of his attempts at fixing up, and using his great eye, after arriving, to look around for refreshments, for he was always hungry. Being a noted character, when it became known that he had "reformed," and that he was patronized by the Dorrises, a great many others took pains to patronize him, and give him work of the kind he was willing to do, for he was still very particular in this respect. When at The Locks, if he threatened to drink too much, Mrs. Dorris took his glass and kept it, although her husband was usually in favor of "turning him on," as Tug expressed it, for he was very amusing when a little tipsy, and kept them in continued laughter by his dignified oddity.

"I will tell him to-day," Tug said, taking the gun into his own hands again. "He must not go into the bottoms unless accompanied by a party, and as he hasn't been over yet, he may take it into his head to go to-day. I will tell him in an hour; he won't be up before that time."

"Do you know, Tug," Silas said, "what I think of you?"

"Well, out with it. Let's have it."

"I think you are a better man than you pretend."

"It's a lie!" his companion replied fiercely, hitting the table a hard blow with his clenched fist. "It's a lie!"

"I have often thought it was very much to your credit that you took such an interest in a hunted man," Davy said, "who is shadowed by a cowardly enemy, but perhaps I am mistaken—I usually am; it's not important."

Tug hung his head in mortification at this suggestion, and for once in his life neglected to be indifferent and dignified at the same time, which was possible with him, if with no one else.

"Whoever accuses me of being a good man," he said finally, "wrongs me. When I made the discovery a good many years ago that I could never hope to become anything, I made up my mind to distinguish myself for shiftlessness. I despise a common man, therefore I am an uncommonly proficient loafer. I am better known in this town than some of your respectable men, and I don't have to work so hard. There are men here, and plenty of them, who have worked all their lives, and who have no more than I have, which is nothing. They expect that there is a great deal in the future for them, but I have sense enough to know there is nothing very great in the future for any of us, therefore I live as my fancy dictates. I am a natural-born vagrant; most of us are, but most of us do not say so. I despise five-cent respectability, therefore I am a dollar vagrant, and will pass for that anywhere. I had enough of good people when I was married to one of them; my wife was a *Good Woman*."

"I hope I haven't offended you," the meek little man said, looking at his fierce companion in alarm. "I didn't mean any disrespect."

"Oh, you needn't take it back," Tug retorted. "You've gone too far. It's all right; but let me tell you the truth for once in my life—I believe I never did before. I expect it will set me to coughing, but I will try it. My wife hasn't a relative in the world that I know of; certainly I never met any of them. The only objection I have to her is that she is *Good*. She is so *Good* that she is a bore; goodness is a fault, and a grave one with her. She couldn't possibly be more disagreeable than she is, and her fault is, she is *Good*. When there is a dry spell, she wants to get up a rain, and whether it rains or not, you are expected to give her credit for philanthropy. When it is too cold, she moans about the poor people who are suffering, and those who are around her must accept this as noble, or be called wicked, or heartless, or something else. She even has a *Good* way of gossiping about people, and I despise her for no other reason than that she is *Good*. I can't tolerate her; she makes my feet cold."

Tug had uttered the word *good* in each instance like an oath, and Davy cowered under his cold stare as though fearing *he* might be *good*, and was about to be accused of it.

"Everything she does is right; everything you do is wrong,—there you have the old women in a mouthful," the outraged husband continued. "She is always jumping on you for not being *Good*, and for your refusal to see goodness in her; and no one around her sees a moment's peace, for she badgers them to death for their neglect to rid the earth of sin, or some other trifling matter like that. She neglects herself in the most shameful manner to moan about Rampant Rum, or the Vitality of Vice, for I never saw her ears clean, and if ever you find her with clean finger-nails, look out for the pigs, for they will fly. If she is a *Good Woman*, then hurrah for the devil. The fat, the lean, the long, the short, the ugly; *they* go into the *Good* business, for I never knew anyone who could attract attention in the ordinary way to engage in it, and when a woman becomes too fat for society, or too plain to be admired, she goes to yelling that she is better than anybody else, and wants everybody to behave, although they may be behaving all right already. The good-looking and amiable ones remain at home, where they belong, and I admire them for it. Had I been a rich man, the old women would have remained with me, and called *that* good, but since I was a friendless devil, and a worthless vagabond, she left me, and called *that* good; I hope she is the only woman of that kind in the world. Look how she treats little Ben! Does she act like a mother toward him? Don't I have to take all the care of him, and look after him, and attend to his bringing up? Is it common for mothers to neglect their own ragged children, and weep over fat and contented people? That's what she does; therefore, if you are a friend of mine, don't call me *Good.*"

Silas was not taking as much interest in the recital as he would have done under other circumstances, for he was thinking of Allan Dorris; but Tug was determined to talk about the "old womern."

"When we were first married," he continued, "I told her some sort of a lie about myself; a simple sort of a yarn about nothing, and only intended to earn cheap glory for myself. In some way she found me out, for she is always poking her nose around smelling for sin; and, until I could stand it no longer and finally left her, she was continually asking me for additional particulars of the fictitious incident I had related. I say she found me out; I don't know it, but I always believed she did, and that she only asked these questions to hear me lie, and gloat over her own virtue. The story I told her was about saving a man's life, and as he afterwards came to Davy's Bend, and knew the old womern, I felt sure that she had found me out. After that she asked me a thousand questions about it, and every time I invented a new lie to go with the first one. Did she do this because she was *Good?* You bet she didn't; she did it to convince herself that she was *Good*, and that I was *Bad*; but I tell you that, average me up, I am as good as she is, and I am perfectly worthless."

Picking up a rickety chair which stood near him, Mr. Whittle smashed it to pieces on the floor, after a tremendous pounding and racket, which was one of his ways of expressing anger.

Silas was very much impressed by this ferocious proceeding, and looked on in meek astonishment until his companion was seated again.

"Isn't it time for you to go to The Locks?" he asked.

"Sure enough," Tug said. "I am going up there this morning. I'll go now."

Without further words, he picked up his gun, and started out, going over the hills to avoid the frequented streets. He had made up his mind to make a full breast of the story, so he walked along leisurely, thinking that he had a genuine surprise in store for his friend.

Arriving at The Locks' gate, he blew the whistle, which was always looking out into Dorris' room like an eye, and waited for an answer. It came soon after; the cheerful voice of Annie Dorris, inquiring what was wanted.

"It's me,—Tug," he answered, "I want to see Dr. Dorris."

"He left an hour ago, to go over into the bottoms," was the reply. "Anything urgent?"

"Oh, no," the man replied, as he swallowed a great lump which came up into his throat. "Nothing urgent; I only wanted him to pull a tooth."

With long strides at first, Tug started for the river, but after he was out of sight from The Locks, he ran like a man pursued, and arriving at the place where the ferry was tied up, making steam for the day's work, he seized the first boat within his reach, and pushed off into the stream. The owner of it called to him to come back, as he wanted the boat himself; but Tug paid no attention, except to row the harder, and soon disappeared under the trees.

CHAPTER XX.

THE SEARCH IN THE WOODS.

From noon until twilight Annie Dorris watched the point on the other shore of the river, where her husband had promised to wave the signal of his return long before nightfall, but nothing did she see save the floating debris of the flood, which looked like tired travellers hurrying forward to find a night's shelter.

Great trees came floating down, with their arms outstretched as if for help, and occasionally these disappeared in the angry water, as human floaters might disappear after giving up in despair, believing it to be impossible to reach the shore.

Boats carrying parties of men came back, one by one, to the town, as the afternoon wore away, and the ferry came in later in the evening, panting like a thing of life after its hard day's work; but no boat with a single, strong rower appeared to cheer the gaze of the faithful watcher.

Everything seemed to be hurrying away from her, and from Davy's Bend, and from the gathering darkness under the trees, save the returning boats, and she thought their occupants appeared to be anxious to reach their own homes, and tell of some horror in the woods. Perhaps some of the rowers had a message to be delivered at The Locks; and when they did not come, the fear found its way to her throbbing heart that the news was dreadful, and that they delayed until they could muster up more courage.

While it was yet light on the water, an ugly night-shade collected under the trees where her husband's boat had disappeared, reaching out with long arms to capture those in the boats, who were hurrying away from it,—a black monster it seemed, fat with prey, watching the town with stealthy care until its people were sleeping after the day's work, and unsuspicious of attack.

As Annie Dorris watched this black shadow grow larger and larger, and become so bold as to approach still nearer to the town, it seemed to her that no one within it could ever escape; and though an occasional boat did come out, it hurried toward the town rapidly, as if in fright, and this encouraged her to hope that her husband had been delayed in some way, and would safely return with wonderful adventures to relate. So she kept up the vigil, and saw the shadow grow blacker as the afternoon became night.

When it was too dark to see even the river, Annie Dorris stood looking out into the night, hoping that her husband had returned another way, and that his footstep would soon be heard on the stair; for she could think of no danger that could befall him, since rowing in the flood was safe, in spite of the strong current. Once she heard a light step on the stair, and she was sure that it was her husband coming up to surprise her, and there was a pause of long duration on the landing; but when she threw open the door in joyful expectation, the quiet darkness looked at her in pity. More than once the footstep on the stair was heard by the anxious and terrified wife, and more than once she hurried to the door to look into the hall; but hope seemed to be leaving the house, and she imagined she heard it in the lower hall, hurrying away.

Returning to the window, she saw such fearful phantoms in the darkness that she ran, bareheaded, into the street, and up the hill to her father's house.

"Annie!" Thompson Benton said, as she ran into his room with starting eyes and dishevelled hair. "Annie, what has happened?"

"Oh, father," she replied, bursting into tears, "my husband has not returned from the bottoms!"

Thompson Benton had been expecting a calamity to befall Allan Dorris; for, while he had grown to honestly admire him, there was always something in his manner which indicated that he was in danger. Perhaps this suspicious dread grew out of the keen relish with which Allan Dorris enjoyed his home; as if every day were to be his last. It may have been the result of the general belief that he remained in the town to hide away from malicious enemies, or knowledge of the pathetic sadness which always distinguished his manner; but, whatever it was, Thompson Benton put on his coat and boots, which he had just taken off, precisely as a man might do who had been summoned on a long-expected errand. He had no explanations of the absence to offer to the weeping wife, but became grave at once, and made his preparations to go out in nervous haste. So, without speaking an encouraging word to his daughter, who had sunk down on her knees beside her father's chair, he left the house and hurried down to the town.

With long strides he reached the river's brink, where a number of boats were tied, and spoke to a few trusty men who were there, some of whom at once put oars into two of the boats, while others hurried back into the town after lanterns and torches.

While they were gone Thompson Benton walked up and down the bank, pausing frequently to look toward the woods, but he said nothing, and paid no attention to those who looked at him curiously for an explanation; for the absence of this grim old man from his home at night was important; it was particularly important now, since it was known that he was only waiting for the return of the men with the torches, to go over into the bottoms.

The news spread rapidly that something unusual was in the air, and when the two boats, rowed by four men each, pushed out into the stream, half of the town was left on the bank to talk of their mission in low whispers, and hope that Allan Dorris would be found safe and well.

Among those who watched the lights in the boats as they were rowed away and finally disappeared under the trees, was Silas Davy, who felt that his neglect to warn Allan Dorris of the shadow which followed him so persistently had resulted in a tragedy at last. The departure of the men at that hour to look for him, and the preparations they had made for the search, were dreadfully significant,—there could be no mistake of that; and Silas wandered along the shore for an hour, hoping to see the boats return, and hear the men talking cheerfully on the water, indicating that his friend had been found. But the longer he watched the woods, the darker they became, and the less prospect there seemed to be that the lights the men had carried would ever reappear, so he resolved to walk up to The Locks, hoping to find Dorris there, and be the first to give the news to the town. But at the gate he met Mrs. Wedge, who anxiously asked him for information of the missing man; there was nothing cheerful in her pale, anxious face, nor in the stillness which hung about the place like a pall.

Silas was compelled to acknowledge that there was so little hope in the town that he had come there for encouragement. He then told her in a whisper of the departure of the men in the boats, and of their carrying lanterns and torches, but Mrs. Wedge did not give him the encouragement he expected, for she put her hands to her face, and Silas was certain that she was crying. When she had recovered her composure, she motioned the little man to follow her, and they walked together up the broad walk, and up the stone steps until they entered the door. There were no lights in the house, and the great mass of stone seemed to be a part of the darkness from the woods. When they were on the inside, Mrs. Wedge carefully closed the door, and said to him softly,—

"Listen!"

A timid step on the stair, going up and coming down in unceasing monotony. Occasionally it stopped on going up, as if it were of no use to look again; on coming down, as if fearing some corner had been overlooked in the search, but it soon went on again, up and down the stair, into the room which was sacred to the empty cradle, and out of it again,—the step on the stair which always gave warning of trouble. Once it came so near them that Silas half expected, as he stood trembling in the darkness, that the ghost of poor Helen would lay hands on him, and inquire in pitiful tones for the little girl who seemed to be lost in the house. But it passed by, and wearily ascended the stairs, only to come wearily down again after a short absence in the room where the light and the life had gone out.

Mrs. Wedge led Silas back to the gate, and, after crying softly to herself awhile, said to him in a voice so agitated that he could scarcely understand her,—

"It has not been heard before since they were married. I had hoped that poor Helen had found rest at last, but her footstep on the stair this night means— I won't say the word! It might be carried by some evil spirit to his wife. The poor girl is at her father's, and I am afraid to look at her. O Annie, Annie!"

Meanwhile the boats pursued their journey into the woods; a man in the bow of each with a torch to direct the rowers. The underbrush was submerged, and they made fair progress toward the line of hills opposite the town, though they drifted about a good deal, for sometimes they were in doubt as to their bearings, as there was nothing to guide them. Occasionally they stopped to listen, hoping that Dorris had disabled his boat, and was safe in some of the trees, but, hearing nothing, they hallooed themselves, each one taking his turn until they were all hoarse. But the rippling water laughed with joy because their voices sounded dead in the forest lake, and seemed afraid to venture out into the damp, noisome darkness.

Finding a place where the current was not so strong, they pulled to a point which they believed to be above the town, calling "Halloo! Halloo!" at every boat's length; but the devilish gurgle in the water continued, and their voices came back to them, like hounds ordered to enter a dangerous lair. Occasionally a waterfowl resting for the night was disturbed, and went crashing through the branches of the trees, but no other sound came to them, and as the hours wore away they looked at each other in grave apprehension.

A few times, in the middle of clearings, they came upon deserted houses, with vagrant water pouring in at the windows, only to creep out at other windows after making a search in the rooms for lives to destroy. But most of the people had escaped to the hills with their farm animals, leaving their household effects to be covered with the reptiles which had been frightened out of the thickets and tall grass, and which clung to whatever offered them safety. Under the trees they frequently found drifts composed of household furniture, bridges, fences, out-houses, logs, stumps, and what not, and the desolation which reigned supreme in that dark, damp place was relieved but little by the glare of the torches, which made the men look like pale-faced spirits rowing about in an eternal effort to escape.

If the men wearied in the search, a look at the earnest, gray-haired old man in the largest boat, who was always straining his eyes in attempting to penetrate the darkness, revived them, and they floated on, pulling to the right or to the left, as Thompson Benton directed, and crying, "Halloo! Halloo!"

in tones which sounded plaintive, and sad, and hopeless. Always an earnest man, Thompson Benton had never before been as earnest as he was this night, and he had called "Halloo! Halloo!" so frequently that when he spoke it was either in a hoarse voice, or in a soft whisper.

At the lower point of the bend in the hills which gave the town its name, a sluggish lake was found, the main current striking diagonally across the river to shorten the distance in its hurry to do mischief below, and the boats found their way into this. While floating around not far from the base of the hills, those who were in the smaller boat suddenly came upon a gravestone, the top of which was only a foot out of water.

"We are floating over Hedgepath graveyard," the man who was in front carrying the torch said to the others. The stone which had attracted his attention seemed to be taller than the others, for it was the only one appearing above the surface; the water covered everything except this rounded piece of stone, which alone remained to mark the resting-place of the dead, providing the dead had not been seized with the universal desire for floating off, and gone away to visit graveyards in the lower country.

He caught hold of the stone to steady the boat, and, throwing his light upon the other side of it, read:—

"Sacred to the memory of—"

The name in whose honor the slab had been raised was below the water, and the man put his hand down into it to read, as a blind man reads raised letters.

"The first letter is A," he said, rubbing the face of the stone with his fingers, "like the alphabet; and the next is L."

The fellow continued rubbing the face of the stone with the tips of his fingers, while his lips moved as he tried letter after letter, and gave them up.

"Hello! Another L!" he said in surprise, at last, drawing up his hand hurriedly on making the discovery, and shaking it violently to throw off the water, but there remained on his wrist a sickening scum, which he hurriedly transferred to the side of the boat.

"I'll read no further," he said, with a frightened look. "I'm afraid it will turn out to be Allan, with a space and a big 'D' following it."

The torch-bearer still held on to the stone while the rowers rested, but the other boat, in which Thompson Benton sat, was busy a short distance beyond them; from one clump of debris to another, as if he only hoped now to find the lifeless body of the one he sought.

"Strange people are buried here," the torch-bearer said, speaking softly to his panting companions, while they rested from their hard work. "Suicides, and those who have died violent deaths; Hedgepath is devoted to them. I've heard it said that this is a rough neighborhood, but the best of their dead are put away further up the hill. If the flood has not drowned out the ghosts, we will see one to-night."

The suggestion of ghosts was not a pleasant one to the rowers, particularly to those who were farthest from the torch, for they looked timidly about as though they were likely to be approached from behind by spirits riding on headstones.

"There is a road running along the edge of Hedgepath, leading from the ferry into the hills," the torch-bearer said, who was the bravest of the lot, because he was directly under the light, "and those who have travelled it at night say that the inhabitants of this place sit on stumps beside the road and want to argue with the passers-by. One fellow who was hanged,—*he* has a great deal to say about the perjured witnesses; and another who was accused of poisoning himself,—he says he found it in his coffee, though he does not tell who put it there; and so many others have horrible stories to tell that travellers usually hurry by this place as fast as they can."

It was not a cheerful subject, but his companions listened with close attention, occasionally casting glances behind them.

"The unknown people who are found floating in the river; *they* are buried here, and those who travel the Hedgepath road at night say these offer them letters, and ask that they be posted. I have forgotten who it was, but somebody told me that he received one of these letters in his own hand, and mailed it, and that soon after one of the bodies was taken up by friends from a distance, and carried away."

The grim joker was interrupted by a hail from the other boat, and the men dipped their oars into the water, and pulled toward it.

Thompson Benton and those who were with him were looking with eager eyes at a boat which was floating a short distance beyond them, within the rays of their torch, and which was rising and falling with the ripples, with both oars hanging helplessly out in the water. The men were waiting in fear for their companions to come up to keep them company before approaching it, and when the two boats were side by side, they were held together, and the outside oars of each were used to row toward the deserted craft, as a party of men who discover a suspicious object in a strange locality might move toward it together.

As they drew nearer, the form of a prostrate man was seen seen—

Dismiss thy husband into the shadows from whence he came, O pretty wife, for he is murdered.

In the bottom of the boat, lying easily on his back, the rowers found Allan Dorris, dead; his eyes closed as if in disturbed sleep, and his face upturned to the heavens. His right hand was gripped on the side of the boat, as if his last wish had been to pull himself into a sitting posture, and look toward the town where his faithful wife was watching for his return. The flash of the torches made the face look ghastly and white, and there was a stain of blood on his lips. Those who looked upon the face saw in it an expression of regret to die, which remained with them as long as they lived; they spoke of it tenderly to their children, who grew up and gave their own children descriptions of Allan Dorris's pitiful face as he lay dead in his boat on the night when the waters of the great flood began to recede. It is said that the face of a sorrowing man looks peaceful in death; it may be equally true that death stamps unmistakable regret on the face of its victim who is not ready.

O, pitiless Death, you might have spared this man, who was just beginning, and taken one of the mourning thousands who watch for you through the night, and are sad because of your long delay. This man desired so much to live that his white face seems to say now: "I cannot die; I dread it—Oh, how terrible it would be to die now!" And his eyes are wet with tears; a touching monument of his dread of thee!

The rough men reverently uncovered their heads as Thompson Benton looked at the dead man in stupefaction, but when he had recovered, he lifted the body gently up, and made a hasty examination. Laying it down again, he looked at the men, and said in a tone which indicated that he had long expected it,—

"Shot in the back."

Lashing their boats together, the rowers gulled back to town without speaking a word; that containing the body of Allan Dorris towing behind, the pathetic face looking up to heaven, as if asking forgiveness. The stars came out as the rowers pursued their journey back to the town, and the storm was over.

Peace to the pathetic dust! In the town on the hill, where the twinkling lights mingle with the stars, waits a weeping woman who knew Allan Dorris well; let her opinion of the dead prevail, and not that of the gossiping winds which have been whispering into the ears of the people.

CHAPTER XXI.

LITTLE BEN.

In answer to a note requesting his presence at The Locks, Silas Davy hurried towards that part of the town as soon as he found relief from his duties at the hotel, regretting as he went along that Mr. Whittle was not ahead of him with his gun, for late events had not been of a cheerful nature, and he felt the need of better company than little Ben, who dragged his weary frame into the hotel kitchen a few minutes before Silas started.

Not that Silas did not love the boy; nor had he any objection to his company on this errand, but with cries of murder in the air, and the reports of guns, he thought he would have preferred a stouter companion in his walk; but as they hurried along, little Ben keeping up with difficulty, Silas thought that perhaps the boy's mild goodness would keep away evil, and protect them both. It occurred to him for the first time that in a storm of thunder and lighting he should like to keep close to little Ben, for though mankind might be unjust to him, the monsters of strength would pity his weakness, and strike elsewhere, therefore Silas came to feel quite content in his company.

Of the shot in the bottoms which had created so much excitement in Davy's Bend, and of the drifting boat which had been found in the flood by Thompson Benton and his men, Silas knew nothing except as he heard these matters discussed about the hotel. Although the people went to The Locks in crowds the day after the body was found, and remained there from early in the morning until late at night, every new arrival being taken into one of the darkened lower rooms to look at the dead man, Silas was not of the number. He was afraid to look at his friend's face, fearing he could see in it an accusation of his neglect to give warning of the shadow, so he remained away, and went about his duties in a dreamy way, starting at every sound, as though he feared that the people had at last found out his guilt, and had come to accuse him for not notifying them of the danger of which he had been aware. The receipt of the note had frightened him, too, and he felt sure that when he entered the presence of Annie Dorris, she would break down, and inquire why he had robbed her of a husband in his usual thoughtless way. Perhaps the sight of little Ben, in his weakness and goodness, would plead for him, so he picked the child up, and carried him on the way as far as his own weak arms would permit.

Mrs. Wedge soon appeared in answer to his ring at The Locks gate, and admitted him into the hall where he had heard the step on the stair on the night when there was alarm because of Dorris's absence in the bottoms. It was dark in the hall now, as it was then, and while Silas waited for Mrs. Wedge to fasten the door at which they had entered, he listened eagerly for the footsteps, and when he did not hear them, he trembled at the sound of his own as he finally went up the stairs behind Mrs. Wedge, followed by little Ben.

Going up to the door leading into the room which had been occupied by his friend, Silas was ushered into the presence of Annie Dorris, who was seated near the window where the shadow had twice appeared. There was a great change in her manner, he noticed at once; the pretty face, which had formerly always carried the suspicion of a laugh, was now distinguished by a settled grief, and it was pale and haggard.

Her pale face was in sharp contrast to the dress of mournful black, and the good fellow who was always trying to do right, but who was always in doubt as to which was right and which was wrong, would have given his life cheerfully to have been a month younger.

While Silas stood near the doorway, changing his hat from one hand to the other in confusion, he noticed that tears started to her eyes.

"Please don't cry," Silas said, walking towards her. "I want to tell you the guilty part I have taken in this dreadful affair, but I cannot muster up the courage when there are tears in your eyes. Please don't cry."

Annie Dorris bravely wiped her tears away at this request, and looked at Silas with a face indicating that if his presence had opened her wounds afresh, she would try and conceal it.

"I am oppressed with the fear that I am to blame for this," he continued, in desperate haste, "and I must tell you, and get it off my mind, even though you send for the sheriff and have me arrested; I cannot contain the secret any longer, now that I am in your presence."

Little Ben had crawled into a chair on entering the room, and was already fast asleep, with his head hanging on his breast, dreaming, let us hope, of kind treatment, and of a pleasant home.

"Within a month after Allan Dorris came to Davy's Bend," Silas said, seating himself near Mrs. Dorris, "Tug and I discovered that he was shadowed by some one, who came and went at night. For more than a year,—until the day before it happened—we saw the strange man at intervals, but Tug said it would unnecessarily alarm you both to know it, so we kept it to ourselves. I am sorry we did it, but we thought then it was for the best. I always wanted to tell you, but Tug, who worshipped you both, would never consent to it until the morning your husband went into the bottoms alone. When he came here, and found that he had gone, he followed him, and has not been seen since. The day before, while rowing in the bottoms, I met the shadow, and when Tug heard this, he came at once to warn your husband not to venture out alone."

Annie Dorris made no reply. Perhaps this was no more than she expected from Silas, whom she had sent for to question.

"The shot which once came in at that window was fired by Tug," Davy continued, pointing to the pane which had been broken on the night of Allan Dorris's marriage to Annie Benton, "and he fired at the shadow as it was looking in at your husband. For more than a year Tug has carried a gun, and has tried to protect you; but he made a mistake in not giving warning of this stealthy enemy. Of late months he has spent his nights in walking around this place, trying to get a shot at the shadow; and though some people accuse him of a horrible crime, because of his absence from town, he is really on the track of the guilty man, and will return to prove it. I cannot tell you how sorry I am to see you in mourning, but I hope you believe I did what I thought was for the best."

When Silas had concluded, they were both silent and thoughtful, and the heavy breathing of little Ben was all the sound that could be heard. This attracted the attention of Silas, and he said, respectfully,—

"Would you mind kissing the boy, ma'am? The poor little fellow is so friendless, and has such a hard time of it, that he makes my heart ache. If you will be good enough, I will tell him of it, and he will always remember it gratefully. Poor chap! I don't suppose he was ever kissed in his life."

Annie Dorris went over to the sleeping boy, and, after kissing him, as had been requested, picked him up, and laid him down on a lounge which stood in the room.

"There was always something fierce and mysterious about my husband," Mrs. Dorris said, after a time; "but both attracted me to him. I could not help it. A hundred times he has offered to tell me his story, but I did not care to hear it; so that now I know nothing about him except that he was the most worthy gentleman I ever knew, and combined all those qualities which my heart craved. I knew when we were first married that some such result as this was probable, but I could not resist him; and I do not regret it now. Three months of such happiness as I have known will repay me for future years of loneliness, and his kindness and consideration are sweet memories, which console me even now while my grief is so fresh. He was manly and honorable with me in every way; and the fault, if there has been a fault, was my own. I am sure that he was a better man because of his misfortune. I believe now that trouble purifies men, and makes them better; and the more I studied him the more I was convinced that there were few like him; that a trifling thing had ruined his life, and that there were hundreds of men, less honorable, who were more fortunate. Even now I do not care to know more of him than I already know. I fear that this is a fault; but I knew him better than anyone else in the world, and his manner was so pathetic at times, and his love for me always so pronounced, that, though I am now a young woman, I expect to spend my life in doing honor to a noble memory."

There was something so womanly in her manner that Silas was convinced that she would live only to honor the memory of his friend. There was inexpressible sadness in her face, but there was also strength, and capacity, and love, and honor.

"I am the one person whose good opinion he cared for," she said again; "and I forget everything except his love for me, and his manliness in everything. It is nothing to me what he was away from here. A single atom in the human sea, he may have committed a wrong while attempting to do right, and came here a penitent, trying to right it; but as I knew him he was worthy of any woman's profoundest admiration, and he shall receive it from me as long as I live. The stream of life leads upwards to heaven against a strong current, and, knowing myself, I do not wonder that occasionally the people forget, and float down with the tide. He has told me that he had but one apology to make to any one,—to me, for not finding me sooner. This was a pretty and an undeserved compliment; but it was evident that in his own mind he did not feel that he had wronged anyone, and I feel so. I have no idle regrets, and do not blame you and Tug. On the contrary, I thank you both for your thoughtful care. When Tug returns, as I am sure he will, bring him here. Who has not wounded their best friends in trying to befriend them? Though you two have grievously wounded me, I recognize the goodness of your motives, and feel grateful."

She got up at this, and started toward the door, motioning Silas to follow. From the dark hall she stepped through the door which Dorris had never entered alive; but he had been carried there dead. A dim light burned near the door, and there was something in the air—a taint not to be described, but to be remembered with dread—which made Silas think of a sepulchre.

On a raised platform, in the room to which the steps of poor Helen were always leading, stood a metallic burial case, with a movable lid showing the face under glass. The face was so natural that Silas thought it must have been preserved in some manner, for his friend seemed to be quietly sleeping, and he could not realize that he had been dead a week. Even before Silas had taken his hasty glance, Annie Dorris had knelt beside the inanimate clay of her husband, and he thought he had better go away—he could think of nothing else to do—and leave her. And this he did, only stopping at the door to see a picture which he never forgot,—the coffin, the sobbing woman, the dim light, and the gloomy hangings of the room.

On being awakened, little Ben shielded his face with his hands, as if expecting a blow, which was his usual greeting on opening his eyes, but, recognizing his friend, he contentedly followed him down the stairs, and out at the iron gate into the street. Davy was not a large man or a strong man, but little Ben found it difficult to follow him, and was compelled to ask his friend to stop and rest before they reached the hotel. When they finally reached the kitchen, they found it deserted, and Silas hastily placed meat and bread before the boy. This he devoured like a hungry wolf, and Davy wondered that such a little boy had so much room under his jacket.

"They don't feed you overly well at the farm, do they, Ben?" Silas inquired.

The boy had turned from the table, and was sitting with his hands clasped around his knees, and his bare feet on the upper round of the chair. After looking at his companion a moment, he thoughtfully shook his head.

"You work hard enough, heaven knows," Silas said again, in a tone which sounded like a strong man pitying some one less unfortunate, but there was little difference between the two, except age, for there was every reason to believe that should little Ben's cough get better, he would become such a man as Silas was.

"I do all I can," little Ben answered, "but I am so weak that I cannot do enough to satisfy them. I haven't had enough sleep in years: I think that is the trouble with me."

That cough, little Ben, is not the result of loss of sleep: you must have contracted that in going out to work in the early morning, illy clad, while other children were asleep.

"I'm going to tell you something, poor fellow," Silas said, "which will please you. While you were asleep up at The Locks to-night, the lady kissed you."

Little Ben put his hand apologetically to his mouth, and coughed with a hoarse bark that startled Silas, for he noticed that the cough seemed worse every time the boy came to town. But he seemed to be only coughing to avoid crying, for there were tears in his eyes.

"You are not going to cry, Ben?" Silas said, in a voice that indicated that he was of that mind himself.

"I think not, sir," the boy replied. "When I first went to the farm, I cried so much that I think that the tears have all left me. I was only thinking it was very kind of the lady, for nobody will have me about except you, Mr. Davy. My father and mother, they won't have me around, and I am in Mr. Quade's way; and his wife and children have so much trouble of their own that they cannot pay attention to me. They live very poorly, and work very hard, sir, and I do not blame them; but I often regret that I am always sick and tired, and that no one seems to care for me."

Little Ben seemed to be running the matter over in his mind, for he was silent a long while. In rummaging among his recollections he found nothing pleasant, apparently, for when he turned his face to Silas it showed the quivering and pathetic distortion which precedes an open burst of grief.

"If you don't care," he said, "I believe I *will* cry; I can't help it, since you told me about the lady."

The little fellow sobbed aloud at the recollection of his hard life, all the time trying to control himself, and wiping his eyes with his rough sleeve. He was such a picture of helpless grief that Silas Davy turned his back, and appeared to be rubbing something out of his eyes; first one and then the other.

"I am sorry I am not able to help you, Ben," the good fellow said, turning toward the boy again, after he had recovered himself; "but I am of so little consequence that I am unable to help anyone; I cannot help myself much. I have rather a hard time getting along, too, and I am a good deal like you, Ben, for, though I work all the time, I do not give much satisfaction."

Little Ben looked at his companion curiously.

"I thought you were very happy here, sir," he said, "with plenty to eat every day. You are free to go to the cupboard whenever you are hungry, but often I am unable to sleep because I am so hungry. You never go to bed feeling that way, do you, Mr. Davy?"

"No," he replied, almost smiling at the boy's idea that anyone who had plenty to eat must be entirely content; "but I am a shiftless sort of a man, and I don't get on very well. I always want to do what is right and fair, but somehow I don't always do it; I sometimes think, though, that I am more unjust to myself than to anyone else. It causes me a good deal of regret that I am not able to help such as you, Ben. If I were able, I would like to buy you a suit of clothes."

"Summer is coming on, sir, and these will do very well," the boy replied.

"Yes; but you were very thinly clad last winter, Ben, and oftentimes I could not sleep from thinking of how cold you were when out in the fields with the stock. If ever there was a good boy, you are one, Ben; but you are not treated half so well as the bad boys I know. This is what worries me, as hunger worries you."

"I am sorry to hear you are poor, sir," little Ben said. "Not that I want you to do more for me than you have done, but you have always been so kind to me that I thought you must be rich to afford it. You always have something for me when I come to town, and I am very thankful to you."

What a friendless child, Davy thought, to consider what he had done for him the favor of a rich man! A little to eat, and small presents on holidays; he had been able to do no more than that; but, since no one else was kind to the boy, these were magnificent favors in his eyes.

"On which cheek did the lady kiss me, Mr. Davy?" the boy inquired later in the night.

"On this one," Davy replied, touching his left cheek with his finger tips.

"I was thinking it was that one," little Ben continued. "There has been a glow in it ever since you told me. I should think that the boys who have mothers who do not hate them are very happy. Do you know whether they are, Mr. Davy?"

"I know they ought to be," he said; "but some of them are very indifferent to their mothers. I have never had any experience myself; my own mother died before I could remember."

"It seems to me," little Ben continued, "that if I were as well off as some of the boys I see, I should be entirely satisfied. I must start home soon, or I will not get there in time to be called for to-morrow's work, and when I creep into the hay, where I sleep after coming to see you, I intend to think that the kiss the lady gave me was the kiss of my mother, and that she does not hate me any more."

For such as you, little Ben, there must be a heaven. The men who are strong in doubt, as well as in the world's battles, come to that conclusion when they remember that there can be no other reward for such as you and Silas Davy, for your weakness is so unfit for this life that it must be a burden which can only be reckoned in your favor in the Master's house where there are many mansions.

"If there were not so many happy children," little Ben said again, "perhaps I should not mind it so much, but I see them wherever I go, and I cannot understand why my lot is so much harder than theirs. My bones ache so, and I want to sleep and rest so much, that I cannot help feeling regret; except for this I hope I would be happy as you are."

Silas Davy is anything but a happy man, little Ben, but, being a good man, he does not complain, and does the best he can, so when the boy soon after started for the farm, and Silas walked with him to the edge of the town, he pretended to be very well satisfied with himself, and with everything around him. Indeed, he was almost gay, but it was only mockery to encourage his unfortunate companion.

"Next Christmas, Ben," Silas said, as they walked along, "you shall have"— he paused a moment to consider his financial possibilities—"a sled from the store."

"*That* is too much," Ben replied, with hope and gladness in his voice. "A sled will cost a great deal, for the painting and striping must come high. I would like to have a sled more than anything else, but I am afraid you would rob yourself in buying it. I am afraid that is too much, Mr. Davy."

"It will not cost as much as you expect, and I can easily save the money between this and Christmas," the good fellow replied. "I have always wanted to do it, and I will, and it will be a pleasure. Remember, Ben, when you feel bad off in future, what you are to get when you come to see me Christmas morning."

"I will not forget, sir."

"When you own the sled, and I have had the pleasure of giving it to you, we will feel like very fortunate fellows, won't we, Ben?" Silas said again, cheerfully, as they walked along.

"We shall feel as though we are getting along in the world, I should think, Mr. Davy," the boy replied.

They had reached the edge of the town by this time, and Davy stopped to turn back. He took the boy's hand for a moment, and said,—

"Remember the sled, Ben. Good night."

"Good night, sir. I will not forget."

Silas had scarcely said good night to him before he was lost to his sight,—he was such a very little fellow.

CHAPTER XXII.

TUG'S RETURN.

A month had passed since Allan Dorris was found floating over the mounds in Hedgepath graveyard, and the waters having gone down in the bottoms, the people were busy in rescuing their homes from the ooze and black mud beneath which they were buried. There had been so much destruction in the bottoms, and so much loss of trade in the town, that the people were all mourners like Annie Dorris and Silas Davy, and it did not seem probable that any of them would ever be cheerful again.

Silas Davy was the only person in the town, save Annie Dorris, who knew the secret of the murder, and he kept it to himself, believing that Tug was on the trail of the culprit, and that nothing could be gained by making the people aware of the mysterious man and his mysterious visits. He was sure that Tug would return finally, when, if he saw fit, he might tell the people what he knew; otherwise they might continue their conjectures, which generally implicated Tug. From the day of the murder he had not been seen in the town, and while it was not openly charged that he had fired the fatal shot, a great many talked mysteriously of his disappearance, and believed that he had something to do with it, for about this time it became known that he had frequently been seen around The Locks in the middle of the night, carrying a gun.

Silas had gone down to the old house by the river, to see if the bed gave any signs of having been occupied, as there was a possibility that Tug had returned, and was ashamed to make his presence known, not having accomplished his purpose. But there was no sign. The dust upon everything was proof enough that the owner was still away, and Silas was preparing to blow out the light, and return to the hotel, when his friend came walking in at the door; ragged, dirty, and footsore, and a picture of poverty and woe, but there could be no doubt that it was Tug, for he carried in his right hand the old musket that had so long been his constant companion. His clothes hung in shreds about him, and bare skin appeared at his elbows and knees; his tall hat was so crumpled that it looked like a short hat, and his hair and whiskers were long and unkempt. There were bits of hay and twigs clinging to his clothing, and Silas was sure that he had been sleeping out at night, and creeping through the brush during the day.

"Tug, my old friend!" Silas said, in a voice trembling with excitement and pleasure. "God bless me; how glad I am to see you!"

Tug sat down wearily in a chair, and laid the gun down at his feet. He was certainly very tired, and very hungry, and very weak, and Silas thought how fortunate it was he had brought a lunch with him, although he had only hoped that Tug would eat it. This he placed before his friend, who pulled his chair up to the table at sight of the sandwiches, and said in a hoarse voice,—

"I've caught an awful cold somewhere. Do you starve a cold, or stuff it? I've been starving it for several days, and I think I'll try stuffing. You don't mean to tell me you have brandy in that bottle, do you?"

It was brandy fortunately, which Silas had been saving for his friend since his departure, but he seemed so tired now that he could not enjoy it with his old relish, for he did not look at it with his usual eagerness, and there was a melancholy air about him which was very distressing to the little man by his side. As Silas watched him, he thought that he discovered that he had grown a dozen years older within a month, and that he would never again be the contented, easy-going man he was before. He was a serious man now, too, a thing he had always despised, and it did not seem possible that he could ever recover from it.

When he had finished his meal, he walked slowly and painfully over to the bed, and, stretching out upon it, remained silent so long that Silas feared he had washed his voice down his throat with the brandy.

"How is Missus Pretty?" he inquired at last, turning to Silas, who sat beside him.

"Very poorly, I am sorry to say," Silas replied, in a husky voice.

This did not encourage Tug to talk, for he became silent again, and although Silas was keen to hear where his friend had been, he was silent, too.

"Have you told her that we were to blame?" Tug asked, after a long pause.

"Yes, I told her everything, but she does not blame us, and asked me to bring you up immediately after your return."

There was the click in the ragged man's throat that usually distinguished him when he was about to laugh, but surely Tug had no intention of laughing now, though he wiped his big eye hurriedly, and in a manner indicating that he was vexed.

"I might have known that it was wrong not to tell Allan Dorris of this enemy," Tug said. "I am usually wrong in everything, but I hoped I was doing them a favor in this matter; for who wouldn't worry to know that they were constantly watched by a man who seemed to have come a long distance for the purpose? They were so happy that I enjoyed it myself, and I wanted to protect them from The Wolf, and though The Wolf was smarter than I expected, I meant well; you know that."

"I am sure of it," Davy replied.

"A man who has been bad all his life cannot become good in an hour, and while I meant well, I did not know how to protect them from this danger. We should have taken them into our confidence when The Wolf first appeared; I can see that now, after it is too late. It was my fault, though; you always wanted to. I'll have more confidence in you in future."

Both men seemed to be busy thinking it all over for several minutes, for not a word was exchanged between them until Silas inquired,—

"Do you suppose there is any danger of the shadow molesting Mrs. Dorris?"

Tug was lying on his back, and putting his hand under him he took from his pistol-pocket a package wrapped in newspapers, which looked like a sandwich. Handing this to Davy, he said,—

"Look at it."

Going over to the table and the light, Davy began the work of unwrapping. There was a package inside of a package, which continued until a pile of newspapers lay on the table. At last he came to something wrapped in a piece of cloth, and opening this he found a human ear, cut off close to the head! He recognized it in a moment,—the ear of the shadow, with the top gone!

He hurriedly wrapped the horrible thing up as he had found it, and while he was about this he felt sure that Tug's journey had not been in vain; that somewhere he had encountered the shadow and killed him, bringing back the ear as a silent and eloquent witness.

When the package had been returned to Tug's pocket, he turned on his side, rested his head on his hand, and told his story.

"Out into the river like a shot; that's the way I rowed that misty morning when I found that Allan Dorris had gone into the bottoms alone. I had no idea where to go to find him, so I pulled over toward the hills on the east shore, where there was a slow current, and concluded to float down the stream. It may have been an hour later, while in the vicinity of the big bend, that I heard a shot below me. Rowing toward it with all my might, I soon came upon Allan Dorris lying dead in the bottom of his boat. Only stopping to convince myself that he was stone dead, I pulled out after his murderer. I knew who it was as well as if I had seen the shot fired, and I knew that he would be making down the river to escape, so I made down the river myself to prevent it. He had the start of me, and seemed to know the bottom better than I did, for when I came into the main current I could see him hurrying away, a good half mile ahead of me. But I was the best rower, and within an hour I was coming within shooting distance, when he suddenly turned under the trees, near the island where we saw him the first time. I lost track of him here for several hours, but at last I came upon his boat, a long distance up the creek, and just when I heard a whistle down at the station. Had I thought of this before, I might have found him there, and brought him back alive, for I have since found out that he signalled the train and went away on it; but it was too late then, so I could do nothing but go over to the station and wait for the next train."

The narrator's hoarseness became so pronounced that Silas brought him the remaining brandy, which he tossed off at one swallow.

"A lonely enough place it was," Tug continued, "and nobody around except the agent, who told me there would not be another train until a few hours after midnight, so I occupied myself in studying maps of the road. I had no money, of course, but I felt sure I could make my way to a certain big town several hundred miles away, which I had once heard Dorris mention, and it had been in my mind ever since that he came from there. Of course his enemy lived in the same place, and the certainty that The Wolf came to the Bend on that road once, and went away by the same route, and the probability that he always came to the Bend from that station by rowing up the river, made me feel certain that the course I had mapped out was right.

"I need not tell you that I had trouble in travelling without money, for there are many people who cannot travel comfortably even when supplied with means in abundance; but in course of time I arrived in the city I once heard Dorris mention, very tired, dirty, and hungry, as you will imagine, but not the least discouraged; for the more I heard about the place,—and I inquired about it of every one who would listen to me,—the surer I was that I would find The Wolf there. The people with whom I talked all had the greatest respect for the city, as they had here for Dorris; this was one thing which made me feel sure he came from there, but there were a great many other evidences which do not occur to me now. I arrived in the morning, and there was so much noise in the streets that it gave me the headache; and so many people that I could not count them, therefore I cannot tell you the population of the place.

"It was so big and gay, though, that I am certain that the Ben's City people would have been impressed as much as I was, though they put on airs over us. A Ben's City man would have felt as much awe there as a Davy's Bend man feels in Ben's City, and it did me a great deal of good to find out that Ben's City is nothing but a dirty little hole after all.

"For two weeks I wandered about the streets, looking for that ear. There were crowds of people walking and riding around who were like Allan Dorris in manners and dress, and I was sure that they all knew him, and respected him, and regretted his departure, for I knew by this time that he came from that place to Davy's Bend. There was an independence and a rush about the town so unlike Davy's Bend, and so like Allan Dorris, that I was certain of it. Several times I thought of approaching some of the well-dressed people, and telling them that I was looking for the man who had murdered Allan Dorris, feeling sure that they would at once offer to assist me in the search; but I at last gave it up, fearing they would think he had taken a wonderful fall in the world to be friends with a man like me.

"One day, about three weeks after my arrival, I met The Wolf on a crowded street. I tapped him on the shoulder, and when he turned to look at me, he trembled like a thief.

"'That matter of killing up at Davy's Bend,' I said, 'I am here to attend to it.'

"He recovered his composure with an effort, and replied,—

"'What's that to me, vagrant? Keep out of my way, or I'll have you jailed. I do not know you.'

"'You are a liar,' I replied, 'and your manner shows it. I am dressed this way as a disguise. I have as good clothes as anybody when I choose to wear them. I am a private detective.'

"I had heard that a great many vagrants claim to be private detectives, so I tried it on him, and it worked well; for he at once handed me a card with an address printed on it, and said,—

"'Call at that number to-night; I want to see you.'

"He had probably heard of private-detectives, too, for I knew he wanted to buy me off; so I consented to the arrangement, knowing that he would not run away.

"When it was dark, I went to the street and number printed on the card, and The Wolf met me at the door of a house almost as big as The Locks, but land seemed to be valuable there, for others were built up close to it on both sides. There was a row of houses just alike, as far as I could see, but different numbers were printed on all of them to guide strangers. The Wolf led the way up stairs, after carefully locking the door, and when we were seated in a room that looked like an office, and which was situated in the back part of the house, he said,—

"What do you want?'

"'I want to kill you,' I replied.

"He was a tall, nervy man, but I was not afraid of him; for I am thick and stout. He laughed contemptuously, and replied,—

"'Do you know this man's offence?'

"'No,' I answered, 'but I know yours.'

"He sat near a desk, and I felt sure that under the lid was concealed a pistol; therefore I found opportunity to turn the key quickly, and put it in my pocket.

"'Now you are in my power,' I said to him. 'You killed Allan Dorris, and I can prove it, and I intend to kill you.'

"A very cool man was The Wolf; and he watched me from under his heavy eyebrows like a hawk, taking sharp note of everything I did, but he did not appear to be afraid. I couldn't help admiring the fellow's nerve, for he was the coolest man I ever saw, and there was an air of importance about him in his own house which did not appear when he was crawling around Davy's Bend. There was something about him that convinced me he was a doctor, like Dorris, though I heard nothing and saw nothing to confirm the belief.

"'I have had enough trouble over this affair already,' he said, 'and I am willing to pay for your silence. You don't know what you are about, but I do, and I know there is more justice in my cause than there is in yours. I have been actuated by principle, while you are merely a vagrant pursuing a hobby. You are interfering in the private affairs of respectable people, sir, and I offer you money with the contempt that I would throw a bone to a surly dog, to avoid kicking him out of my way.'

"'I am not a respectable man myself,' I answered, 'but I know that it is not respectable to shoot from behind. I give you final notice now that I don't want your money; I want your life, and I intend to have it. Back in the poor town I came from there is a little woman whose face I could never look upon again were I to take your money, and I intend to be her friend and protector as long as I live. I believe the money you offer me belongs to Dorris; for you look like a thief who believes that every man is as dishonest as yourself, and has his price. Even my rags cry out against such a proposition.'

"He was as cool as ever, and looked at me impudently until I had finished, when he said,—

"'I want to step into the hall a moment.'

"He knew I was watching the door to prevent his escape, and acknowledged that I was master of the situation by asking my permission.

"'To call help, probably,' I said.

"'No, to call a weak, broken woman; I want you to see her. Whatever I have done, her condition has prompted me to.'

"I opened the door for him, and he stepped into the dark hall, where he called 'Alice!' twice. I was so near him that he could not get away, and we stood there until Alice appeared at the other end of the hall. It was the little woman we had here one night! But though she was dressed better than when we saw her, she was paler; and when she came down the dark hall, carrying a candle above her head to light the way, I thought I had never before seen such a sickly person out of a grave.

"When she came up to us I saw that she was panting from her slight exertion, and we stepped into the room together. She did not know me, and looked at me with quiet dignity, as if she would conceal from me that she was weak and sick.

"'Does he bring news of him?' she asked, looking from me to The Wolf.

"The woman was crazy; there was no doubt of it. Had she not been she would have fallen on her knees, and said to me, as she did the night she was in this room, 'Gentlemen, in the name of God!' for I was determined to make way with a person who was probably her only protector.

"'Does the gentleman come from him?' the pale woman asked again.

"She is the only person who ever called me a gentleman, and what little compassion I had before vanished.

"The Wolf paid no attention to her talk, and I thought he was accustomed to it; perhaps she was always asking questions to which no reply could be given. She was not a young woman, and there was something about her— probably the result of her sickness—which was so repugnant that I almost felt faint. If she had walked toward me, I would have run out of the house, but fortunately she only looked at me.

"'If you came here at his request,' the little woman said, as she stood in the middle of the room, 'take this to him for me. I have been writing it for two years; it will explain everything.'

"I thought the man was pleased because she had commenced the conversation so readily; for he appeared to be in good humor, as though she were saying exactly what he had desired she should to impress me.

"'When they told me he was contented in his new home,' she continued, 'I was satisfied, and I want him to know it. He had life, and vigor, and energy, and no one ever blamed him but Tom and me. This letter says so; I want you to take it to him. When I discovered that he disliked me, and would always neglect me, it was a cruel blow, though he was not to blame for it, for other men have honestly repented of their fancies. I could not think of him as a bad man for no other reason than that he was dissatisfied with me; for all the people were his friends, and he must have deserved their friendship. I suppose a man may form a dislike for his wife as naturally as he forms a dislike for anything else—I have reason to *know* that they can—and not commit a graver offence than one who happens to dislike any other trifle which displeases him. I would have told him this myself had he not kept out of my way so long; it is all written in this letter, and my name is signed to it. I commission you to give it to him.'

"She took from her bosom and handed me a crumpled piece of paper, on which nothing was written, but I carefully put it in my pocket, to humor her strange whim.

"'I am satisfied now, since I have heard that he is contented, and if Tom is willing we will never refer to the matter again. He is a good man; even Tom says that between his curses, and why not let him alone? Tell him that Alice gave you the letter with her own hands, and that she will not live long to annoy him. Tell him that Alice rejoices to know that he is contented; for Tom has told me all about it, and since my sickness it has been a pleasure for me to think that a worthy man—and he is a worthy man; for no one can say aught against him except that he could not admire me, which does not seem to be a very grave offence, for no one else admires me—has found what his ability and industry entitles him to,—peace. Peace! How he must enjoy it! How long he has sought it! I can understand the relish with which he enjoys it.'

"The Wolf was not pleased with this sort of talk; it was not crazy enough to suit him, and he looked at her with anger and indignation in his ugly face.

"'I never said it before, Tom,' she continued, evidently frightened at his wicked look, 'but I must say it now, for I cannot remember the hate you tried to teach me; I can only remember that a man capable of loving and being loved buried himself with a woman he could not tolerate, all from a sense of duty, and looked out at the merry world only to covet it. I have forgotten the selfishness which occupies every human heart; it was driven out of my nature with hope and ambition, and I am only just when I say that he deserved pity as well as I. He was capable of something better than such a life; and was worthy of it. I might have been worthy; but I was not capable, and was it right to sacrifice him because I crept while he ran? Do we not praise men for remedying their mistakes? You know we do, and I only praise him for it; nothing more. The truth should always be written on a tomb; this house is like a tomb, it is so cold and damp, and I must tell the truth here. I am cold; why don't you build a fire?'

"She put her hand into the flame of the candle she carried, to warm it, but it did not burn, very much to my surprise; and she looked at me with quiet assurance while she warmed her hands in this odd manner. As I watched her I noticed that the wild look which marked her face when she first appeared was returning; her craze came back to her, and she put it on with a shiver.

"'Your feet are resting on a grave,' she said to me again, after staring around the room awhile, and as coolly as she might have called my attention to muddy boots. 'Please take them off. It may be *his* grave. I have brought flowers to decorate it; an armful. Stand aside, sir.'

"I did as she told me, and, advancing toward where I sat, she pretended to throw something on nothing out of her empty hands.

"'I came across a grave in the lower hall this morning, Tom,' she said to The Wolf, pausing; and she said it with so much indifference that I thought she must have meant a moth. 'Of course they would not be together: I have never expected that. The grave in the hall was shorter than this one, and it was neglected. But this one,—this shows care. And look, Tom! The flowers I threw upon it are gone already!'

"There was surprise and pain in the little woman's voice, and she pretended to throw other flowers from her withered hands on the mound her disordered fancy had created.

"'They disappear before they touch it!' she said. 'I almost expect it to speak, and protest against any attention from me. And it is sinking; trying to get away from me! How much his grave is like him; it shrinks away from me. I'll gather them up; I'll not leave them here!'

"Out of the air she seemed to be collecting wreaths, and crosses and flowers of every kind, and putting them back into her arms.

"'I will put them on the neglected mound in the lower hall, for no one else will do it. How odd the fair flowers will look on a background of weeds; but there shall be roses and violets on my grave, though I am compelled to put them there. Open the door, Tom; my strength is failing. I must hurry.'

"The door was opened, and she passed out of it, and down the dark hall, staggering as she went. When she reached the door through which she came at The Wolf's call, at the lower end of the passage, she turned around, held the candle above her head again, and said,—

"'Be merciful, Tom; I request that of you as a favor. You were never wronged by him, except through me, and I have never been resentful except to please you. Let the gentleman return and deliver the letter I gave him.'

"Opening the door near which she stood, she disappeared.

"So Tom was the cause of all the trouble? I resolved as we stepped back into the room that he should regret it, and I think there is no doubt that he does."

Tug turned on his back again, and seemed to be considering what course he had better pursue with reference to the remainder of his story. At last he got up from the bed slowly and painfully, and walked over to the cupboard where his law-book was kept, which he took down and opened on the table. After turning over its pages for a while, pausing occasionally to read the decisions presented, he shut up the book, returned it to the shelf, and went back to the bed.

"I am too much of a lawyer," he said, "to criminate myself, pardner, and you'll have to excuse me from going into further details. But I can give you a few conjectures. In my opinion the pale, ugly little woman without a mind, but who looked respectable enough, was once Allan Dorris's wife, but I don't know it; I heard nothing to confirm this suspicion except what I have told you. The Wolf was her brother (a man with an uglier disposition I never laid eyes on), and I shall always believe that Dorris married her when a very young man; that he finally gave her most of his property and struck out, resolved to hide from a woman who had always been a burden and a humiliation to him. It is possible that he was divorced from her a great many years before he came here, and that she lost her mind in consequence; it is possible that he had nothing to do with her; but I give you my guess, with the understanding that it is to go no farther. I am not in the habit of telling the truth; but *this* is the truth: I know no more about his past history than you do; but while in the city I came to the conclusion I have just given you."

There was another short silence, and Silas became aware of the fact that Tug was breathing heavily, and that, for the first time since he had known him, he was asleep in his own house at night.

CHAPTER XXIII.

THE GOING DOWN OF THE SUN.

Two years have passed since the great flood in the river, which is still told about with wonder by those who witnessed it, and Tug Whittle is now living in the detached building at The Locks, which was occupied so long by Mrs. Wedge, that worthy lady having long since taken a room in the main house.

Little Ben, released from his hard work at Quade's, is growing steadily worse, in spite of the kindness shown him by Mrs. Dorris and Mrs. Wedge. A victim of too much work is little Ben; but he is as mild and gentle as ever, and spends his days, when he is able, in wandering about the yard, and keeping out of the way, for he cannot forget the time when every hand was against him.

Mr. Whittle has become an industrious man during the two years, and is as devoted to Mrs. Dorris and her little child as it is possible for a man to be. The day after Tug's return to the Bend from his tramp to the lower country, he called on Mrs. Dorris, and related his story as he related it to Silas Davy, and going into the little detached house after its conclusion, he did not come out again for two days and nights; and it was supposed that he was making up for lost sleep. After his appearance he was fed by Mrs. Wedge, and at once began to make himself useful around the place. In a little while they learned to trust him, and he soon took charge of everything, conducting himself so well that there was never any reason for regretting the trust reposed.

Allan Dorris had died possessed of several farms in the adjoining neighborhood, and these Mr. Whittle worked to so much advantage, with the aid of tenants on each, that in a financial way Mrs. Dorris got on very well; for Mr. Whittle wanted nothing for himself except the privilege of serving her as he did.

Very often he was absent from The Locks for weeks at a time, looking after the farm affairs, and he seldom visited his mistress except to give accounts of his stewardship, which were always satisfactory. He had been heard to say that it was his fault that she was a widow; therefore he did not care to see her except when it seemed to be necessary, for her modest grief gave him such pangs of remorse that he wanted to take the musket, which he still retained in times of peace, and make away with himself. Therefore he spent much of his time in managing her affairs, which called him out of town; and he became known as a tremendous worker,—to rival his record as a loafer, Mr. Whittle himself said; but Silas Davy knew, and even the people admitted it, that he was greatly devoted to his young mistress, and that he had no other aim in life than to make her as comfortable as possible in her widowed condition.

Occasionally he came to town, on an errand, after nightfall, and returned to the country before day, as little Ben had done, and usually they only knew he had been around the house at all by something he had left for their surprise in the morning. If he found anything in the country he thought would please Mrs. Dorris or little Ben, he went to town with it after his day's work on the farm, and left his bed in the detached house before day to return.

Besides the harm he had done Mrs. Dorris, the wrong he had done his son was on his mind a great deal, and he avoided the boy whenever it was possible. He was ashamed to look into his face, though he was always doing something to please him. His rough experience on the farm had forever ruined the boy's health, and his father was continually expecting to be summoned from the field to attend his funeral.

Tug was still rugged and rough, and unsociable with those with whom he came in contact in the field or on the road, but he loved those in The Locks, from Mrs. Dorris down to the baby, with a devotion which made him a more famous character than he had ever been as a vagrant. He had become scrupulously honest and truthful, as well as industrious; and those who marvelled at the change were told by the wiser heads that Tug had something on his mind which he was trying to relieve by good works.

Silas Davy no longer had reason to regret that he was unable to buy little Ben a suit of clothes, for little Ben was well clothed now, and comfortably situated, except as to his cough; but in other respects the clerk had not changed for the better.

He was still employed at the hotel, and still heard the boarders threaten to move to Ben's City; for Davy's Bend continued to go slowly down the hill. He still heard Armsby boast of his fancy shots, and of his triumphs in the lodge; and, worst of all, he still heard patient Mrs. Armsby complain of overwork, and knew that it was true.

He occasionally went to The Locks to see Mr. Whittle,—usually on Sunday evening, when that worthy was most likely to be at home,—and as we come upon them now, to take a last look at them, it is Sunday evening, and Tug and Silas are seated on a rude bench, in front of the detached house, with little Ben between them.

"I have come to the conclusion, Mr. Davy,"—Tug is wonderfully polite recently, and no longer refers to his companion by his first name,—"I have come to the conclusion that there is only one way to get along; it is expressed in a word of four letters—work. Busy men do not commit great crimes, and they know more peace than those who are idle; therefore the best way to live is to behave yourself. I don't know whether I can behave myself enough from now on to do any good, or not; but I intend to try."

"I think you can, Tug," Davy replied. "You have been very useful during the past two years."

"But I have been very useless during the past forty and odd," Mr. Whittle continued, looking at little Ben as though he were evidence of it. "I have changed my mind about everything, with one exception, within a few years,—except that I do not believe a certain person is good, I have no opinion now that I had a year ago,—but on this I will never change. My acquaintance with Dorris and his wife has taught me a good many things which I did not know before. His bravery taught me that bravery comes of a clear conscience, and his wife's goodness and devotion teach me to believe that a dead man is not so bad off, after all. Did you know that she expects to meet her husband again?"

Tug waved his hand above his head, intended as an intimation that Mrs. Dorris expected to meet her husband in heaven, and looked at Silas very gravely, who only nodded his head.

"She seems to *know* it," Tug continued, "and why should I dispute her? How much more do I know than Annie Dorris? By what right do I say that she is wrong, and that I am right? She is good enough to receive messages, but I am not; and it has occurred to me that I had better be guided by her. I have never been converted, or anything of that kind, but I have felt regret for my faults. I have done more than that. I have said aloud, as I worked in the fields, 'I'm sorry.' I have frequently said that,—may be only to myself, but may be to the winds, which are always hurrying no one knows where. Who knows where they may carry the sound when a wicked man says, sincerely, 'I'm sorry?'"

Sure enough, who knows? May it not be to heaven?

"I have heard her play hymns on the organ which I felt must be songs of hope, the words of which promised mercy, for they sounded like it, and she does not play them for amusement; I believe it is her offering for the peace of Allan Dorris, and a prayer could not go farther into heaven than her music. I have known her to go to the church with the little baby, and I should think that when the Lord hears the music, and looks down and sees Annie Dorris and the child, He would forget a great deal when Dorris comes before Him."

Silas had heard the music, too, and he agreed that if it could have been set to words, they would have been "Mercy! Mercy!"

"I am too old a crow to be sentimental," Tug said again, "but I have felt so much better since I have been working and behaving myself that I intend to keep it up, and try and wipe out a part of my former record. If I should go to sleep some night, and not waken in the morning as usual to go away to work, very good; but if I should waken in a strange place, I should like to meet Allan Dorris, and hear him say, 'Tug, I have reason to know that erring men who have ever tried to do right receive a great deal of consideration here; you have done much toward redeeming yourself.'"

Silas was very much surprised to hear his companion talk in this manner, and said something to that effect.

"I am surprised myself," Tug answered, "but the devotion of Annie Dorris to the memory of her husband has set me to thinking. The people believe that Allan Dorris was buried in The Locks' yard, by Thompson Benton, but I know that his iron coffin still stands in the room where you saw it. I think his clay feels grateful for the favor, for it has never been offensive like ordinary flesh. The lid has been shut down never to be opened again, but when I last looked under it, I saw little except what you might find in the road,—dust."

The chill of the evening air reminds them that it is time for little Ben to go in, but the two men remain outside to look at the sunset.

"The people of this town," Mr. Whittle continued, after the boy had disappeared, "are greatly amused over the statement that when an ostrich is pursued, it buries its head in the sand and imagines that it is hid. I tell you that we are a community of ostriches; I occasionally put a head into the sand myself, and so do you and all the rest of them. When little Ben is near me, I try to cause him to forget the years I neglected him, by being kind, but he never looks at me with his mild eyes that I do not fear he is thinking: You only have your head in the sand, and there is so much of you in sight that I remember Quade. Therefore I keep out of his way whenever I can. Do you think his cough is any better?"

"I am afraid not, Tug," Silas replied. "I was thinking to-day that it is growing steadily worse."

Tug looked toward the setting sun and the church, and the solemn tones of the organ came to them; Annie Dorris was playing the hymn the words of which seemed to be "Mercy! Mercy!"

"Word will be sent to you some day," Tug said, as if the music had suggested it, "that little Ben is—" he paused, and shivered, dreading to pronounce the word—"worse. I wish you would get word to me some way, without letting any one know it; I want to go away somewhere. Then you can come out for me, and tell them on your return that I could not be found. It is bad enough for me to look at him now; I could never forget my sin toward him were I to see him dead. Of course you will go with him to the cemetery, with Mrs. Dorris and Mrs. Wedge and Betty; and I would like to have the baby at poor Ben's funeral, for he thinks so much of it, but it will be better for me to stay away, though I want them to think it accidental. When I return, you can show me the place, and on my way to and from the town I will stop there and think of the hymn which Mrs. Dorris plays so much."

The sun is going down, and it seems to pause on the hill to take a last look at the town. Perhaps it is tired of seeing it from day to day, and will in future travel a new route, where objects of more interest may be seen. Anyway, it lingers on the hill, and looks at the ragged streets and houses of the unfortunate town down by the river, which is always hurrying away, as if to warn the people below to avoid Davy's Bend, where there is little business, and no joy.

When its face is half obscured by the hill, the sun seems to remember The Locks, with whose history it has been familiar, and looks that way. So much shadow has gathered around it already from the woods across the river that objects are no longer to be distinguished: nothing but the huge outlines. At last the sun disappears behind the hill, but a friendly ray comes back, and looks toward The Locks until even the church steeple disappears; and Davy's Bend, and The Locks, with its sorrow and its step on the stair, are lost in the darkness.

Milton Keynes UK
Ingram Content Group UK Ltd.
UKHW010849010724
444982UK00005B/469